RETURN TO SOL:
ATTACK AT DAWN

THE ORION WAR – BOOK 12

BY M. D. COOPER

M. D. COOPER

Just in Time (JIT) & Beta Readers

Scott Reid
Chad Burroughs
Timothy Van Oosterwyk Bruyn
Gareth Banks

Print ISBN: 978-1-64365-055-5

Cover Art by Andrew Dobell
Editing by Jen McDonnell, Bird's Eye Books

TABLE OF CONTENTS

FOREWORD

Surprise! Chances are that if you picked up this book on release, you expected to be reading the final book in the Orion War series, but that's not exactly what's in your hands right now.

I started writing this story at the exact point I left off in *Race Across Spacetime* with Tanis, Tangel, Sera, and the others arriving at New Canaan…but what ended up happening was that a whole bunch of other characters clamored for attention, and just wouldn't be quiet!

If you recall, at the very end of *Race Across Spacetime*, the group at the galactic core skirted around the edge of Sagittarius A* to reach a gate, which they used to jump to New Canaan. Unfortunately, in doing so that close to so much mass, they skipped ahead through time by a month, arriving at their destination to find it under attack by what Tangel described as 'everyone'.

But what happened during that lost month? Last we saw, Orion had fallen, and the Hegemony was on the run. Joe and Jessica had just routed a Sirian assault on Kapteyn's Star, and, at this point, Rika is solidifying her hold on Genevia after killing the Nietzschean emperor. Lastly, Corsia is earning victory after victory in the Trisilieds, while the Hoplite fleets mop up Orion Guard defenders in the PED.

All of that is to say, who could be attacking New Canaan? How could a force so large that it triggered the recall of all ISF ships to their home system be on their doorstep?

Which is the story the characters were demanding I tell.

Joe, Katrina, Jessica, Cheeky, and the all rest have been up to a lot over that month, and they insisted I tell you about it. At first, I thought it would just be a short, initial segment in the book, but here I am still not done wrapping up the first week since Joe and Jessica routed the Sirians at Kapteyn's Star, and I have a full-length novel, with more to write!

I *could* have put it all into one volume, but even making this the longest Aeon 14 book to date, there wasn't any way to tell the story properly without rushing the ending, and so *Return to Sol* has become a two-parter.

I do want to make it clear that this is not half a story that is going to leave you hanging—at least, no more than is usual for an Orion War book. There is a full story arc within these pages, as well as the events that will bring us to the doorstep of the final conflicts in the war.

There was a bit of concern in my mind about breaking this book into two separate volumes, but I ran a poll on the Discord server and in the Facebook group, and in both places, the response from readers was unanimous: two books. A few even suggested three.

So here you have it, *Return to Sol: Attack at Dawn*, soon to be followed by *Return to Sol: Star Rise*.

Now, it's time to let slip the dogs of war.

Malorie Cooper
Danvers, 2020
mdcooper@thewoodenpenpress.com

PREVIOUSLY...

A lot went on in the previous book, *Race Across Spacetime*. We started with Tanis and Angela coming to in a pinnace and wondering where they were, and ended with a jump from the galactic core to New Canaan, only to find that the system was under attack.

Excepting Earnest and Finaeus's journeys through time, the entire book took place over four days, with Sera mounting a rescue to save Tanis and Angela, while ascended AIs hunted them in the New Sol System.

Ultimately, Tanis and Angela were captured and taken to the core. At the same time, Finaeus and Earnest jumped backward in time with the express purpose of saving Tangel from her demise at the end of *Starfire*. They and Tangel then jumped to the core and aided in Tanis and Angela's rescue.

In those days, Joe and his daughters traveled back to New Canaan, not wanting to remain in New Sol once it was clear that Tanis and Angela were no longer there.

There, the ISF had been upgrading I-Class supercarriers with EMG/DMG weaponry capable of firing through stasis shields. Given the fact that the ascended AIs had given stasis shield technology to the Hegemony of Worlds, this proved to be rather useful when Sirius attacked Kapteyn's Star.

That battle ended with Joe bringing the *Carthage* to Kapteyn's Star, and, aided by starfire from Star City, they drove the Sirians back.

Elsewhere, other battles have been raging in the Milky Way Galaxy. Corsia, who launched an attack against the Trisilieds Kingdom several books ago, has been seeing progress with her efforts there, and Svetlana's Hoplite force has been sweeping through the Perseus Expansion Districts, distracting the Orion forces.

Now, with those campaigns drawing to a close, all eyes are turning to the inner systems of the Hegemony of Worlds, the desire to decisively end the war growing in everyone's minds.

A sentiment the Hegemony has picked up on, increasing their desperation and need to score a final victory before the Orion War reaches its conclusion...

KEY CHARACTERS

Bob – Bob is Bob, no additional introduction is needed.

Caldwell – Colonel Caldwell of the ISF commands sixty-seven ships under TSF Admiral Svetlana in her Hoplite fleet.

Camille – Crew aboard Katrina's ship, the *Voyager.*

Carl – Head engineer and first mate of the *Voyager.*

Cary – Tangel's biological daughter. Has a trait where she can deep-Link with other people, creating a temporary merger of minds, and is able to utilize extradimensional vision to see ascended beings. Recently, she's been aboard the *Perilous Dream*, having assumed the role of Widow A1.

Cheeky – Captain of *Sabrina*, and longtime friend of Sera. Cheeky was once a human woman, but is now a recreation of her mind as an AI in a mostly human body.

Corsia – Former captain of the *Andromeda*, Corsia is now admiral of the ISF's Twelfth Fleet, currently operating in the Trisilieds Kingdom.

Diana – Empress of the Scipian Empire

Darla – Tanis's first AI, Darla is an ancient AI with mysterious ties to Hades, the first AI to reach the galactic core.

Earnest – Designer of the *Intrepid* and a host of other ISF technology, Earnest is New Canaan's foremost scientist.

Elena – Former Hand agent and Sera's ex-lover. Double agent for Orion who attempted to kill Tanis at Alexandria.

Faleena – Tangel's AI daughter, born of a mind merge between Tanis, Angela, and Joe. Widow designation F11.

Finaeus – Brother of Jeffrey Tomlinson, and Chief Engineer aboard the *I2*.

Gil – Gil is the ship's AI aboard Jessica's flagship, the *Lantzer*.

Greer – Admiral Greer commands the TSF forces focused on ending the Orion War in the Inner Stars. He first encountered the *Intrepid* and her crew at the Ascella Watchpoint, and joined in the conflict on the side of New Canaan during Orion's first attack on the star system.

Iris – The AI who was paired with Jessica during the hunt for Finaeus, who then took on a body (that was nearly identical to Jessica's) after they came back.

Jason – Jason Andrews is the first captain of the *Intrepid*, and governor of the New Canaan colony. Jason has a long and storied career spanning thousands of years to pre-FTL days, when he pioneered trade routes between near-Sol stars.

Jen – ISF AI paired with Sera.

Jessica Keller – ISF admiral who has returned to the *I2* after an operation deep in the Inner Stars to head off a new AI war. She also spent ten years traveling through Orion space before the Defense of Carthage—specifically the Perseus Arm, and Perseus Expansion Districts.

Joe – Admiral in the ISF, commandant of the ISF academy, and husband of Tangel.

Katrina – Captain of the *Voyager*, Katrina has had a long and storied life. Originally born into Luminescent society, she's been a spy, a traitor and rebel, a governor's wife, and then governor herself. Later, she was a refugee, a captive, a warlord, and a marauder. The list could go on for several novels.

Kerr – The I-Class *Carthage*'s multinodal AI.

Kirb – Crew aboard the *Voyager*.

Krissy Wrentham – TSF admiral responsible for internal fleets fighting against Airtha in the Transcend civil war. She is also the daughter of Finaeus Tomlinson and Lisa Wrentham.

Leory – COO of the Sirian Hegemony. The Hegemony used to have a CEO, but after they were conquered by Sol, they were denied the use of that title.

Lisa Wrentham – Former wife of Finaeus Tomlinson, she left the Transcend for the Orion Freedom Alliance when Krissy was young. Head of a clandestine group within the OFA known as the Widows, which hunts down advanced technology and destroys it. Former Widow designation A1.

Malorie – Woman whose brain was placed in a spider-like body by Katrina after a rather complex series of events in the Midditerra system. Malorie and Katrina started off as enemies, but are now close friends. However, Malorie rather enjoys her body and behaving as much like a large, red, rather terrifying spider as possible.

Misha – Ship's cook aboard *Sabrina*.

Nance – Engineer aboard *Sabrina* who once held an ascended AI's shard.

Ophelia – Captain of the *Carthage*, Ophelia's first major command was as captain of a cruiser, where she served with distinction in the Battle for Victoria.

Peabody – Captain of the *Starblade,* Peabody's first major command was as captain of the *Antares,* where he served with distinction in the Battle for Victoria.

Petra – Hand Regional Director based in Alexandria, capital of the Scipian Empire. After the great unveiling, Petra also became the ambassador from the Transcend to Scipio. She is now also the consort of the Scipian empress, Diana.

Prime – An AI who went insane due to unethical experimentation in the 32nd century, Prime was thought to have been killed at Proxima by an AI named Eric, but a backup of the unstable AI escaped.

Rachel – Captain of the *I2*. Formerly, captain of the *Enterprise*.

Saanvi – Tangel's adopted daughter, found in a derelict ship that entered the New Canaan System. Widow designation E12.

Sabrina – Ship's AI and owner of the starship *Sabrina*.

Sabs – An autonomous shard of *Sabrina*, Sabs is a clone of the ship's AI, but has grown into her own person.

Sebastian – Rear Admiral serving under Svetlana.

Sera – Director of the Hand and former president of the Transcend. Daughter of Airtha and Jeffrey Tomlinson.

Symatra – SAI Admiral in the ISF, Symatra played a critical role in the Defense of Carthage, and commanded Cary and Saanvi during the conflict.

LMC Sera (Seraphina) – A copy of Sera made by Airtha containing all of Sera's desired traits and memories. Captured by Sera and the allies during their excursion into the Large Magellanic Cloud.

Valkris Sera (Fina) – A copy of Sera made by Airtha containing all of Sera's desired traits and memories. Captured by ISF response forces who came to the aid of the TSF defenders during the siege of Valkris.

Svetlana – Admiral in the TSF in command of a Hoplite fleet operating behind enemy borders in the Perseus Expansion District.

Tanis – Not to be confused with Tangel's former human identity, Tanis is the oldest of Jessica, Trevor, and Iris's AI children. She resides at Star City.

Tangel – The entity that resulted from Tanis and Angela's merger into one being. Not only is Tangel a full merger of a human and AI, but she is also an ascended being.

Terrance – Terrance Enfield was the original backer for the *Intrepid*, though once the ship jumped forward in time, he took it as an opportunity to retire. Like Jason, he was pulled into active service by Tangel when New Canaan became embroiled in the Orion War.

Trevor – Husband of Iris and Jessica Keller. Originally from the Virginis System, Trevor is now a commander in the ISF, and serves with his wives aboard the ISS *Lantzer*.

Troy – Initially the AI pilot of the *Excelsior*, a heavy mining rig, Troy sacrificed himself to save the *Intrepid* at the Battle for Victoria. Later, Katrina found him on Victoria's moon. Eventually, he ended up as the ship's AI in her vessel, the *Voyager*.

Usef – Usef has worked his way up from a lieutenant serving in the fledgling ISF on Victoria, to one of the space force's most renowned officers. At present, he is in command of a special operations battalion.

Uriel – Leader of the Hegemony of Worlds, Uriel has turned from an elected official to a dictator who styles herself the 'hegemon'. She rules from High Terra in the Sol System.

Virgo – An AI upgraded by Myrrdan to take over the *Intrepid*, Virgo was the rogue AI responsible for much of the sabotage on the *Intrepid* that led it to the near-disaster at Estrella de la Muerte. The corrupted node Virgo inhabited was too dangerous to attempt to purge or store, so Bob and Earnest ejected it from the *Intrepid* in interstellar space.

MAPS

For more maps, visit www.aeon14.com/maps.

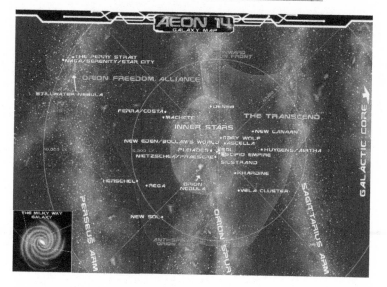

PART 1 – WHY SO SIRIUS

THE ROUTE

STELLAR DATE: 05.11.8950 (Adjusted Years)
LOCATION: ISS *Lantzer*, Inner System
REGION: Kapteyn's Star System, Alliance Controlled Territory

The *Lantzer*'s bridge crew broke into cheers as the final Sirian cruiser began to gout plasma, twisting in half as one of the main engines died under atom beam fire.

"That's the last of their capital ships," Jessica said as she rose from her command seat and stretched her arms. "A couple of corvettes and destroyers got away, but I count this as a win. Good work, everyone."

Trevor did the same at the weapons console, twisting his back side to side before ambling over to Jessica and wrapping her in a tight embrace. "Serves those bastards right."

"You have no idea." Jessica's voice was laden with grim satisfaction. "Sirius is a blight on the galaxy, so much can be laid at their doorstep."

Iris approached, and the pair opened their arms to include her in the embrace.

"So, what do you think is next?" the AI asked. "Do you think Joe will really order a strike on Sirius?"

"It's the logical next step," Jessica replied. "Not only that, but it will take the pressure off Kapteyn's Star—and I know he feels as strongly about this system as I do."

"I'm with you there," Karma said. "I still think of Tara as home as much as Troy."

<Well, I imagine you're going to find out what's next,> Gil said. *<The* Carthage *is hailing us.>*

The trio broke their embrace, and Jessica stepped to the fore, switching the holotank from a view of the battlespace to the image of Admiral Joseph Evans.

Something had changed in her good friend since last she'd seen him. For the first time, he looked the part of a grim-eyed military man who had seen too much of war. She never thought she'd see the day when hints of the cocksure pilot would no longer sparkle behind his eyes, but it seemed it had finally come.

"Good work, Admiral Keller." Joe's voice was as weary as his visage let on. "We may not have wiped them out, but we sent a hell of a message. One that will take a week to arrive through the dark layer."

"And what's next?" she asked. "Are we going to regroup?"

"At the gates," Joe replied. "We're jumping to Sirius."

"Yes!" Iris thrust a fist in the air. "About fucking time!"

Joe nodded and crossed his arms. "I'm sending drones in to find their interdiction buoys. If we can find enough, we'll rail-shot them from here and then jump straight down to Incandus."

"Too bad Markus isn't here to see this." Jessica ran a hand down her cheek. "I bet he would have loved to see Brilliance Station burn."

"Don't count your space rubble before it's smashed," Trevor cautioned. "Sirius is a hell of a stronghold."

The lavender-skinned woman nodded. As one of the oldest colonized star systems in the galaxy, Sirius had rarely suffered defeat in war, while also remaining largely insular. The latter was the only silver lining, as most places they spread their odious 'Luminescent Society' caste system to did not fare well under it.

"Our plan is not to take or occupy the whole system," Joe

said, sending a wide view of the space around Incandus, the white dwarf star in the binary system. "But we're going to hammer every military target around Incandus and Radius, stripping their defenses bare."

"And just leave them for whatever wolves may come by?" Trevor asked.

"Or until we have time to deal with them after the war," Joe said with a shrug. "Honestly, once we unseat the Hegemony, I'm rather hoping that we can have them form a new government, and deal with this mess themselves."

"Really?" Jessica gave a caustic laugh. "I wouldn't trust them to form a responsible government if all of humanity depended on it. No, when we're done with Terra, we need to make sure that Sirius isn't a threat to anyone ever again."

Joe cocked an eyebrow. "Do you really want to be in the business of policing the galaxy?"

"Do you want to be in the business of fighting wars like this every few centuries?" she countered.

The man on the holo sighed. "I just want to retire."

"Didn't you already do that once?" Iris asked.

"Hush, you." He gave a soft chuckle.

"I'll rally my fleet," Jessica told him, changing the topic. "I'll leave a few on patrol while the rest form up at the gates. Do we need to deal with S&R?"

"Scipio's going to jump a few recovery platforms in for that," Joe replied. "Though feel free to lend any aid you can, so long as you're ready to jump to Sirius in thirty hours."

"Piece of cake, sir." Jessica gave him an impish wink. "Almost like we know how to ply the black or something."

A hint of light came to Joe's smile, and he nodded. "Good, glad to hear it, Admiral."

The holotransmission terminated, and Trevor let out a heartfelt sigh. "I have no idea how he does it."

"Which part?" Iris asked.

"Soldier on," he replied. "There's a man who just never stops."

Jessica nodded, smiling as a few memories came to mind. "He comes off as an easygoing guy, but he's always pushing forward. Somehow, he just makes it look effortless."

"I suppose we should do our jobs now," Iris said as she returned to her station. "We have a fleet to ready."

"Sure as hell do," Jessica replied. "Karma, get me all-fleet. It's time to bring justice to Sirius."

THE ORION FRONT

STELLAR DATE: 05.12.8950 (Adjusted Years)
LOCATION: Hale's World, Hale's Beacon System
REGION: Midway Cluster, Orion Freedom Alliance Space

"Admiral!" a woman called out, feet dragging as she ran through the deep snow, cheeks red from the cold. "A courier ship is inbound; we've received word from Command!"

Svetlana twisted to the side, her skis blowing a plume of snow into the air as she came to a stop a few meters from Lieutenant Raini.

It had been some months since the last few QuanComm blades linked to New Canaan and the *I2* had burned out, leaving Svetlana's Hoplite fleet to their own devices, deep in Orion space.

"How long till they dock? Did they send a data burst?" She pulled her goggles up and set them on her forehead.

"Just a few hours, ma'am, they didn't know if the system was safe enough to broadcast their presence. There is a burst, but most of it is for your eyes only. I did get word that New Sol has fallen, though!"

The admiral pulled off a glove, wiping a bit of melting snow from her cheek while she tried to process the information. "Well, shit…that's some amazing news!"

"Yeah!" Raini was grinning ear to ear. "Does that mean our mission here in the PED is over?"

Svetlana looked around at the snowy slope lined with towering pines. "I suppose it might be. I hope our efforts here had a part in weakening New Sol. I guess we'll know more soon."

"Yes," the lieutenant nodded rapidly. "They have fresh QC blades as well, so we'll be able to get up-to-date news. I know a lot of people have been getting nervous, operating off the grid for so long."

Svetlana nodded. Though she couldn't blame anyone for losing track of her force. After the victory in Sullus, they'd continued their rampage across the Perseus Expansion Districts until arriving at Hale's World, where she'd granted her tired crews a furlough in the relatively peaceful system.

Anyone attempting to follow the fleet would have had to hunt through fifty lightyears of space in order to find the Hoplite force. Despite her crew's growing unease, Svetlana hadn't minded being cut off from the lines of communication or resupply. Their situation was not unlike the ancient Greeks whose namesake her fleet bore: alone, cut off, but still unstoppable, deep within the heart of an enemy empire.

She was certain those Greeks would have stopped for some skiing as well—if such a thing had been done in ancient Mesopotamia.

"Well, I suppose my reprieve is over," Svetlana said to the lieutenant. "Was there anything else?"

"Uhhh…" The woman appeared uncertain. "There's a message for Colonel Caldwell, but I can't find him anywhere."

Svetlana nodded in the direction of the nearby lodge, and pushed off with her poles, going slow so the lieutenant could follow after. "Did you check the southern isles?" she asked once underway.

"The…you want me to check the entire islands, ma'am?"

She couldn't help a laugh in response. "No, Lieutenant, an ISF shore leave shuttle went down there this morning. Check with them. I recall the colonel saying he enjoyed coral reef exploration."

"Really?" Raini was struggling to keep up, slogging through the deep snow, so Svetlana slowed.

"That's what I heard. Don't hold me to it. I can also pass the message to him."

"No, ma'am." The lieutenant drew herself up. "I'll hunt him down. I wouldn't burden you with that."

The admiral smiled at the junior officer. "That's good to hear, but if you can't find him before long, let me know. He shouldn't be that far out of touch."

Svetlana caught a brief flash of consternation on Raini's face. Despite her words, she too had been out of Link range. One of the lodge's 'features' was that there was no wireless signal outside of designated areas. She could have connected to the orbital satellite network, but the admiral wanted to at least get down the slopes a few times before duty called once more. The fact that she'd done two whole runs before someone found her struck her as rather surprising.

It only took the two women a few minutes to reach the lodge, where the local staff greeted them with an enthusiasm that was so effusive, Svetlana suspected it wasn't remotely genuine.

Or maybe they really are this happy to get out from under Orion's thumb.

Though there were pockets of military presence, much of the Perseus Expansion Districts had virtually no Orion Guard presence. Local systems were left to fend for themselves, albeit with a strong undercurrent of fear that any misstep would bring the Guard swooping in to deliver swift and unpleasant retribution.

The sentiment was so pervasive that, at first, Svetlana had believed Orion's hammer must fall with some regularity, but though her fleet analysts had spent some time searching for recent police actions by Orion in systems they'd passed through, such events were few and far between.

The entire oppression of the PED was managed through a well-orchestrated propaganda campaign.

A damn sight cheaper than actively policing the PED.

Once inside the lodge's large foyer, the lieutenant bid

Svetlana farewell and went ahead to the dining room, which had been claimed as the junior officers' lounge. The admiral instead stopped at the coffee bar and ordered a latte, settling on a stool while connecting to the low-bandwidth network the lodge possessed.

She hopped onto the planetary network, and then connected to the TSF fleet in orbit of Hale's World.

<Admiral Sebastian. I understand we finally have word from the home front.>

<We do indeed, Svetlana.>

He sounded tired, and she didn't blame him. Even with weeks spent in the dark layer between systems, there had been little real downtime for the fleet personnel.

I guess I should let him come down and have his R&R before we have to leave.

Sebastian had insisted she go first, and nothing she'd been able to say—aside from a direct order—would sway him. He was a good man, which was exactly why she didn't want him burning out.

<Apparently, this poor courier has been trying to catch up with us for almost a month.>

Svetlana couldn't help a soft chuckle. *<Poor bastards. I bet it must be something to solo your way through the PED, traveling through whatever chaos is in our wake.>*

<Yeah, the captain seemed a bit put out about how long it took to find us.>

<Glad he survived the ordeal,> she rolled her eyes, knowing with how the courier corps prided themselves on short, efficient runs, he'd likely been chafing at the delay. *<Instruct them to dock with my ship first. I'd like to chat with the captain.>*

<Already did so. You on your way up?>

The admiral heaved a heavy sigh. *<Yeah, should be aboard the* Cossack's Sword *in thirty.>*

<Excellent.> The rear admiral's grin translated readily into

his mental tone. *<I can't wait to get dirtside. They have some beautiful jungles down there I'd like to spend some time in.>*

<Really? I never took you for a big nature buff.>

<Always new things to learn, I suppose,> Sebastian said with a languid wink in her mind. *<I'll hold off on getting lost in the flora and fauna until you say the word.>*

<Appreciated.> Svetlana downed the rest of her latte, and slid off the barstool. *<Talk to you soon.>*

<You got it, Admiral. Sebastian out.>

Having anticipated interruption, Svetlana hadn't even unpacked her bags before hitting the slopes. While on the way up to her room to retrieve them, she called down to the valley's port for one of the waiting fleet pinnaces to pick her up.

The crew chief informed her he could have a bird at the lodge in ten minutes, and she thanked him, sighing at the shame it would be to leave so soon. She glanced out a window in the hall, her gaze lingering on the white slopes stretching to the low-slung clouds.

"I'll be back," she promised, adding a wink for good measure.

A creak in the floorboards behind her caught the admiral's attention, but the reflection in the glass showed an empty hall. An instant later, her HUD's Link strength icon displayed zero signal.

Years of training kicked in, and she ducked, lashing out with a booted foot as something whistled through the air over her head. Her blow struck an invisible enemy, and Svetlana rolled backward, looking for something she could throw at the stealthed foe.

A garbage can was at her left, and she grabbed it, flinging it down the hall, dumping papers and food across the floor as it sailed through the air, only to be knocked aside.

Gotcha!

A banana peel was stuck to the attacker's chest, and while it didn't tell the admiral exactly where the next blow would come from, it was better than nothing.

Her combat HUD had activated automatically, and Svetlana's predictive systems painted a rough outline of a person in the hall.

Rising to her feet, the admiral eased backward down the hall, quickly pulling her winter jacket off and wrapping it around her left arm.

"Bring it, bitch." She had no idea if it was a man or a woman, but the epithet seemed appropriate.

"Gladly." The single word hissed from the enemy, and Svetlana's blood pressure spiked.

It's a fucking Widow!

If she were armed and armored, the admiral wouldn't be overly concerned. Widows were, after all, just women—mostly. But with only a pulse pistol and nothing but the skinsuit she'd worn for warmth on the slopes, she wouldn't stand a chance against the clone.

Wait…why hasn't she just shot me?

"Admiral?" Lieutenant Raini's voice came from the far end of the hall. "Your—"

The woman's voice cut off as she came into view and saw the trash strewn across the floor, save for a banana peel floating in the air.

"Look out," Svetlana shouted as the Widow turned on the newcomer, and a lightwand flashed.

Not caring that it would do little harm, the admiral drew her pulse pistol and fired three bursts at where she guessed the woman's head to be.

A hiss of annoyance came from the creature, and then Raini joined in, firing on the banana peel.

Her second shot knocked it off, but Svetlana could tell from the lightwand's position that the Widow was still facing the lieutenant.

"Hey, bitch," she shouted, glad that the epithet fit so well.

Her predictive analysis showed the enemy turning to her left, lightwand in her right hand, still directed at Raini, who was backing away.

Without much thought, Svetlana unfurled her jacket and dashed toward the Widow, flinging it at her head a moment before slamming into her, sending them both to the ground. She kept her weight atop the invisible attacker as best she could, but the Widow's arm came up, lightwand flashing toward the admiral's head. Raini suddenly landed on the woman's outstretched arm, her knees pinning it to the ground.

The Widow whipped the lightwand around, the electron beam slashing across the lieutenant's thigh.

Raini screamed, but didn't release her hold. Svetlana twisted and brought her pulse pistol to the Widow's neck, firing once to let her know she was serious.

"Drop the lightwand, or we find out how many blasts it'll take to turn your neck into pulp."

The wand fell to the floor, lighting the carpet on fire.

"Asshole," the admiral muttered as Raini grabbed it and thumbed the weapon off.

The blade's glow disappeared, but the lieutenant convulsed as an electric shock hit her.

The Widow bucked beneath Svetlana, so she fired another round at the enemy, but missed and splintered floorboards instead. In the process of trying to gain purchase, the woman pushed Svetlana off, and she rolled overtop the burning carpet before quickly scampering out of the way.

The next thing Svetlana knew, the window shattered, and the Widow presumably went through it.

"Are you OK?" She crouched next to Raini, whose thigh was sheared off nearly to the bone. "Nevermind. Stupid question."

A moment later, the wireless network was back, and the admiral tapped into the lodge's emergency channel.

<I need a medic with biofoam now! Second floor. Main hall!>

Raini slumped forward in her arms, and Svetlana held the woman close, glancing around, not entirely certain the Widow was gone.

A minute later, the medic arrived, and the hunt for the attacker was on.

NAIL, MEET HAMMER

STELLAR DATE: 05.14.8950 (Adjusted Years)
LOCATION: ISS *Andromeda*, approaching Holden
REGION: Jewel Star System, Trisilieds Kingdom

"Weapons, full spread on that target!" Corsia called out while noting a ship for her crew, and nodding with grim satisfaction when the *Andromeda's* beams lanced out and cut deep into the hull of a Trissie cruiser.

Her fleet had been fighting in the Trisilieds Kingdom for months, taking system after system, decimating every defense the Trissies possessed, and cutting off the supply lines that were keeping the inner systems of the Hegemony of Worlds in ore and exotics.

<*Mother*,> Sephira chastised. <*Are you slipping? I can manage the* Andromeda *without you giving firing orders to the crew.*>

Corsia laughed and shook her head. Even for an AI, it was easy to sometimes fall into old patterns while concentrating on other things.

<*That's 'Admiral' to you*,> Corsia replied. <*Or are **you** slipping?*>

Sitting in the ship's command chair, the admiral's daughter gave her a knowing smile, and the AI shifted her focus back to the view of the battlespace that filled the holotank.

Though she didn't need the visual to manage the battle—her own internal view being every bit as detailed—Corsia had found that the second view, compiled by the tactical NSAIs, could provide valuable insight that she didn't always consider on her own.

More than once since she'd led her fleet into the Trisilieds, battles had been won by an edge as slim as one gained from a second view of events.

After so many near-wins—and a few losses—the ISF's Twelfth Fleet was closing in on their goal: the Trissie's capital system. But first, they had this final bulwark to drive through, a major starbase orbiting a brown dwarf a little over a lightyear from the capital.

Normally, brown dwarfs were lonely travelers, typically only dragging a few smaller bodies through space with them. But not this one. Named Jewel, it had accumulated a significant number of companions. Two ice giants drifted around the small system's perimeter at seven and ten AU, and within that, a veritable sea of smaller bodies made their home amidst a series of barely-stable orbits.

The current battle took place above a band the locals called 'The Sea of Glass', a band of ice and frozen gas that stretched around Jewel, just over three AU from the star.

In most systems, such a dense asteroid belt wouldn't remain stable, but in the Pleaides, there was enough interstellar debris that the system was constantly replenished by extrasolar objects settling into the belt.

Despite the fact that they were fighting a war in it, Corsia was fascinated by the Jewel. Without a stellar wind of any note, and a much smaller magnetic field than fully convective stars possessed, the brown dwarf's system was a strange mix of stellar and interstellar phenomenon.

All of it beautiful.

<Angelique?> The admiral reached out to the colonel in command of the 9801st fleet division. <I think there might be a reserve holding behind that worldlet plowing through the Sea of Glass.>

There was a dozen such dwarf worlds in the belt, each creating a narrow kirkwood gap in the ring. Because the orbit of each proto-planet took years to complete, many of the gaps closed up before the next year, and the small objects had to gouge their way through time and time again.

Some accreted matter from the process, and others lost it. The world in question was of the latter type, slowly being worn down by its journey through the sea.

<*Nothing anomalous on scan,*> the colonel replied. <*What makes you think that?*>

<*It just seems like an ideal location. Break off a wing to investigate.*>

A year ago, if Corsia had known she would be considering making decisions based on what amounted to little more than intuition, she probably would have blown a core. But somehow, having a smaller body—one that wasn't an entire starship—had given her a different view of situations, along with a 'gut feeling' she hadn't expected.

Sometimes the AI wondered if that was what Tanis's advantage had always been. Nothing more than a better perspective.

<*On it, ma'am,*> Angelique replied. <*I'll keep you apprised.*>

Corsia sent an acknowledgment to the woman, and turned her focus back to the bulk of the battle. The ISF ships were fighting the Trissies occupying a debris field spread around a small planet named Holden. Unlike the Sea of Glass, this debris field was not natural, but the leftover flotsam and jetsam of mining and refining for a major ship-building operation.

Based on the number of yards orbiting Holden, she suspected that a goodly number of ships the ISF fleet had done battle with over the prior months had seen their hulls laid here.

Likewise, once the Holden Yards were in ISF hands, they would use them for refit and repair before moving on to Car Almor, and hopefully bringing a swift conclusion to this front in the war.

But first, she had to take them, and there were over a hundred thousand enemy ships surrounding Holden—more than a challenge for the nine thousand in the Twelfth Fleet.

A dozen more enemy markers disappeared on the holo, and Spencer—the fleet coordination officer—let out a small cry of joy. "That's it for their outer defenses."

"Not even sure why they set it up," Corsia replied. "Ten thousand light hulls aren't going to pose a serious threat to us, even *without* stasis shields."

Sephira shook her head in mock dismay. "It's like each time we come up against a new fleet commander, they just don't believe that our shields can weather so much punishment."

"I'm more than happy to reeducate them," Corsia gave her daughter a predatory grin.

Ahead, a group of enemy ships eased away from Holden, boosting out in a wide arc. The force consisted of at least a thousand cruisers and ten times that many destroyers.

Corsia drew vector projections, measuring probabilities as the cone of uncertainty narrowed.

"They're going to come around us," Sephira said. "Seems they have learned something after all."

Ships operating with stasis shields had one vulnerability: they had to maintain openings in the field around their engines to allow reaction mass to exit. By their very nature, fusion engines destroyed incoming beams and railfire, but concentrated proton beams could penetrate the engine wash, and damage a shielded ship.

Luckily, engines were also a weak spot for conventionally shielded ships, and enemy commanders hadn't realized that it was the *only* place they could damage the ISF vessels.

"They might just be attempting a pincer," Corsia replied, frowning at the display. "If they maintain their current burn pattern, they'll be in position to fire on us in twenty minutes."

"And we'll still be ten minutes from effective range on the defenders around Holden," Sephira said, finally rising from her seat and walking to the holotank to stand beside Spencer. "What do you propose?"

The fleet admiral tapped a slender rose-gold finger against her chin. "Let's wait till they're at the apex of their arc, and then spool out the AP drives and burn hard for Holden."

"That'll reduce our engagement time on the first pass," the ship's captain replied. "But draw this out a lot longer."

Corsia glanced at her daughter, unable to hold back a feeling of pride in the competent ship commander she'd grown to be.

The admiral and her human husband Jim had several children, some organic, some SAI. All served in the ISF, but only one was on the current mission to overthrow the Trisilieds Kingdom, and that was Sephira. She had served aboard the *Andromeda* for years, but eight months ago, had been promoted to captain when Corsia advanced up to fleet admiral.

Initially, she had been far less sure of herself, in no small part due to operating in the shadow of her mother while at the helm of one of the most storied ships in the ISF.

Now, however, Sephira had come into her own. A competent captain who wasn't afraid to voice her opinion and suggest tactics—most of which were sound and insightful.

"It certainly will," Corsia replied. "However, if there are more enemies waiting below in the field of glass, we'll alter vector and pass through the ring to engage those enemies before coming back up around."

"That seems...risky," her daughter said after a moment. "What if the force below the ring numbers those above? We'll be caught between them."

"Not at the *v* we'll have reached by then."

Spencer gave Corsia a questioning look. "You're not suggesting we disengage, are you, ma'am?"

"Not at all!" Corsia shook her head. "If they do have an

equal force below the ring, then we'll spread out and hit other targets throughout the system. If the Trissies operate like they have in other systems, they'll send at least some ships to defend those targets."

"Divide and conquer." Sephira nodded. "I like it."

"Granted, it'll be hard to do when we're outnumbered forty to one. If we didn't need resupply so badly, I'd just order atom beams on the shipyards and then move on."

"Taking and holding ground is such a pain," Jim said as he strode onto the bridge. "We've gotten a bit spoiled, haven't we?"

Corsia gave him a warm smile. "That we have. But New Canaan can't get us resupply for another few weeks, and I don't want to give the Trissies that long to regroup, so we do this the hard way."

"Think there *will* be a point where you might say 'fuck it' and just blow Holden?"

The admiral shrugged. "There's always a point where blowing everything up is the right play. Today, the goal is not to reach that point."

While talking to her husband and daughter, she disseminated the orders to her fleet's five divisions to spool out AP drives and increase delta-*v* with Holden to twenty thousand kilometers per second, with burns to begin in five minutes.

Sephira passed the orders on to her helm officer, then returned to her command chair to review targeting options with her weapons team.

As befit its place, the *Andromeda* was at the center of its division, at the leading edge of the Twelfth. Far from the largest ship in the fleet, the vessel made up for its lack of size with extreme agility.

Corsia had assigned her own ship a Trissie cruiser as its target, one she suspected might be an enemy command vessel.

When the ISF ships made their pass, they'd have seven to ten seconds to fire on their targets. With such a narrow window, fire control needed to preprogram the attack in careful coordination with helm.

As much as Corsia wanted to pay attention to the specifics of the *Andromeda*'s part in the battle, her focus couldn't be so narrow.

Ahead, Holden had four major shipyards, each sitting in geosynchronous orbit around the planet, tethered via a space elevator. While a cost-effective way to supply a ship-building operation, it ensured that the yards couldn't move to avoid any incoming attack.

Because of that, the Trissie fleets were arrayed around the planet at higher orbits, divisions formed into overlapping umbrellas of protection, focused on defending the yards far more than their own numbers.

Corsia knew all too well what it was like to use ships as shields to defend stationary targets. The ISF and Transcend fleets had done just that two years prior, when the Trisilieds and AST fleets had attacked New Canaan.

Payback's a bitch.

Given the slow orbits the defense fleets were moving in, it was easy to select targets for the ISF ships to hit. Each division would focus all fire on a dozen cruisers under one of the moving umbrellas, concentrating fire on those ships before striking at targets of opportunity afterward.

Based on data accumulated from prior engagements, the destruction of sixty of the enemy's largest ships was all but guaranteed.

It was a pittance when measured against the full might of the Trisilieds force, but Corsia's goal was to show that the ISF fleet could wear away the enemy pass after pass, while not losing a single vessel of their own.

"Helm, make ready for max thrust," Sephira called out,

drawing Corsia from her strategy back to the physical world.

"Let's hope it causes them to overextend," the admiral said, setting a display to show the enemy fleet division that had broken off to come around behind the ISF ships.

Inside her mind, she kept another view up, the scan feed from the wing Colonel Angelique had dispatched. They were still three light seconds from passing through the ring. Given their current v, the ships would get a clear view of the enemy forces—if any were present—in thirty seconds.

Readouts on the bridge's main display shifted as the AP drive fired, relativistic exhaust from antimatter annihilation degenerating into gamma rays pouring out of the ship's engine nozzle.

The ISF fleet surged forward, their increase in velocity sending them ahead of the Trissie flanking maneuver. Corsia watched with interest as the eleven thousand ships that had been burning hard to come around behind her fleet had to pivot and increase their own burn to catch up.

Projections were tight, but her gut instinct paid off yet again as it became clear the enemy's maximum burn wouldn't be enough, and they'd pass harmlessly behind the ISF ships, over a hundred thousand kilometers distant.

"Well timed," Jim said, nodding with approval. "Any sooner or later, and I think they would have been able to compensate."

"It's those cruisers," the admiral said, flashing a smile. "They anchored their strike force around them, but they have too much mass to shift vector fast enough. The destroyers could have matched us, but I guess whoever is operating that force decided it wasn't worth sending them in alone."

"Smartest move they've made all day," Jim replied. "Now if they'd just surrender. We have a lot of work to do, and it would be nice if the Trissies would just get out the way and let us do it."

"Funny how it doesn't work that way," she replied. "They seem to want to defend their territory."

He snorted. "What's left of it."

"Makes me wonder how much of a fleet they're going to have left to defend Car Almor," Corsia said. "We didn't expect them to have this much of a force here to begin with. It's possible their capital is almost undefended right now."

"Too bad we don't have gates," Sephira chimed in. "Then we could skip this fight and just go right for their heart."

"The whole point is to destroy their fleets and fleet-building capability, though." Corsia glanced at her daughter, who gave a wry nod.

"Sure. Any other enemy, and I'd believe you. But after what the Trissies did on Carthage…the people they killed…. We all know this one is personal."

Corsia pursed her lips and shot her daughter a half-serious glare. "Maybe, but we still have our objectives. They're the priority."

Sephira winked and nodded. "Of course, Admiral Corsia."

Conversation died out as the fleet neared its targets, and the admiral ensured that each of the other five division commanders had their targets set.

A moment after she'd reached out to Angelique, the colonel's scouting wing completed its transit through the Sea of Glass, and got a clear view of the far side.

There were no ships to be seen anywhere, just empty space.

Corsia sent an order for the wing to fan out and run a detailed scan sweep of the surrounding area. Since they were already out of the main fight, there was no reason not to be thorough.

"Do you think they might have ships in stealth?" Jim asked. "Not the easiest thing to do with all the particulate matter in this system."

"Not unless you have almost no delta-v within the stellar

plane."

"If that's the case, then any ships down there will take nearly an hour to get up to Holden," Jim replied. "Not a huge threat."

She nodded. "True enough. Still one I'd like to know about, though."

The fleet-wide display showed five minutes until the engagement with the Trisilieds defenders, and once again, conversation fell off as personnel concentrated on their tasks.

Corsia grew only dimly aware of the bridge and crew around her as she spread her attention across the entire battlespace, finding herself wishing she had Tanis and Angela's ability to take the whole thing into her mind.

An errant thought sparked into existence, a curiosity as to whether or not the pair would be able to do that anymore, now that Tangel was gone and they were separate people once more.

Then the time of the battle was upon them, and she pushed the idle curiosity away, watching as the five ISF divisions began to fire their beams at the targeted cruisers.

In her division, groupings of two hundred and fifty ships each fired on one cruiser, destroying four in the first two seconds. Next, they sent relativistic beams streaking out at another four. Then the final four were torn apart with three seconds to spare.

Once the primary targets were destroyed, individual wings began to pick off smaller targets, light cruisers and destroyers, until the ISF fleet passed beyond a nominally effective range.

The ships in Corsia's fleet all rotated, turning their engines away from the Trisilieds defenders, firing to slow and shift vector to come around in a broad arc to make another pass.

Just over a hundred thousand kilometers away, the enemy flanking fleet, tagged as 'EF1' on the tactical display, shifted their vector again, continuing to tail the ISF fleet. The enemy was accelerating, and Corsia's ships were slowing down, which meant it would only be a matter of time before they came in range of one another.

Based on her projections, they would be within effective firing range for over five minutes—a lifetime, in a battle like this.

<Colonels,> she said, reaching out to Angelique and Crys directly. <I want you to fire a full spread of grapeshot in a cone around the EF1 Trissies. Time it to reach them at the mark I'm passing you. Do it with the silent sabot rounds, I don't want them to know what we're doing.>

<Understood,> Crys said in a knowing tone, while Angelique sent a nonverbal acknowledgment.

Next, Corsia sent orders to the ships in her division to load up sabot burst rounds in their railguns, and ready to fire on her mark.

Across a hundred and fifty thousand kilometers of space, the five thousand ISF ships stared down twice their number of Trisilieds vessels. From an observer's viewpoint, it would appear as though the ships were slowly approaching each other, while in reality, one was traveling backward, slowing down, while the others were boosting at maximum thrust.

Twenty thousand railguns fired.

The tactic was such a staple for ISF fleets that Corsia was continually surprised by its effectiveness. Though Tanis had first used it against enemies to tremendous effect in Bollam's World twenty years ago, few militaries had adopted it since. Despite being pleased at how well it still worked, the enemy's inability to adapt annoyed the admiral.

Sure enough, when the sabot canisters of grapeshot began exploding amidst the EF1 ships, they followed the textbook response of spreading out to lessen the likelihood of hitting the chaff.

A maneuver that put them right in the path of the fire

41

coming from Crys's and Angelique's divisions.

Dozens of smaller ships lost shields, some venting atmosphere and billowing flame into space. The larger ships all managed to weather the barrage, but many had drained energy reserves to deflect the impacts.

<All ships, maximum burn. Make for marked targets in EF1,> Corsia ordered.

The ISF fleet had been slowly decelerating, ships angled slightly to bring them around Holden, but now, every vessel shifted vector, driving straight at the enemy.

Corsia expected the Trissies to change vector the moment it became apparent what was happening, but they didn't. Their ships were still widely spaced, too far apart to easily bring concentrated fire onto the ISF ship's stasis shields. Not that such a small number of ships posed a significant risk anyway.

In the two minutes it took to close with the enemy, only a few of their destroyer wings formed into closer groupings; the cruisers in the center of their formation seemed unsure of what to do, several closing together, while others fell back, increasing the space between themselves and other ships.

"Maybe they think we'll fire more grapeshot?" Jim offered.

"I wouldn't blame them," Corsia replied. "It wouldn't be the first time we've done something like that."

"What *is* your plan?" Sephira asked. "The division doesn't have any orders."

The admiral tapped a finger on the rim of the holotank. "I'm still debating."

The two fleets were just crossing the hundred-thousand-kilometer mark when Corsia gave a curt nod and delivered orders for each division to target cruisers only.

The colonels acknowledged, and beams lanced out from the ISF ships, lighting up enemy shields, even as the Trissies did the same. A large percentage of the enemy ships brought their fire to bear on the *Andromeda*, striking the cruiser's shields and causing the secondary CriEn to activate.

"Bastards," Sephira muttered, leaning back in her seat and shaking her head.

The concentrated fire meant that it wasn't possible to open up holes in the shield to fire through, restricting any action the flagship could take. Helm jinked the ship side to side, but the enemy shifted their fire to follow it across the battlespace.

Corsia switched her main data feeds to come from nearby ships, relaying the data through the *Andromeda's* aft comm arrays.

Six Trissie cruisers had already been torn apart, and a dozen more had taken damage. The fleets were now within eighty thousand kilometers and continuing to reduce delta-*v*. She passed orders to all five divisions to ready drones.

If we can completely destroy this force, maybe the remainder will surrender.

It wasn't the first time Corsia had hoped for such an outcome. Though the Twelfth Fleet had lost ships and people as it battled the Trisilieds defenders in system after system, most of the deaths had been on the enemy's side.

Few would object to winning battle after battle, but combat was beginning to feel more like slaughter. After the Trissies lost the first four systems, and realized they stood little chance against the ISF fleet, they began to retreat rather than fight. That had gone on for a few dozen systems, where most of the 'battles' were little more than destroying ship-building facilities after giving ample warning for everyone to clear out.

That had changed the closer Corsia's fleet drew to Cor Almor. The enemy had made desperate last stands, fighting far beyond any point where they stood a chance of winning.

In some of the recent battles, the ISF's strategy had shifted to drawing the Trisilieds ships away from strategic targets so they could be destroyed as quickly as possible without any prolonged fights.

But that wasn't an option in the Jewel system. The Twelfth Fleet needed time at dock before the final push, and waiting weeks for New Canaan to throw them a bone wasn't going to cut it.

Despite that, Corsia still hoped to be able to show the enemy that they stood no chance. Even if it meant ending a hundred thousand lives.

Since when did **that** *become the lesser of two evils?*

Beamfire danced between the two fleets, relativistic photons and protons tearing through the black, causing the plasma and stellar dust in the region to glow brightly.

The ISF ships continued to shrug off the attack without issue, but the Trisilieds didn't fare so well. A ship was falling out of the fight almost every second. Though that seemed like a lot, at the current rate, it would still take three hours to destroy the EF1 group, with ten times their number still orbiting Holden.

<*Deploy drones,*> Corsia ordered as the range between the fleets decreased to twenty thousand kilometers.

Few of the ISF fleets could manage mass drone deployments; there just weren't enough AIs in the fleets to manage them. The Twelfth was different in that most of the ships were managed by AIs, which meant that dropping and controlling a million drones was a simple task.

She wondered what the enemy commanders must think when five thousand scan signatures turned into a million.

Some of them must literally shit themselves.

AIs spread across the fleet directed the drones toward smaller targets, while the ISF ships continued to direct their fire toward the largest ships. A grouping of eighteen cruisers began to move 'up' through the enemy formation on a vector to exit the battlespace, and Corsia brought her division's rail destroyers to bear against them.

The destroyers—little more than two concentric rings with

engines mounted to the larger ring—kept a million pellets racing around their circular rail tracks, able to spew them out a dozen apertures, emptying a full track in a matter of seconds.

It only took a minute for the destroyers to move into position, and a hundred million pellets streaked into space at over a quarter the speed of light.

The cruisers only had a second to respond, and Corsia was surprised to see that eight managed to jink out of the way, only taking moderate damage. Of the others, six suffered catastrophic shield failure and were torn apart, and four took minor damage.

"Not bad," Jim said, an eyebrow cocked. "That was some fast maneuvering."

"Not fast enough," Corsia shook her head, glaring at the holo as she sent the order for the rail destroyers to unload their second rings at the enemy.

The destroyer captains focused their fire on the eight that were trying to get away, creating a field of fire around the cruisers that put them in harm's way no matter whether they jinked or stayed on course.

Following the second salvo, only five cruisers were moving under their own power, and the admiral turned her attention back to the rest of the battle, knowing that the rail destroyers could finish the job without her supervision.

Elsewhere on the battlefield, the drones were careening about the enemy ships in swarms, the leading edge disabling shields on one destroyer after another, while the second wave targeted key systems on each enemy ship, leaving them dead in the water.

"Better hope this works," Jim muttered. "We only have one full flight of those things left. If we don't convince the rest of the defenders that this isn't a fight they can win, we're going to have to do things the hard way."

"What else is new," Sephira said. "At least they've finally

stopped directing all their fire at us."

Corsia glanced at her daughter and chuckled. "Don't like being sidelined, do you?"

"Would you?"

"No, I suppose not."

The admiral turned back to the holotank, watching as the division commanders split their drones into smaller groups, spreading out through the enemy fleet and engaging nearly every ship within.

Unlike the capital ships in the Twelfth Fleet, the drones did not possess stasis shields, so before long, a million had been taken out of the fight. By then, the two fleets were within a thousand kilometers of one another, and the ISF ships began to deliver a withering rail barrage.

Corsia had opted for the most direct intercept vector, which meant that the two fleet formations would pass right through one another, thirty thousand starships broadsiding one another for at least twenty seconds.

While few ships were within a hundred kilometers of each other, and the formations were spread out over ten thousand kilometers, the space felt like a much smaller volume, with the ISF ships jinking madly before cutting engines. Once thrust was cut, each ship went 'full bubble', wrapping the entire vessel in shields, weathering punishing fire from the enemy fleet without exposed vulnerability.

Once the ships of the Twelfth were several thousand kilometers behind the enemy, they lowered forward stasis shields and rotated, once again boosting toward the enemy. The delta-v was such that even with the ISF ships now in pursuit and boosting at full power, the distance between the fleets continued to grow.

"You won't get away that quickly," the admiral whispered, a smile forming on her lips as the Trissie ships cut thrust and rotated, turning their engines away from the pursuing vessels.

While the capital ships had passed by one another, the drones had continued to wear down the ships comprising EF1. The defenders had deployed their own drones and fighters, but they only numbered in the tens of thousands; hardly a match for the AI-controlled attack craft.

"Half their cruisers are destroyed or disabled," Spencer commented. "Forty percent of the destroyers."

"No enemy survives the loss of half their forces while the other side loses none," Jim said in a quiet voice.

Corsia only had to glance at her husband to know he felt the same way she did about the wholesale slaughter they were forced to undertake.

She reached out and clasped his hand, squeezing it before activating a comm to broadcast a message for the enemy.

<*This is Fleet Admiral Corsia aboard the* Andromeda.>

"Great, paint a target on us," Sephira muttered from her command chair.

<*We have no desire to kill you, aiming simply to remove your ability to be a threat to us. If you abandon your ships, we will not fire on your escape craft. Do not make for Holden, but Tieranon. We will allow you safe passage and ensure all craft reach that station. Any escape craft attempting to reach Holden will be destroyed.*>

A goodly number of escape craft were already moving away from the battlespace, most toward Holden. A few seconds after she spoke, several began to change course, while the bulk continued toward Holden.

Without pause, a swarm of drones separated from the main battle and dove toward the lifeboats. It didn't take long for the remainder of the escape craft to change course as well.

"Surprised they haven't responded," Jim said.

"Pretty sure we took out their flagship and most of the division command vessels."

He shrugged. "Sure, but usually there's one or two captains who feel free to respond and tell us how we'll never win, and they'll fight to the end. You know…the usual spiel."

"Do I ever. Maybe it's because we're only a few light seconds from Holden. They're hoping whoever is in charge there is going to send aid."

Jim widened the view on the holotank to include the worldlet that was their ultimate objective. "I'm surprised they haven't, to be honest."

"Let's hope it's because they now see this is a lost cause."

As the pair spoke, the ISF ships had continued to wear down the enemy, taking out hundreds more. That seemed to push the defenders over the edge, and escape pods began to pour out of the destroyers and, soon after, the cruisers.

True to Corsia's word, no ISF craft fired on an escape pod, and, provided no weapons were active on the ships they'd abandoned, those vessels were left alone. At first, it was just a few hundred ships that were bleeding lifeboats, but after a minute, all but a smattering of remaining ships followed suit.

The drone swarms made short work of them.

"I'm kinda shocked they didn't—"

Sephira's statement cut off as one of the cruisers exploded of its own volition.

"Scuttle?" the admiral asked with a laugh. "I honestly expected them to do so almost immediately. I mean, I would have."

"That's because our ships can't be captured," Jim replied. "Their ships aren't anything special. The Trissies know there's no strategic advantage in us taking their hulls."

Corsia glanced at her husband. "Or so they think. Flinging a hundred thousand fusion-powered kinetics at their home system could have some marked benefits."

It wasn't the first time they'd used salvage in the fight against the Trisilieds. At the beginning of the campaign, thousands of engines stripped from Nietzschean ships had been jumped into systems on the perimeter of the Pleiades, and used to distract and misdirect the enemy.

Admittedly, none had been used as weapons.

"They wouldn't make it far," Sephira replied. "Though I suppose they would point out for us where the enemy defenses are set up."

"Precisely," the admiral replied. "Then we can move in under stealth and take them out."

"Let's finish this fight first," Jim said, nodding to the holotank, and the space where the last of the EF1 ships had been abandoned and destroyed.

"Spencer," Corsia said, glancing at the FCO. "What did we lose?"

"Ten percent of our drones. Half of the surviving ones need repair, the other half at least need new batts."

"Expected." The admiral nodded for him to continue.

"Four hundred and seventy ships took fire through shield openings. None are severely damaged, though three hundred and thirty-two are no longer combat-capable."

It was a larger number than she'd expected, but after eight months in the field, and dozens of engagements since their last refit, many of the ships were already running on backup systems.

"Reform the fleet," she instructed. "Put us back on a vector to re-engage the defense forces at Holden. I want to be there in fifty minutes."

"Aye, ma'am."

The FCO set to his task, directing his team to begin a deeper assessment as to the status of each division and their ships.

As always, that was one of the things Corsia appreciated most about him. Just because a ship didn't take direct fire in an engagement, other failures could have occurred. By the time the *Andromeda* was back within striking distance of its target, she'd know the status of each vessel in the fleet, down to any loose bolts and low coffee supplies.

"Nothing from them," Jim said, gesturing at the ships blanketing Holden with their overlapping orbits.

"Sweep the drones ahead," Corsia said to Spencer. "Make sure we're not going to walk right into grapeshot."

"Shit," the FCO muttered. "I don't know why I didn't think of that."

"Probably because it doesn't matter," Sephira replied. "Trissie grapeshot can't penetrate our shields."

The admiral folded her arms. "Sure, but I'd like to deploy cooling vanes. We need to bleed off all excess heat before the next engagement. It's going to be a doozy."

Jim snorted. "A doozy?"

"Yeah, you got a problem with my vocabulary?" Corsia gave him a wink, but knew it wasn't as jaunty-looking as she'd hoped.

He gave an emphatic nod. "Yeah, I sure do."

The deadpan stare he gave her lasted several minutes before Jim burst out laughing.

"OK, sorry, I think it's cute. Carry on with your doozies."

Spencer stifled a laugh, and Corsia's brow lowered, a level stare directed at her husband. "I feel like you're undermining my authority here."

He shrugged. "You're the one who said 'doozy'. Pretty sure nothing can undermine your authority more than that."

Sephira rolled her eyes and tried to look busy, while other crew on the bridge did their best to hide smiles.

<You do so much better at that, now,> Jim commented privately.

<Than when?>

<Well, certainly before you got an organic body,> her husband said. <But your personal presence has really improved in the last few months. Before this command, you were one of the most respected captains in the ISF. Now you're reaching Tanis-like levels of loyalty

from the crew.>

Corsia passed a laugh from her mind to his. *<Let's not get carried away. Tanis-level loyalty is not the sort of thing that comes easily.>*

He shrugged. *<I did say 'reaching', not 'achieved'. Maybe you still have decades of work ahead of you.>*

<I feel like that was a bait and switch. I'd almost made it, and now I have decades?>

<Well, I was worried I was going to give you an inflated ego.> Jim gave her a wink, then glanced at the forward display. "Oh, there it is, we're getting a message from Holden."

The admiral blew out a long breath and squared her shoulders before putting the feed on the main holotank.

A pair of women appeared—twins, from the looks of it— the only distinction between them was five stars on one's lapel, and four on the other.

"Admiral Corsia of the Twelfth ISF Fleet," the five-star said. "I am Admiral Emiria of the Kingdom of Trisilieds. You have shown some cunning, making it this far into the kingdom, but you'll go no further."

Corsia shrugged. "Cunning and significantly superior technology. Out of curiosity, how do you plan to stop us? Or am I going no further because King Somer is going to offer his surrender?"

The round trip was over fifteen light seconds, and their response was preceded by expressions of annoyance when listening to her reply.

Emiria cleared her throat. "You will get no surrender from the Trisilieds. We'll fight to the last against your tyranny. And even though you have your stasis shields, we know we can wear you down, shoot around your engines. You can't prevail against the force waiting for you at Plieone. There's no point in continuing."

Corsia glanced at Jim, then Sephira. *<What could they have*

there that will slow us down?>

<A million ships?> the captain suggested. *<That would be a major pain in the ass.>*

<I'm going to call their bluff,> the admiral said. "Well, we're going to continue anyway. First, were going to take Holden from you. I'm giving you this one opportunity to abandon your ships and make for Tieranon, or suffer the same fate as your other ships have."

<Weak, Mom,> Sephira chuckled.

<Quiet, child,> Corsia shot back. *<We really don't have any aces up our sleeves.>*

<Not even our reserve?> Jim asked.

<Well, yeah, of course, but that's still just a slugfest—only one where we have slightly better numbers.>

He gave her a knowing look. *<I get that you don't want to have to wipe them out, but what choice do we have? We have a mission, and we're almost at the end of it.>*

<I still have an option.>

The response came back from Admiral Emiria before Jim could say anything.

"You're going to have to come and do the deed, then. We're not going to abandon our ships without a fight."

"You could run," Corsia suggested. "We'll only give chase for a bit. Less, if you go the opposite direction of Plieone."

<You're so flip, Mom,> Sephira snorted.

<Just tired.>

<And no, you can't use pico,> Jim added. *<It's against the law.>*

The admiral shrugged. *<Parliament retconned the law. Its use is allowed in cases where there would be severe loss of life—the Evans Clause.>*

A smirk crossed her lips as she imagined what Jason Andrews must have done to ram that through the legislative body. By New Canaan's own law, what Joe had done in the A1 System when he fired picobombs at the Orion fleet had been a war crime. But imprisoning one of the ISF's most storied heroes wasn't the sort of thing that would fly with the military.

Corsia was of the opinion that pico weaponry should have been legal all along, but there was still concern that resorting to so-called superweapons would only escalate things further.

Not that I can imagine how much 'further' they think things can escalate. We're in a galactic war now. Unless we plan to jump to Andromeda and start slugging it out there, too, it's as big as it's going to get.

<Yeah, but that law is for us, if *we* face extreme loss of life,> Jim countered, and Corsia took a second to realize her husband was referring to the Evans Clause.

<It doesn't say that,> she replied. <Launching a dozen picobombs could end this without any more of these people dying.>

<Other than the ones aboard the ships the pico hits,> Sephira clarified.

"We won't stand down, we won't retreat," Admiral Emiria spoke, ending the private conversation. "You're going to have to get your hands bloody if you want to win this fight."

"As if they aren't already," Corsia said. "Very well. Have it your way. I'll see you on the banks of the River Styx."

She severed the connection and turned to Sephira. "Captain Sephira. I'm authorizing you to load twenty-four RMs with picobombs."

A look of consternation crossed her daughter's face, but there was no hesitation in the captain's response. "At once, Admiral."

LAST FLIGHT UP

STELLAR DATE: 05.12.8950 (Adjusted Years)
LOCATION: Hale's World, Hale's Beacon System
REGION: Midway Cluster, Orion Freedom Alliance Space

"I leave you alone for one day," Colonel Caldwell said as he strode into the lodge with a squad of ISF Marines at his back. "Can't you just have a proper holiday for once?"

Svetlana shrugged and took a sip of her coffee before replying. "It was over, anyway. Courier arrived, and I was about to head up and have a chat."

"Yeah, well, now you've gone and ruined shore leave for all of us." He gave her a wink while speaking. "Which is fine, I suppose. I'd already caught sight of all the two-tailed fish I needed to see in one life…those things are friggin' weird."

"Get it right, Colonel, that's a one-headed fishes, not a two-tailed fish." Svetlana chuckled. "Ol' Scorry strikes again."

"Who?"

"I'll tell you another time," she replied. "We've established a perimeter and are running active scan across the grounds. If the Widow is still here, we'll find her."

The ISF colonel frowned. "What makes you think she'd still be around?"

"She didn't go for the kill right off," the admiral replied. "She wants me alive, which means she'll try again."

Caldwell heaved a sigh. "That logic only works if she hasn't changed her mind. Maybe they figured your hide's too thick for anything but a killshot."

"Well *that's* not comforting." She rolled her shoulders, working out a kink. "I suppose I can't guess at a Widow's intentions. Like, not even a little bit. Things creep me the fuck out."

"I can imagine," he nodded. "I've only seen vids of them during briefings, and that was enough."

"Then you know how they operate," the admiral replied, giving him a knowing look.

"Yeah. In teams." He glanced back at his Marines, who had moved through the room with careful precision, looking for any sign of a stealthed enemy in the lobby. "Which is all the more reason for you to get back up to the *Cossack's Sword*. We can handle the hunt down here, along with General Lorelai, of course."

Svetlana pursed her lips, not wanting to leave the scene, but also knowing that keeping herself from being caught or killed by a Widow was more important.

For the mission, and me personally.

"OK." She nodded reluctantly. "Lorelai is already on her way down. I'm pretty sure she'd have bundled me into a shuttle as her first action, anyway."

"What makes you think she didn't tell me to do it?" Caldwell gave her a wink.

The admiral coughed and shook her head. "I suppose I should have expected that. OK, my pinnace awaits. I'll head back up to the *Sword*."

"Good. It's clear, by the way."

"My people already scanned it, Colonel."

The man gave an unapologetic shrug. "Our stealth tech is better than yours. Figured it couldn't hurt to have another look. Last thing we want is a hitchhiker getting aboard your flagship."

"Fair enough." She shouldered her bag, which someone had fetched from her room. "You'll let me know the instant you learn anything?"

The man placed a hand over his heart. "Without fail."

Svetlana sketched a salute before turning and walking out of the lodge.

A hundred-meter slope ran down to a landing and parking area, the space now dotted with TSF soldiers and ISF Marines, some patrolling the area, others setting up active scan beacons. She strode past them all, lost in thought as she made her way to where the pinnace awaited.

A pair of ISF Marines stood near the entrance, chatting with several TSF chiefs. As soon as the group saw her, they straightened and saluted.

"You all looked thick as thieves there," the admiral said as she returned the salute. "I assume the pinnace is clear?"

"Inside and out," the ranking CWO said. "We're good to go."

"Excellent," she replied. "Then let's do just that."

Upon entering the pinnace, she saw Raini sitting in one of the crew seats, the biofoam on her leg wrapped in a thick, white bandage.

"Shit, Lieutenant, what are you still doing here?"

"Oh, you know, ma'am." The woman's voice contained a strange, wistful quality. "Just counting the rainbows above your head."

"Painkillers?" Svetlana asked as she took a seat across from the lieutenant.

"The best," Raini gave a serious nod. "Nano to dull the nerve signals, plus something to distract the mind from the fact that half my leg is gone."

The admiral laughed, glancing at the trio of chiefs as they filed onto the craft. "It'll be back in no time. Not even half a day in the tube."

"Uh huh," Raini said in a sing-song voice. "Into the tube I go, I go, I goooo."

Shaking her head, Svetlana tapped into the fleet network via the pinnace's comm array. No longer limited to the lodge's reduced signal, information flowed into her mind. She ran a quick check on the fleet status, reviewing ship positions and civilian activity to be sure all was well.

Sebastian would have let her know if anything was awry, and while she didn't consider herself the micromanaging sort, there was a calm that could only come from knowing that she had a proper grasp of the situation derived from her own analysis.

Other than the fact that the civilians seemed not at all bothered by a foreign military having taken up residence in their system, availing themselves of the world's resort and recreational facilities, nothing seemed out of the ordinary at all.

Hale's Beacon definitely ranks as the strangest system we've made it to thus far in Orion space.

When she had jumped her fleet to Hale, she knew it was primarily a resort system, filled with amenities that people came from a hundred lightyears to enjoy. Even so, it was one that possessed its own militia, a force just shy of the maximum that Orion allowed systems in the PED to field.

Svetlana had come into the system expecting a fight, though she'd hoped to convince them to stand down. But instead of finding themselves faced with an enemy force at the system's edge, the TSF fleet was met with service ships and the system's president aboard his military's flagship, issuing them a victor's welcome.

As it turned out, word of the Hoplite fleet's victories against the Orion Guard forces had spread far and wide throughout the PED in the past eight months, and dozens of systems were declaring their independence from Orion—Hale's Beacon being one such system.

And so, after some brief ceremonies and discussions on currency to be used in trade, the TSF and ISF ships were granted permission to travel to Hale's World, where the crews began to enjoy some much-needed shore leave.

Though Svetlana was happy for the reprieve, she'd not

trusted the locals at all when they first declared their intentions to be peaceful. She still wasn't entirely certain as to what their ultimate goals might be, but it had seemed like a shame not to avail themselves of the hospitality.

Even so, more than enough crew remained aboard the ships to keep them operational, and a dozen vessels were always above the planetary capital.

A part of Svetlana had worried that the show of force would send the wrong message, but the rest of her didn't care. Her fleet's mission in the PED was to distract the Orion Guard, to divide their attention, and weaken their reserves—not make nice with the local systems.

Not that the admiral hadn't done her best to have the best of both worlds. She felt as though the Hoplite fleet had left most systems better off than they'd found them.

However, she now had to solve the mystery of Widows on Hale's World.

As she considered the enemy's endgame, the pinnace lifted off from the lot and sailed over the lodge as it threaded the peaks while gaining altitude. Svetlana half-expected a surface-to-air missile to streak out from the woods below and strike the craft, but no threat appeared, and she drew a deep breath, grateful for the lack of excitement. Before long, the blue skies outside the craft turned black, revealing stars hidden by the glow of the world below as the pinnace approached a cluster of ships in geosynchronous orbit.

The *Cossack's Sword* lay in their midst, the admiral's home for nearly the past year. Being in close quarters surrounded by enemies had created a strong sense of family on the ship, and though she wished her holiday hadn't been cut short, a part of her was eager to be on the other side of the ship's hull.

The thoughts brought up memories of the Vale. It had been years since she'd been home and seen her children or grandchildren. The idea that perhaps the war with Orion could be over gave the admiral hope that she'd be able to see her grandkids before they were too old for her to pick up and hug.

<Ten minutes,> the chief at the pinnace's helm called back.

She nodded absently. <Thank y—>

The admiral's utterance was interrupted as something hit the pinnace. A rending sound reverberated through the hull, centering directly above Raini, where a hole began to open. Svetlana reached behind herself and pulled a pulse rifle off the rack, firing into the opening before she'd even unbuckled her seat's harness.

For a moment, the admiral saw a ghost of a figure, and fired again, a soft grunt rewarding her efforts.

Then movement out of the corner of her eye drew her attention toward the rear of the craft. Something hit her in the face, and brilliant light flared, only to be replaced moments later by darkness…then nothing at all.

A SIRIUS DECISION

STELLAR DATE: 05.12.8950 (Adjusted Years)
LOCATION: ISS *Carthage*, orbiting Victoria
REGION: Kapteyn's Star System, Alliance Controlled Territory

"Krissy doesn't think we should hit Sirius," Joe said as Jessica stepped off her pinnace in the *Carthage*'s cavernous A1 dock. "She thinks we should save our strength for Sol."

"Last I checked, we don't answer to her," the lavender-skinned woman said. "She's probably one of their best tacticians, but we've spent more time dealing with Sirius than just about anyone."

Joe pursed his lips and nodded. "Sure, five thousand years ago."

"C'mon," Jessica shook her head and crossed her arms. "You know they haven't changed. Their descendants in Bollam's World held the same shitty values, and Sirius itself still maintains their fucking 'Luminescent Society' with their slaves and light worship and all that crap."

He hadn't expected so much vehemence from her, but he supposed that after swearing to protect Kapteyn's Star, seeing so much chaos and destruction come at the hands of the Sirians while she'd been forced to retreat had been more than Jessica could handle.

"If it makes you feel any better, we're not going to follow her lead on this," he said as they walked across the deck toward the lift bank. "Jason has backed our plan, and we're going to make the jump as soon as the S&R ships arrive to help clean things up around Victoria."

"I'm not shocked," Jessica's lips formed a thin line. "He's taken more shit from Sirius than any of us."

"Surprised he doesn't want to come with," Joe replied,

nodding in agreement. "But I suppose someone needs to guard the home front."

"And wait for Tanis and Sera to return."

Joe bit his lip, nodding in agreement. "Yeah…for me…I can't handle the waiting anymore. I just need to be doing something."

"And the girls?" Jessica asked.

"Back at New Canaan. The *I2* is still at New Sol, supporting Krissy as she figures out what the hell to do with an empire the size of Orion."

Jessica snorted. "Give me a pitched battle any day over that shit-show."

"I hear you there. Remember when I was just an ace pilot, and you were only a detective?"

"Ace pilot?" she asked with a laugh as a lift car arrived, and the pair stepped in. "I think 'cocky flyboy' is a far better description for what you were."

"Oh?" he chuckled. "Well, then, 'oversexed cop' is what you were."

She held up a finger and shook her head. "Agent, not cop. Don't go getting those confused."

"You've been both over the years."

Jessica sighed, recalling other roles she'd filled, her thoughts flitting back to her own children, wishing she could do more than exchange a few words over the QC with them. "I've been pretty much everything."

"Shoe saleswoman. Ever done that?" he asked with a wink.

A smile danced across her lips. "Admiral Evans, you won't trip me up that easily. Yes, I've done even that."

"Shit…that's the most esoteric thing I could think of."

"You need to bolster that imagination of yours."

The lift doors opened, and she followed Joe out into a maglev station, then boarded a waiting car that took them forward to the bridge.

Jessica had never been aboard the *Carthage*, and though there were small deviations from its template, the *I2*, they were minute, and, in a way, it felt like being back aboard the ship that had been her home for many decades.

Her thoughts drifted to Tanis, and she found herself fervently hoping that the other woman would return soon. They'd always sworn to grow old together, sit on a porch and watch their children's children grow up.

Not that we'll ever grow old anymore....

It was a thought that had been rattling around in her brain more and more as the allies closed on their enemies' homeworlds.

What am I going to do after this is all done?

The old promise to Tanis still held sway; she really *did* want to spend a decade or so on the world of Carthage, actually relaxing for once in her life. But after that...Star City.

Even though it had been a decade since she'd lived there with her children, she'd spent decades in the world inside The Dream, and it beckoned to her—not to mention what lay beyond.

Now that she knew what Star City truly was, who lived there and what it had become, she wondered what purpose there really was to humanity's eternal struggles.

The people within the dyson sphere possessed the machinery of ascension: a surefire way to elevate humans to the next phase of existence. Consistently, predictably. It rendered all other purpose and struggle moot.

And yet, if peace wasn't achieved in the galaxy at large, even Star City was doomed to fall.

A never-ending battle between chaos and order.

The pair rode in silence until the train stopped at the bridge station, and they exited, walking the short distance to a conference room that mirrored the *I2*'s.

Within sat Ophelia, the *Carthage*'s captain, as well as Alyse, the ship AI's avatar.

"Captain," Jessica nodded to the woman in greeting before smiling at Alyse. "Glad to see you're doing well in your new position."

"You too, Jessica. Your liberation of Kapteyn's Star means more to me than you can know."

"I think I have an idea…plus what we found on Tara."

"Yes!" Alyse said with an infectious grin. "We'd all resigned ourselves to the belief that the Sirians had utterly destroyed what we built here, only to find that some made it to Procyon and beyond, while others seem to have disappeared…."

Joe nodded as he filled a coffee cup at the counter. "It's an enticing mystery, but not what we're here for today."

Jessica selected a glass and filled it halfway with the red wine from the decanter on the table before taking her seat. "But believe you me, it's a mystery that we'll solve at some point."

Everyone expressed agreement, waiting for Joe to sit and take a long draught of his coffee.

"I plan to destroy Sirius," he said after setting the cup down. "Utterly. It only seems fair."

"Do you mean that you'll raze their worlds?" Ophelia asked, eyes wide.

"No, those we'll leave for the Noctus. But the Lumins will see their stations destroyed and their cities leveled. Once we crush their militaries, we'll give the civilians time to evacuate our targets and exit the system. If they remain, they'll die. It's time we wiped these people from the galaxy."

"Are you sure?" Jessica asked, a little surprised by the vehemence in his voice. She shared his sentiment entirely, but had counted on him being the voice of reason that would keep them all from going too far overboard.

"I'm not planning genocide or anything," he said, brows

lowered. "But they won't have a place to call home when we're done."

"Given the ships that escaped Kapteyn's Star, their forces will number close to half a million," Ophelia warned. "How will we take them on without this turning into a protracted fight? You know they'll eventually use the Noctus as human shields, threatening to kill them all in order to bring us to heel."

Joe steepled his fingers. "We're authorized to use picotech."

"Shit," Jessica whispered. "You really want to give it to them."

"I do," he replied. "Governor Andrews is also on board with this. He'll get it approved by parliament before the deed is done."

Jessica stared into her friend's eyes, wondering at the cold fire that burned within. Something had changed in him in recent months, since his daughters had left on their mission aboard the Widow ship.

She supposed she knew what it was, as it burned within her as well.

We just need this war to end.

It had only been two years since Orion—aided by the Hegemony and Trisilieds—launched its attack on New Canaan, but so much had happened in that spread of time that it felt like a thousand lives. Add to that the twenty years spent searching for Finaeus Tomlinson, and the return trip, and the struggle was beginning to feel eternal.

TO END ALL WARS

STELLAR DATE: 05.14.8950 (Adjusted Years)
LOCATION: ISS *Andromeda*, approaching Holden
REGION: Jewel Star System, Trisilieds Kingdom

The shuttle eased into the *Andromeda*'s main bay, settling gracefully on the cradle's arms. The small craft was clean, but still bore the look of a vessel that had been worn and battered over decades of service.

Corsia walked toward the ship as the ramp extended, pulling up its service record only to find that the craft's hull had been laid on Luna ten years before the *Intrepid* had left Sol.

"How in Jove's red splotches did something so old end up in my fleet?" she asked aloud as the shuttle's door opened to reveal Colonel Angelique.

"Beats me," the woman said as she ambled down the ramp. "It's as solid as they come, though. Thing takes a lickin' and keeps on tickin'. Plus, someone saw fit to furnish it with stasis tech, which made it just the thing to use for your little roundup."

"You got all four?" Corsia asked, though she knew that there was no way Angelique would have shown up if she hadn't.

The colonel nodded as she reached the base, and turned to watch a group of techs, each carrying a CriEn module. "You sure about this, Admiral? You already have four aboard. Won't this do funky-bad things to spacetime?"

Corsia snorted a laugh. " 'Funky-bad, Colonel?"

The woman shrugged. "I do actually understand the deleterious effects on the local stability of spacetime that arise from drawing on too much vacuum energy, I just prefer my simpler description. The universe wants to be smooth...even in vacuum. Eight of these on your ship will make it unsmooth."

"Sorry," the admiral inclined her head as the specialists from the shuttle handed the cores over to Jim's team of engineers, who would take them to their designated locations. "I'm a bit out of sorts. I'm still getting used to the physiological feedback loops one gets from an organic body."

"I thought you'd be used to those by now, ma'am," Angelique replied.

"I spent a long time hooked up to this ship." Corsia gazed around the bay. "Something you may not be aware of is that ships create those feedback loops just like a body. It takes time to adjust to the differences."

The colonel cocked an eyebrow. "Are you telling me that ships can feel stress?"

"Absolutely. And remember, 'feeling stressed' is your brain's interpretation of data from your body. Your body doesn't have a feeling about the stress, it's having a specific physiological response to conditions. The same is true of a starship."

A grin formed on the other woman's face. "I'm going to start asking my chief of engineering how my ship 'feels'. I bet he'll love that."

"Send him my way if he doesn't."

"So, back to my question about funky-bad things...."

Corsia placed a hand on the colonel's shoulder. "We'll be traveling so fast that localized disturbances will be minimized."

Angelique sighed. "If you say so...just don't die. I don't want the responsibility."

"Even if it comes with a shiny star on your lapel?" the AI asked.

"Hell no," the colonel shook her head. "Once you get above colonel, all the fun gets sucked out of the job."

"Really?" Corsia smirked. "Look what I'm about to do."

The other woman's face became serious, and she heaved a sigh. "You're about to take an incredible burden on your own shoulders to save the rest of us...and the enemy. We won't forget it."

"You'd do the same," Corsia replied.

"I would." Angelique gave an assertive nod. "Still will. You say the word, and we'll stick those cores on my ship, not yours."

"No," the admiral squared her shoulders as she shook her head. "My history—this ship's history—adds a layer of protection you wouldn't have. Don't worry, we'll all kick back in a bar on Carthage once this is over. Swap lies and laugh about how the kids don't get what we went through."

"Imma hold you to that." Angelique placed a hand on top of Corsia's before giving her a nod. "Good luck, Admiral."

"Thanks. We're gonna need it."

* * * * *

Jim remained below in engineering, watching over a sea of holodisplays, with his teams spread throughout the ship, ready to take action if things went awry.

Sephira stood next to the holotank, while Corsia sat in the command chair, hard-Link cable connected to the base of her skull.

"I really should be the one to do it," the captain said. "You're too important to risk."

"Is there an echo?" the admiral asked with a laugh. "It has to be me that flies the ship, Sephira. Not only because I need to take the blame, if it comes to that, but because I have more experience with this."

Her daughter arched an eyebrow. "With shredding spacetime?"

Corsia shrugged. "Bob and I had a number of long conversations about the effects. He knew how to mitigate them, and though he didn't share a lot of details, I believe I know what to do."

"That makes me feel so much more confident, Mom."

The admiral straightened and addressed the crew over the general shipnet. <*Thank you all for volunteering to stay on for this. It means a lot to me that you're doing this, and officially, you're all under orders, so if there's blow-back, it'll fall on me. The vector is locked in, we're boosting in t-minus two minutes.*>

Section heads sent back acknowledgments, every one of them without reservation.

Other than a smattering of confirmations of readiness and fleet status reports, the bridge was silent the final minutes before the *Andromeda* surged forward from the ranks of the Twelfth Fleet.

"Engines at maximum burn," Helm reported. "Spooling out the AP nozzle."

"Very good," Corsia replied as the vessel dove toward Holden, shifting above the ISF fleet so as not to hit them with engine wash. "Burn at marker A."

"Aye, ma'am," Helm reported, then paused several seconds. "Burn initiated."

The ship picked up speed, the delta-v with Holden climbing above ten thousand kilometers per second, passing eleven thousand a few seconds later.

Ahead, the small planet was little more than a dot on the forward display, markers showing the positions of fleets and shipyards. Population estimation sat at over one hundred million people all told—small for most worlds, but not such a small number for Corsia to weigh in the balance.

"Targeting our wing," she announced aloud as the distance to Holden fell under ten light seconds.

A marker changed from red to white on the display. A

hundred ships that would cease to exist in five minutes.

"AP drive at one-hundred-twenty-percent rated output," Helm said, the woman's tone steady. "Increasing annihilation at Mark B."

"Good," the admiral replied, noting that Jim had signed off on the output increase.

A fleeting thought crossed her mind that it would be a damn shame if *they* blew up instead of the enemy, but to survive the concentrated firepower of a hundred thousand enemy craft, they needed as much velocity as possible.

<*Are we loaded?*> she asked the chief responsible for ordnance.

<*Yes, ma'am. The warheads are primed, and the missiles are in the tubes. We're ready to fire on the designated marker.*>

<*I'll send the launch command. You've done your part.*>

There was a moment of hesitation, and she knew he was debating challenging her.

<*I applaud what you're thinking, Chief Carr, but this has to be me.*>

<*I…I understand. I hope it works, ma'am.*>

<*Me too.*>

As they had spoken, the ship passed five light seconds, now traveling over thirty thousand kilometers per second. By the time it reached Holden, the *Andromeda* would be moving at over 0.1c.

At two light seconds from its target, the stasis shields began to flare from impacts.

"Railshots, ma'am," Scan announced. "Looks like they're flinging a lot of mass at us."

"Should we enable a jinking pattern, ma'am?" Helm asked.

Corsia shook her head. "No. We don't want to lose v. Unless the kinetic energy rises above the loss in delta-v, stay on course."

"Understood, Admiral."

"That's already a hell of a lot of weapons fire," Sephira commented as the forward scan became occluded by the brilliant flare just a dozen meters in front of the ship's nose.

"Deploy scan probes and relays," Corsia announced, her voice far calmer than she felt.

Using probes and relays to get a view of space ahead of them would make for a one-second delay, but there was no way around it.

Flying blind into the jaws of death.

The Trissie fleet formations were still in place over Holden, their overlapping umbrellas of protection shielding the shipyards and the world below from the ISF, and any marauders. The target formation was slowly passing between the world and the *Andromeda.* One minute from its demise.

The ISF ship passed within one lightsecond's distance, and the enemy ships opened fire. Half a million beams struck the single ship's stasis shields, matter being annihilated against the impenetrable barrier.

"Enact your pattern," she ordered the helm officer.

As the *Andromeda* approached the planet and its defenders, Corsia altered her perception of time, increasing her sampling rate, speeding up her mental processes, until each second was like an hour.

Though it was unlikely that the enemy knew what she had planned, it was equally unlikely that they would expect it to be beneficial to them. As such, picket forces were boosting to intercept the *Andromeda*, engine flares stretching out a thousand kilometers as fleet divisions repositioned.

"Pattern has us in the pocket," Helm announced, the words reaching Corsia's ears with extreme lethargy.

She didn't respond, as slowing down her thoughts to be something that could be put into words would be too distracting at the moment.

Enemy fire intensified, relativistic particles striking the

stasis shield with more energy than a red dwarf star emitted in an hour. The energy blasting back at the Trisilieds fleets was its own sort of weapon, blinding them as much as the *Andromeda*.

Throughout the ship, all eight CriEn modules drained zero-point energy from space around them, funneling unimaginable amounts of power into the stasis field generators and graviton emitters, keeping the bubble in place around the ship.

She performed a careful dance with their power draws, taking measures to shift draws by the nanosecond, finessing the energy flows to keep spacetime itself from destabilizing around the ship.

Based on Corsia's projections, they were seven seconds from the apex, the point where the largest number of enemy ships would be able to fire on the *Andromeda* with maximum efficiency.

Already, quantum-level fluctuations were taking place around the CriEn modules, picoscopic rifts in what normally appeared to be a smooth vacuum between atoms, all supported on the quantum foam.

Her breath caught as she worried that she'd bitten off more than she could chew.

If spacetime tore apart, it could very well swallow the enemy fleets and the planet they encircled in a reality rift that would —

Would what? Will it be a doorway into another universe? Higher dimensions? Or is it just raw annihilation?

No matter what, she hoped not to find out. Her goal was simple: kill as few of the enemy as possible while still forcing them to stand down.

Then the *Andromeda* reached the apex, and the rifts grew from pico to nanoscale, then they became microscopic. Through them, she could see a new sort of nothing...and everything.

Am I seeing what Bob sees? Is that ascension?

Then the ship passed beyond the peak intensity, enemy fire dropping off precipitously as the *Andromeda* passed into their fleets' ranks.

From the apex of enemy fire to the time to launch her own weapons lay a span of seventeen microseconds. They passed by in near-agonizing sluggishness, until the moment came, and Corsia watched the twenty missiles fly from the *Andromeda*'s rear tubes.

It was twice as many as needed, but two were vaporized the moment they passed beyond the ship's shields, and three more only survived another second.

Fifteen found their marks, antimatter-pion engines firing coherent streams of gamma rays as they tore through space toward the ships Corsia had targeted.

The vessels that would soon be no more were a grouping of light and heavy cruisers, a few destroyers mixed amongst their ranks. Twenty thousand souls.

The warheads erupted, each flinging a hundred tiny rods at the targets, dozens of the deadly rounds being destroyed by point defense beams, but still too few. The weapons would hit.

With the *Andromeda*'s v compounded with their own, the rods hit shields at over half the speed of light. Flares of energy as bright as any nuclear blast lit up space, burning down on the planet below.

By now, the ISF ship was tens of thousands of kilometers past Holden, and Helm brought them about, burning the engines to bring them back toward the Twelfth.

Corsia kept her focus on the hundred enemy vessels they'd targeted, watching with grim satisfaction as the ships began to dissolve. Every single one of them.

"I read picoswarm on each of the targets," Scan announced, the words taking a hundred times longer for the man to speak than it did for Corsia to parse the source data.

Ship's optics tracked the event, along with the drones Corsia had released, feeding the image of a hundred ships dissolving while escape pods began firing from the far sides of the vessels.

It only took a few minutes for what had once been solid matter to be ground down into subatomic particles, dust in the interstellar wind.

"Hail them," the admiral ordered Comm.

It took several minutes for Admiral Emiria and her sister to answer, both visibly shaken.

"You..." the woman whispered. "You swore never to use that."

"I did?" Corsia placed a hand on her chest. "I recall no such oath."

"You know what I mean," the other woman hissed. "Your own people declared it a war crime."

The ISF admiral shrugged. "In extenuating circumstances, it's allowed. But I hope it serves up the message you need to hear: we're going to win. No matter how long it takes, you can't stand against us."

Even as she spoke the words, half of Corsia's thoughts were on what she'd seen through the rifts, the wonders that lay beyond the bounds of spacetime.

When all of this is over, I need to talk to Bob. I need to understand.

"Will you just grind us to dust with your picoweapons?" Emiria asked in a hoarse whisper, her question barely heard by the AI.

"I will," Corsia said after regaining her focus on the here and now. "Unless you do as I've ordered. Abandon your ships and make for Tieranon. There doesn't need to be any more death."

The Trisilieds admiral straightened, a look of resignation in her eyes. "Very well. We'll do as you order. I value the lives of my people enough not to lose them in a pointless slaughter."

The ISF admiral nodded, a feeling of weariness settling over her. "Finally, you understand what's been going on for the past eight months."

The enemy cut the connection, and Corsia leant back in her seat as the bridge erupted with cheers.

Finally. We'll get to go home.

ENHANCEMENT

STELLAR DATE: 05.12.8950 (Adjusted Years)
LOCATION: Unknown, Hale's Beacon System
REGION: Midway Cluster, Orion Freedom Alliance Space

Consciousness returned to Svetlana cyclically, waves of lucid thought followed by collapse back into the inky blackness that enveloped her mind.

Eventually, a threshold was crossed, and the admiral managed to secure a tenuous toehold on the world beyond her mind. Her ears managed to deliver sound into her brain in a way that began to make sense, and the feeling of being in a relatively small room settled over her.

There was a hum in the air, low, throbbing. It was the sound of a fusion engine bonding atoms together; vibrating the bulkheads to produce its unique tone like a single, massive speaker.

Other machines were closer, their sounds crisp, pitches higher, reaching her ears over shorter distances. Air hissed in through vents overhead, then a scrape…like a foot pivoting.

"I see you're finally joining us," a woman's rasping voice said, drawing out the sibilant sounds like a snake with bronchitis. "I'm glad. I need you to be fully conscious for the next phases, and it's better if you come out of it on your own."

The admiral drew a deep breath, daring to test her voice, but not her eyes. "What are you doing with me? What phases?"

"What am I doing?" the woman asked, a note of sardonic mirth coming along with the words. "Just a little bit of payback. I'm going to do what I should have all those years ago."

Svetlana finally opened an eye, waiting what felt like

forever before it became acclimated to the bright room. When her surroundings finally became clear, she was not surprised by the sight that met her gaze.

A Widow, encased in her form-fitting black armor, like a human-shaped beetle, bent on her destruction. That, however, was not as concerning as the room, which was clearly a ship's medbay.

"Did you hit me in the head that hard?" the admiral asked.

"No." The Widow shook her head. "Well, yes, but that's not why we're here. I'm making some...alterations."

The word was delivered in such a way that Svetlana knew it had to be bad news. Worse than bad news.

"Are you making me into a Widow?" She whispered the question, unsure of how she'd deal with the answer.

To her relief, the woman gave a derisive laugh. "Of course not. That's not how it works. There's no reason to do so... you're so inferior to even the least of my daughters that I don't think such a thing would be possible. No, I have a different plan for you, Admiral Svetlana. I'm going to turn the tables on those meddlesome girls and their mother with delusions of godhood."

"What are you talking about?" Svetlana demanded. "What meddlesome girls?"

"Good, I didn't think you'd heard the details of what happened at New Sol yet."

"I heard that Orion has fallen. Kirkland is in custody." Svetlana didn't bother to hide her smile. "Your side lost."

"*My* side?" The Widow barked a laugh. "I was never on Kirkland's side. He was just a vehicle, a convenient stooge. But you see, they all think I died at New Sol when the *Perilous Dream* was destroyed." The ebony figure leant closer. "But I was not. I live, and if I cannot be the power behind the throne in Orion, I'll destroy the thrones of others." She straightened, laughing softly. "I'm told revenge is very cathartic."

A fear-laced realization formed in Svetlana's mind. "You're *her*. You're Lisa Wrentham."

"There is no Lisa Wrentham," the Widow said as she turned away, busying herself with something outside of Svetlana's field of vision. "She died millennia ago. I am A1."

Cold sweat formed on Svetlana's forehead. "What are you doing with me?"

"With you?" A1 cocked her head to the side. "Nothing yet. Right now, I'm doing things *to* you."

The admiral didn't press for clarification, certain she didn't want details, but the other woman provided them nonetheless.

"You might have heard about how Tangel's daughters infiltrated my hive, replacing me with Cary, the abomination's daughter. Those three girls brought about the fall of Orion in a way that I had, admittedly, not foreseen. To put it bluntly, they pissed me the fuck off. Destroying their mother is still paramount, and to do that, I first need to infiltrate New Canaan. Of course, *I* can't do that, but you can, Admiral Svetlana."

The admiral gritted her teeth. "You'll not turn me. I have the best neurological and mental protections the TSF has to offer. I'll die before you have your way with my mind."

A1 waved a hand in dismissal. "Girl, I devised half of those protections. Trust me, there are many ways I can worm into your mind. The best part is, you won't even know what I've done until it's too late."

"They'll stop—" Svetlana's utterance was cut short by A1 snapping a finger. She *thought* the end of the sentence, but her mouth was no longer receiving orders from her brain.

"I'm sure you were going to make some sort of desperate threat that's really just a plea in disguise, but it's not really going to have an impact on me, so let's just leave you mute for now, OK? Not like you have anything interesting to say, anyway."

Inside her mind, the admiral railed against A1, desperate now as fear began to take hold. But it was no use. Bit by bit, she could feel things change in her mind, subtle shifts in her memories, core axioms, and beliefs. The problem was, as soon she felt the shift, the new thought patterns felt entirely normal, and the admiral couldn't even tell what had changed.

The process seemed to go on forever, but finally, A1 straightened and gave a nod of satisfaction.

"You may be unremarkable, Admiral Svetlana, but your brain is well behaved. That was a smashing success. Now, for this next part, you can take a little nap. No need to wear you out."

The room and all sound winked out of existence as though someone had simply snatched them away from reality. A moment later, she wondered what it was she had just been dreaming about, the memories fading as she woke up on a hard slab in a small, nondescript cell.

Her internal mods were still entirely offline, not even a date stamp showing on her HUD. Leaning over, the admiral scratched another line on the wall, marking the fourth time she'd woken from what she believed to be her nightly slumber.

Sebastian, Caldwell...you bastards better come get me out of here soon...I don't want to end up wherever these bitches are taking me.

THE OP

STELLAR DATE: 05.14.8950 (Adjusted Years)
LOCATION: ISS *Daring Strike*, Hale's Beacon System
REGION: Midway Cluster, Orion Freedom Alliance Space

Caldwell cursed under his breath as another batch of probes sent back a report containing little more than the temperature of empty space.

In the two days since Admiral Svetlana had been taken by Widows—or what everyone assumed were Widows—they had not found a single sign of the ship that had made off with her.

Though Orion stealth tech was inferior to the ISF's, finding a stealthed ship in a fifty-AU sphere of space was no small task. It could take years, and that was far more time than the searchers had. Even while maintaining stealth and a slow burn, the Widow ship could reach the closest jump point in one more day.

Then the admiral would be gone.

Every ship in the combined Hoplite fleet was scouring the routes to the closest points, Caldwell's cruiser amongst them. They'd deployed every probe in their possession, spreading eyes through the black in the hopes of picking up a gravitational waver, a spectrum shift, a minute occlusion, *anything*.

He was about to check on the ship's fab shops—which were building new probes as fast as they could strip unnecessary mass from the ship—when the scan officer spoke up.

"I've got something. A fusion drive just twenty light seconds from our position."

Caldwell was on his feet in an instant, striding to Scan's

station. "What's remarkable about that?"

"We've not picked up any ships on that vector since the search started, sir."

The colonel dragged a finger along his jawline. "That certainly smells like a stealthed ship making a final push to their jump point. What's their burn profile match, Lieutenant?"

"Nothing on record," the man replied. "Neither ours, the TSF's, or the local logs."

"Not that we can put much trust in the locals," Caldwell replied as he crossed his arms. "Pretty sure anyone on this ship could hack one of their beacons and seed bad data through their network."

The scan officer nodded. "Do it all the time, sir." He frowned at his console. "I have secondary readings from probes, and triangulation."

"Helm," the colonel turned to the ensign in the center of the bridge. "Get us there. Fastest course and burn profile."

"Aye, sir." The woman gave a curt nod. "Punching it to the max."

Caldwell saw that time to zero relative v was fifty-seven minutes—if the target didn't try to get away—and rose from his seat.

"Keep me apprised of any changes," he said, walking to the bridge's exit. "XO will be up here shortly."

"Aye, sir," the OOD replied. "We'll have hawk's eyes on that ship. Are you going over?"

Caldwell nodded. "Damn right I am. Svetlana saved our skins more than once on this little safari…it's time for me to repay the favor in person."

Thirty minutes later, he stood in the *Daring Strike*'s forward starboard bay with a platoon of ISF Marines, every one of them loaded for bear. The ship they were breaching was somewhere in the neighborhood of a large corvette, just over two hundred meters from prow to engine bells.

A platoon was probably overkill, but it would give them the ability to cover all egress from the ship, and ensure that no one would get away.

"You all know the target," Caldwell said as he paced in front of the platoon. "Getting Svetlana out alive is paramount. Nothing else matters. Enemy capture and intel are secondary objectives."

The Marines gave grim nods, none contesting the colonel's words—not that they would have wanted to. They'd all heard stories of the Widows and what they were capable of. Mercy was not on the menu.

Lieutenant Abby added a few words, and then Platoon Sergeant Rygis bellowed the men and women onto the two waiting dropships.

As was protocol, Caldwell boarded the same shuttle as Rygis, while the lieutenant stepped onto the other. The colonel stared off into the distance as the shuttle's rear door closed, willing himself to focus on the task at hand, to push all other concerns from his mind.

"Gotta check your seals," Rygis said as she approached him. "This thing leaks atmo like a sieve, so the moment we hit the black, we'll be leakin'."

"Seriously?" he asked while donning his helmet. "Why hasn't that been fixed?"

The sergeant shrugged. "Was on the docket, but something about making probes to search for a TSF admiral…"

Caldwell chuckled, then switched to the Link. *<OK, got me there.>*

<Sorry, sir, it's my job to keep the CO honest—no matter who it is.>

He held still while she checked his armor's seals. *<Wouldn't have it any other way, Staff Sergeant. If you didn't, how would I know what to do?>*

<You wouldn't, sir. Everyone knows that once you get above major, the Corps requires you to turn off half your brain.>

<Oh? What about officers below that?>

Rygis winked. *<So far as I can tell, the Corps doesn't issue brains to junior officers.>*

The colonel groaned and then checked Rygis's armor over before taking a seat.

Rygis walked up and down the rows once more, then sat next to the pair of squad sergeants, heads bent together.

Caldwell considered listening in on their conversation, but decided not to. They didn't need the old man making them any more nervous than an assault on a Widow ship already would be.

Not that they were green by any stretch of the imagination, but months of being out in the ass-end of nowhere, with no support lines and no R&R, was weighing on everyone.

<We're five minutes from intercept,> Lorne said to the colonel. *<They've tried to out-maneuver us, but they don't seem to have any antimatter, so it's just a matter of time.>*

<So much for us sneaking up on them,> Caldwell replied. *<Not that I'd really hoped for such a thing.>*

Lorne laughed. *<We're dumping a thousand-kilometer plasma trail out our ass, sir. They can see us from New Canaan.>*

<Good, maybe they'll send more bacon. I could use a BLT when this is over.>

<So could we all, sir. I've dropped a countdown on your combat net, bay doors are opening.>

Caldwell passed an acknowledgment, moving the counter ticking down to zero to the edge of his vision. He pulled up an external optic feed, tapping into a view of the Widows' ship.

The vessel was a flat oval, tapered a bit at one end to make it look something like a squished raindrop. The hull was nearly matte black, barely reflecting any light, even with active stealth systems turned off.

A nagging fear hung in the back of the colonel's mind, a worry that if the enemy ship were to kill engines and re-enable stealth, they'd never find it.

Don't invent impossible scenarios, he scolded himself.

The enemy ship was too hot now to hide. Its engines would bleed photons and ions for some time, even if the fusion process was halted.

His shuttle would approach the front of the enemy ship, and latch onto the craft's hull near a scan and comm cluster. The breach should be quick and efficient. Even if there were dozens of Widows aboard, they wouldn't be able to hold out against heavy Marines for long.

<*Any response to hails?*> Caldwell asked Lorne, knowing that if there had been, he'd be the first to know.

<*Nothing, though their weapons are coming online. They know they can't shoot at us, but they'll probably try to shoot at you.*>

Despite being bruised and abused, the Marine assault shuttles had their own stasis field generators, though no CriEns to power them. It was a strategic risk to put such valuable tech on ships that could be captured, but Caldwell didn't doubt the black-box-tech's tamper proofing. Even if he did, lives were more important than tech—that was something he believed in firmly.

Especially with there being so few New Canaan lives in the universe.

There was a small flutter in the a-grav beneath his boots as the shuttle lifted off its cradle and eased out of the bay doors. The other craft followed, both remaining within the *Daring Strike*'s shield, waiting for the optimal time to venture out and close the final gap between the ships.

<*Slipping out of the bubble,*> the pilot called back.

Caldwell watched from the *Daring Strike*'s feeds as the shuttle that bore him moved away from the ISF cruiser and boosted toward the Widow ship. The other shuttle followed after, and once both were clearly committed to the maneuver, weapon coverings slid aside on the Widows' ship and fired on the ISF assault craft.

The beams were shed harmlessly by the stasis shields, and after a few more volleys, the enemy ship ceased firing, likely waiting until after the shuttles latched on—which would require them to disable stasis shielding.

No such luck, Caldwell thought with a callous laugh.

A minute later, the shuttles reached the Widow ship's shields, the enemy wisely disabling theirs before stasis met gravitons. That event tended to blow the graviton emitters on the ship emitting them, and it showed that the Widows had been paying attention to the Hoplite fleet's action in the PED.

It was, however, not a great benefit to the enemy to disable their shields.

The moment they were down, the *Daring Strike* opened fire, making targeted strikes and destroying the Widow ship's weapons. With the risk of enemy fire removed, the two assault shuttles touched down, grappling the hull and disgorging Marines.

As much as he missed being in the van of an assault, Caldwell held back, waiting for Staff Sergeant Rygis to give the all-clear. Once she had, he exited the craft, maglocks holding his feet in place.

All around him, ISF Marines were moving across the hull, taking out comm and scan nodes, while keeping an eye peeled for hullcrawlers or any other type of automated defense.

Nearby, a fireteam was breaching the forward airlock, and Caldwell joined Rygis in observing their progress.

<By the numbers,> he said, nodding in approval.

<LT is already through hers.> Rygis jerked a head toward the rear of the Widow ship.

The colonel laughed. <It's not a competition.>

<You sure about that, sir?>

<OK, maybe a little bit of a competition....>

The Marines completed their airlock breach, opening the outer doors and setting up a grav shield on the hull to hold the ship's atmosphere in before breaching the second door.

There were risks in 'cutting open the can', as the Corps called it, but when dealing with an enemy as dangerous as Widows, sending in Marines two at a time through an airlock was a non-starter.

With the grav shield in place, the fireteam moved forward, first trying to open the interior doors via the control panel, but when that failed, two of them pulled plasma torches from their thigh pouches and proceeded to cut their way in. Behind them, the other two members of their team went prone, weapons drawn and aimed at the future opening.

Another team was set up on the hull, ready to add their beams to the mix should the enemy choose to defend the chokepoint.

As the torches made their final pass, Caldwell crouched behind the remains of a sensor bulge, his own rifle unslung as he watched the breach through the team's feeds.

The Marines had left four small sections of the doors uncut, and placed small charges on each before disabling their maglocks and moving to the top of the airlock and also going prone. If anyone was inside, they were going to have to pick which pair to deal with first...something that would likely be their last decision.

<Hit it!> Rygis ordered once the fireteam was in position.

Charges detonated with soundless puffs of smoke—at least, that's how it seemed from Caldwell's position—and the remains of the airlock door fell inward and landed on the deck, revealing an empty corridor that ended in a T, four meters in. The sides were lined with EV gear and what looked like several weapons lockers.

<Grav is online,> the fireteam leader announced on the

combat net before rising from the deck and advancing inside.

The moment the Marines stepped over the threshold, they fired light-refracting powder into the air. It would eliminate their ability to use stealth, but with Widows possessing their own advanced stealth capability, it was better to remove that technology from the playing field altogether.

They released microdrones, which flew to the T-intersection, and when it showed as clear, the pair advanced to that position and set up a mobile grav shield, while the other two members of their fireteam moved into the ship.

In short order, both squads, barring one fireteam guarding the shuttle and egress, were inside the ship. Four fireteams moved forward, while three worked their way across the ship to the port side.

While the vessel wasn't huge, it could easily hold hundreds of people. Something that made the lack of contact all the more unusual.

<*Status, Abby?*> Caldwell called back to the platoon's lieutenant.

<*We spotted one of those black bitches, but she ran off. Luckily, we're just smart enough not to race into an ambush. Our contact point and her direction of movement are marked on the combat net.*>

The colonel took a look. <*Seems like they're trying to draw you right into engineering.*>

<*Probably a lovely killbox there. We're looking for sections that look like a brig or a medbay…so far, just storage bays.*>

<*OK, keep me apprised. Rygis is going to port, and I'm taking a squad toward the bridge.*>

The lieutenant chuckled. <*She's already ditching you, is she, sir?*>

<*Pretty much. Caldwell out.*>

Abby signaled the same, and he turned his focus back to the corridor he was moving through.

Microdrone reconnaissance revealed that the ship had six

decks that ran its entire length; the center four had six corridors running the length of the vessel, while the upper and lower had four. The Marines of his squad split up across three of the decks, moving forward in search of the bridge.

With our luck, there won't even be one on this ship. Who knows how Widows operate?

They were getting close to the bow when the fireteam on the second deck reported in.

<Sir, I think we've found it,> their leader reported.

Caldwell tapped the man's feed and saw that the Marines had reached a foyer that was half the width of the ship, with three doors leading forward.

<Either that, or the mess hall,> he replied. *<I'll bring my team up, and we'll take a peek.>*

<Understood, sir.>

The team Caldwell was accompanying doubled back to a ladder and climbed up to the next level, firing a few more rounds of refractive powder into the air before advancing forward.

<Fuckin' creepy,> one of the women on the team muttered as they advanced down empty halls.

The colonel had to agree. He wondered if there was anyone other than the one Widow aboard. After Admiral Evans and his daughters had disrupted their operation, the division had to be in significant disorder. It was entirely possible that the woman they'd encountered had simply gone rogue, and was looking for leverage as Orion began to unravel.

A minute later, his team reached the bridge foyer, where the first fireteam had set up charges on the doors before taking cover behind pillars evenly spaced throughout the room.

<What's the word, Corporal?> Caldwell asked.

<They've got E-shielding on the doors. We can't get nano through, so we're gonna do it the old-fashioned way.>

<Works for me,> he replied, nodding for his team to cover

the other two doors in case whoever was inside tried to flank the breachers.

Once everyone was in position, the Marines set up a quick countdown, and then the door blew inward. A private leant out and tossed a ball through the smoke and into the bridge. The device shot probes out in every direction, creating a map of the space while furnishing visuals.

At first, it appeared empty, but then the multiple probes flagged three possible stealthed enemies.

One of the Marines shifted and took a shot, firing a rail-accelerated pellet through the door to hit one of the shapes. The round ricocheted off empty air, confirming enemy presence.

"This is your one chance to surrender!" Caldwell shouted. "We don't give two shits about this flying turd, so the next things we'll toss in will be grenades."

"Hold your fire," a voice hissed from inside. "We're coming out."

The colonel didn't believe for a second that the assassins would give up without a fight.

Before he could reply, the other two doors opened up, and weapons fire streamed toward the Marines.

<End them,> he ordered his Marines, a grim smile forming on his lips as rocket-propelled grenades flew into the bridge, tearing the space apart.

The first fireteam advanced, lobbing refraction powder rounds into the smoke-filled room before stacking up at the door.

A second later, shots rang out, and one of the Marines went down.

<Get me eyes on that shooter!> the corporal yelled as he and his team dropped.

<Marked!> Caldwell replied, pointing out where the attacker had fired from.

It was at the far end of the foyer, from behind one of the columns.

The second fireteam split up, two Marines advancing on that position while the others covered the doors and their comrades.

The colonel moved forward to support them, spotting movement through the middle bridge door as he passed by. A round hit his shoulder, and he dropped, rolling out of the line of fire—he hoped—before sending a stream of kinetics into the ruined room.

Two Marines from the first team slipped through their door, and a brief flurry of rounds were exchanged within the bridge before the corporal marked an enemy down. They continued to move through the bridge while Caldwell glanced back at the private crouched next to the downed man.

<How is he?>

<Punched through his armpit, sir. Holed his lung, but the suit's patched him up. He's out, though. Want me to revive?>

<Not yet, let's get this mess tidied up first.>

<You got it, sir.>

Caldwell moved toward the far door, one eye on the column further down the room where the fire had come from, and the other on the door. When he reached it, he pressed against the bulkhead and lobbed a passel of nano through.

For a moment, he thought he'd missed, as the feeds from the nanoscopic bots showed the foyer he was in. Then he realized what had happened, and ducked as an electron beam streaked through the space where his head had been a moment earlier.

He fired into the entrance, the shots streaking through empty air. Luckily for the colonel, the Widow was covered in his nanobots, and he used them to tag her location on the combat net.

A marker lit up two meters from him, and he rolled away

while two of the Marines from the second team opened fire. The first few rounds ricocheted off the Widow's armor, but then a railshot cracked her chest plate, and Caldwell added his own electron beam to the mix, the blue-white bolt of lightning flashing from his weapon to burn a hole in her torso.

At the far end of the foyer, a brief exchange erupted between the Marines and the enemy hiding behind the column, followed by the pair marking a kill on the combat net.

<We're clear in here, as well,> the first fireteam's leader announced from the bridge. <I don't think the warranty is going to cover this mess, though.>

Caldwell rose and walked to the downed Marine, who was pushing himself into a sitting position. <You still combat-effective, Private?>

<Yes, sir, I am,> he said before rising to his feet. <Breathing hurts like fuck, but it's nothing compared to eating the chow in our mess.>

The colonel laughed. <Good to know. I want you to take it easy. Don't go rushing to the van. You've got a big 'shoot me here' marker on your side.>

<Understood, sir.>

Caldwell was about to walk into the bridge when Staff Sergeant Rygis reached out.

<We found her, sir! She's awake and well.>

A marker appeared on the combat net, two decks down and near the port-side hull.

<I'm on my way.>

A fireteam was moving toward the bridge on the next deck down. The colonel met up with them, and they worked their way toward Rygis's position.

Upon arrival, he couldn't help but smile with relief to see the admiral sitting on a featureless slab in a room that only contained a small san unit.

"Looking good, Admiral," he said in greeting. "Had a nice

little rest?"

Svetlana laughed. "Yeah, no one would leave me alone on the ski slopes, so I had to arrange a little kidnapping to get my R&R. You know how it is."

"Sure do," he replied. "Are you alright? Did they do anything to you?"

"Just a bit of light interrogation. Nothing serious. They didn't bring out the sharp-sharp knives, if that's what you're asking."

"Not exactly, but thanks for clarifying."

<She's good to move,> the corporal checking Svetlana over announced.

"Alright, then," Caldwell twirled a finger. "Let's get you back on Allied decks, Admiral."

"No argument here. I assume you're still going to scour this tub?"

The colonel nodded vigorously. "Just as soon as we get you off of it, we'll scrub it clean."

She rose and nodded at the door. "What are you waiting for, then? I need a fucking cup of coffee already."

SERVED COLD

STELLAR DATE: 05.14.8950 (Adjusted Years)
LOCATION: ISS *Voyager*, Victoria
REGION: Kapteyn's Star System, Alliance-Controlled Territory

The *Voyager* flashed into space a thousand kilometers above Victoria, a world Katrina had sworn she'd never lay eyes on again.

A lot of old promises are coming undone...

"Now that's a hell of a sight," Carl said, gesturing at the *Carthage*, which was lining up with the fifteen-kilometer-wide ring that was in the final stages of construction.

"Go big or go home," Katrina said with a soft laugh. "That's always been their motto."

"The ISF?" he asked, a brow cocked as he regarded her.

"Well, back when I met them, there *was* no ISF, they were just colonists."

Carl's brows lowered. "Not so sure about that, Kat. I think they were always the ISF, they just didn't know it."

<*I don't know what you're talking about,*> Troy grumbled. <*I certainly never signed up to be part of any damn military.*>

"How's that working out for ya?" Camille asked as she ambled into the cockpit and took a rear seat. "Did I pick up that update correctly? The Sirians have stasis shields?"

"Yeah." Katrina breathed the word. "No idea *how*, but I bet we'll find out before long."

"My money is on ascended AIs," Carl said.

"If the Core Devils had stasis shields, they would have used them on their own ships," Camille scoffed. "But Jessica took three of their ships out with the *Lantzer*."

"She's angling to make that hull as storied as the *Andromeda*." Katrina chuckled.

<*Got a long way to go before they stack up against the* Voyager,> Troy countered. <*We've got hundreds of years on them.*>

"It's not a competition, Troy." Camille shook her head, laughing as she spoke.

<*Like hell it's not. You don't know Corsia like I do, she takes a fuck-ton of pride in the* Andromeda. *She'd not take kindly to someone with a stronger legacy. This* **is** *an ISF hull, after all.*>

"I guess it is," Camille mused. "But this ship is older than the ISF now, so they can suck it. We win."

"In real-time, sure." Malorie's voice was a soft hiss, and Katrina jumped as the spider-woman materialized overhead.

"Shit," Carl muttered. "I kinda wish we never got stealth gear this good. Either way, I agree with Camille. *Voyager* trumps ISF in age."

Katrina shook her head. "I'll be sure to tell Corsia that when next we see her. We win the 'most awesome' award by virtue of years, so she can suck it."

<*I want to be there when you do,*> Troy said.

A comm signal touched the *Voyager*'s arrays, and Katrina accepted it, Jessica's warm voice entering her mind.

<*Wasn't sure you'd make it in time for the party.*>

<*Are you kidding? You know there's no way I'd miss this. Even if I did have to stare down at Victoria. All worth it for the chance to slam a missile into Brilliance Station.*>

Jessica chuckled. <*A worthy cause, that's for sure. I suppose if anyone can lay claim to that right, it's you.*>

<*As the only one who has set foot on that floating ball of self-importance, I feel like I do.*>

<*Careful,*> the admiral warned. <*You'll summon Jason. He's been there too.*>

<*He has?*> Katrina's brow furrowed. <*When was that.*>

<*Sorry, it's a story he prefers not to share. I only found out when a piece of intel came up during an investigation once. Not like it's a competition, though. We all have plenty of reasons to hate the*

Sirians.>

Long-forgotten memories wormed their way into Katrina's mind. Thoughts of the atrocities performed by her father and other members of Luminescent Society, how they'd treated the Noctus, the image of Markus's assistant—*Shit…what was his name?*

Try as she might, Katrina could no longer remember. Somehow, that felt like more of a crime than anything else she'd done in her long years roving across the stars.

<So, where do we slot in?> she asked. *<We with you?>*

<Your choice,> Jessica replied. *<Joe's commanding the* Carthage *and the* Starblade*. Both have DMGs now. They're going to hit the fleets while we take on softer targets.>*

Katrina sighed, leaning back in her chair, which earned a curious glance from Carl.

"Talking to Jessica," she told him before responding to the admiral. *<I can't believe they have stasis shields. I wonder if they have their entire fleet equipped with them?>*

<Not all the ships they sent here did,> Jessica replied. *<Intel we picked up is a little…unnerving.>*

<Oh?> Katrina wondered what the admiral was unwilling to say.

<We don't have independent confirmation, but they might have millions of ships at Sirius.>

<Millions?> she nearly choked on the word. *<How in the fucking stars did they get so many?>*

Jessica gave a rueful laugh. *<Hoarding, from what we can tell. Centuries of buildup without helping others.>*

<When you put it that way, it makes perfect sense.>

<So yeah, you'll probably want to join in with my division. We're gonna punch straight through to Brilliance and Incandus. If they do have stasis shields of their own, we'll make them engage us at close range around their most valuable assets.>

A plan began to form in Katrina's mind. *<I'm with you, then.*

What's our strategy? Military targets only?>

<We have to cripple them. That means their entire military industrial complex. We'll do what we can to avoid civilian casualties—especially Noctus, but Sirius has used them as human shields for far too long.>

Katrina clenched her hands into fists, battling memories that brought both guilt and anger to mind. Once, she'd been one of the oppressors, but that had changed after meeting Markus. She'd helped his people flee, and, to a certain extent, she had been trying to compensate for the sins she'd committed beforehand.

Plus all the ones I committed afterward.

She drew a deep breath, steadying her nerves before responding. *<I want to storm Brilliance. That's where we'll find the division SVPs who put the screws to the Noctus.>*

<You sure they're still there?> Jessica asked. *<It's been a while.>*

Katrina gave a caustic laugh. *<Not for me. I stop by to assassinate a few of them every decade or so.>*

<This does not surprise me. I've gotta split, there are a few things demanding my attention.>

<Sure,> Katrina's laugh turned kind. *<Jessica, the big admiral and all her responsibility.>*

<Don't remind me. I miss the good ol' days.>

<Don't we all. Let me know where the Voyager *slots in.>*

<Will do. And I'll sync you up with whoever leads the assault on Brilliance.>

Jessica disconnected, and Katrina leant forward, elbows on armrests. "This is gonna be good. Those assholes won't know what hit them."

"Think so?" Carl asked. "They'll outnumber us ten thousand to one. That's going to be one hell of a slugfest."

"With two I-Class super-carriers?" Malorie chittered and shook her head. "Each one of those things is like a thousand cruisers—especially now that they have fuckin' DMGs."

Carl frowned. "What the hell does DMG stand for, anyway?"

Katrina shrugged. "Dark matter generator?"

"They don't create dark matter, though," he countered.

"It stands for 'damage'," Camille said with a knowing smile.

"Seriously?" Katrina asked. "What the hell kinda name is that?"

"Have you seen those things fire? They do damage."

"Still doesn't seem like enough," Carl said. "The Sirian fleets aren't going to line up all nice for the ISF."

"That's why I'm so excited about this," Katrina replied with a laugh. "The ISF is sick of this war. I think Sirius hitting the Kap again was the last straw."

"You think they're going to use picoweapons." Camille's mouth stayed open after she finished speaking, eyes sparkling in wonder.

Katrina shrugged. "Take your pick of superweapons. They've got quite the assemblage of the things now. They could bring in Exaldi, neutronium bullets, you name it."

"Fuck," Carl muttered. "What if they fired neutronium slugs at Lucent? That white dwarf would go up like a supernova."

"Sure would." Katrina took a moment to imagine what that would be like for the Sirians, to see everything they'd ever built permanently erased. "But that would kill the Noctus. Not to mention the havoc the shockwave would wreak on nearby systems…like the one we're in."

"And Sol," Camille added. "Still, I agree that it would be rather satisfying."

<You all have been pirates for too long.> Troy's tone was mildly condescending. <You can't just destroy entire star systems.>

"We know," Katrina sighed. "But *sometimes*, it would be nice if we could."

* * * * *

"You sure she's OK to do this?" Iris asked from Jessica's side as they stood at the back of the *Lantzer*'s bridge, reviewing fleet status reports. "Being back on Brilliance has got to be hard for Katrina."

Jessica sighed and nodded. "Yeah, I imagine. Apparently, she's been back there a few times, though."

"Oh?" The AI cocked her head. "I suppose she's dealt with the past to some extent, then."

Jessica fixed her wife with a level stare. "She said she assassinates some SVPs each time she passes through."

Iris's mouth formed a circle, and after a minute, she uttered, "Oh."

Silent judgment passed from the AI, and Jessica groaned. "What am I supposed to do? Tell her she can't come to Sirius with us? It's her home system."

"That's exactly what you should do."

"She'd just go anyway. Then I'd have to deal with her running around unchaperoned."

Iris snorted a laugh. "You going to send her a minder?"

Jessica crossed her arms, hip cocked. "I was thinking about it."

"Oh *fuck* no. I'm not going down on some station to pew-pew a couple of asshats in glowy suits—no insult intended—while you get to have the battle of a lifetime up in space."

Jessica increased her skin's glow, and lowered her brow before winking at Iris. "Just kidding. You know I need you up here. We've got two more divisions, and there's a lot to coordinate. Plus, I don't think we're going to need to put boots on deck in a lot of stations, so I'll send someone special to keep an eye on Katrina."

"Oh? Who?"

"Well, Usef's battalion is available...."

Iris grinned. "Oh, heck yeah. Now I kinda want to go along!"

"Hey, whoa! You promised to pew-pew in space with me."

"A girl can change her mind."

"No." Jessica shook her head. "No she cannot."

"Pretty sure she can."

"Not when her superior officer says she can't."

Iris flashed a grin. "You're like my boss-wife. I need to find Trevor, and get him to make a ruling."

Jessica laughed and placed a hand on Iris's shoulder. "Times like this, I really wish you were still inside my head."

"So that you can make me do what you want?"

"No, because I miss this sort of back and forth, I know there's no reason we can't do it now, but it seems to happen less and less."

Iris's expression grew serious. "We could, you know."

Jessica glanced around the bridge, realizing that Karma and Lucida were watching them.

<Could what? Merge like Tanis and Angela?>

<Or not merge. It's possible—Finaeus thinks that the Transcend's method for dealing with Kronos disease could be extended to keep human and AI minds distinct in a longer-term implantation.>

A lump formed in Jessica's throat, and she swallowed it back down. <And you'd do that? For me?>

Iris placed her hand atop Jessica's. <For us. I miss it too.>

"Great," Jessica muttered. "The eve of battle, and now you've got me all weak in the knees."

Iris reached out and stroked Jessica's cheek. "I'm giving you something to fight for."

"Oh, don't you worry about that. I'm not dying in Sirius.

No fucking way."

HOP, SKIP, AND A JUMP

STELLAR DATE: 05.15.8950 (Adjusted Years)
LOCATION: ISS *Carthage*, Victoria
REGION: Kapteyn's Star System, Alliance-Controlled Territory

The *Carthage* was at the forefront of the ships lined up at the gates, its crew running through final rounds of system checks before the relatively short hop across the ten light years to Sirius.

Joe surveyed the shift crew as he entered the bridge, noting the somber mood. While no one in the ISF had been a part of the harrowing journey from Sirius to Kapteyn's Star five thousand years ago, no small number of those refugees' children were now serving in the fleets.

Many of them likely recalled their parents' stories as though they'd just heard them yesterday. They'd know about how the Sirians had pursued the *Hyperion* across ten lightyears just to exact punishment on the Noctus for daring to flee a life of oppression.

Though the oppressors were also long gone, the recent attack on the Kap had shown that the Sirians had changed little in the intervening millennia.

"Admiral Symatra," Joe said in greeting as he approached the AI's holographic projection, which stood brooding next to the holotank. "How do things look?"

"Like shit," she muttered. "Not sure how I let you rope me into this mess."

<Same way as always,> Kerr said. <How do you think I got saddled as the AI for this beast?>

"What are you talking about?" Symatra scowled. "You were purpose-born from Bob's mind. Joe didn't strong-arm you into this."

<No, but I got the 'We need you, there's no one else who can do the job', speech.>

Symatra cocked an eye at Joe. "I never got sweet-talked like that."

"That's because there was no need," he replied with a shrug. "You're one of the ISF's best tacticians, and you love being in the thick of things."

"I blame my mother," the AI groused.

"Which one?" Joe asked with a laugh.

"Like you have to ask. Angela has to be the most reckless AI that ever was."

Thoughts of Angela led to thoughts of where she and Tanis might be. He wished nothing more than to be in pursuit of his wives along with Sera, but he knew there was nothing to be done for it right now. The best medicine was distraction. Lots and lots of distraction.

"So, we've established that we look like shit, can you elaborate?" he asked the captain.

"Well, like always, I get stuck with the sorry leavin's," she said, gesturing at the holotank.

The display showed a thousand rail destroyers arrayed around the *Carthage* and *Starblade*. The ships had the 'nearly complete' look that had become a hallmark of the ISF fleet, especially the ones under the command of AIs.

<I can manage them if you want,> Kerr said with a soft chuckle.

"You just keep your eye on that black hole in your belly," Symatra shot back. "Let's make sure that thing doesn't tear us apart."

<No problem at all. Thing's barely an inconvenience.>

The AI glanced at Joe. "Can you tell him not to be so blasé about that?"

He couldn't help but chuckle. "You say it like carting around a black hole is the most dangerous thing we're doing right now."

"It's the most dangerous to *us*."

"Are the destroyers suitable?" Joe asked, steering the conversation away from the questions he knew Symatra wanted to ask—namely, exactly *what* weaponry they were permitted to use.

Despite his absolution for decimating the A1 defense fleet using picobombs, they technically were still forbidden except with the express approval from legislature.

"They're green across the board. A little light on ablative plating here and there, but they'll do."

"And the fighters?" he asked the ship's AI. "Are we fully replenished there?"

<We will be by the time we jump,> Kerr said.

"Speaking of which…" a smile formed on Symatra's lips. "Drone message just came back from our breach team. The interdiction network will be down on schedule."

Joe's lips drew into a thin line as he contemplated the impending battle. "Good. Let's begin final jump prep."

PART 2 – FIRESTORM

PUNCHING A HOLE
STELLAR DATE: 05.15.8950 (Adjusted Years)
LOCATION: *Sabrina*, Outer System
REGION: Sirius System, Hegemony of Worlds

"You told them *what*?" Cheeky barked at Fina. "We haven't even breached the control station."

"We're almost docked." Fina gestured at the forward display, which showed the station growing larger by the second.

"I think you forget that I'm captain now," Cheeky said through clenched teeth. "Just because I still helm *Sabrina* doesn't mean I'm not in charge."

Fina had the good grace to purse her lips and appear apologetic. "Sorry. I guess being back aboard has me falling into old patterns."

*<I feel like **I'm** the one who needs to be cloned,>* Sabrina said. *<Then each of you can have me.>*

"Then what'll I do?" Cheeky asked, glancing at the overhead before returning her focus to holding her approach vector. "How will I love three of you?"

<You'll just have to find a way. Or we can clone you—wouldn't be hard, to be honest. All the clones!>

"Fuck no," Nance shook her head. "I like being the only one of me. Besides, then there'd be three Mishas."

A cough came from the comm board. "You know I'm right here."

"Oh!" Nance glanced at him, eyes wide in surprise. "Sorry

103

about that, I had no idea."

"Fuck, Nance," Cheeky muttered. "Can you let it go already? That was four nights ago."

"Let it go?" The engineer shook her head vehemently. "Stars no. He made my favorite cake, and then put raisins—*raisins*—in it. I mean, seriously. I might take months to get over this."

"Your loss," the cook said. "I was planning to make another when this job is done—and we're all out of raisins."

"Uhhhh." Nance turned a sweet smile toward him. "Maybe I could find it in myself to forgive you."

<*I like how you still refer to official missions for the ISF as 'jobs', Misha,*> Sabrina said with a chuckle. <*It's been years since we've been flying under our own flag.*>

"Old habits and all that."

"Plus, you suck at staying in character," Nance added. "With most of our work being a little on the sub-rosa side, it's best that we all think of missions as 'jobs'. Less worry about slip-ups."

"Who are you accusing of slip-ups?" Misha demanded. "You want that cake or not?"

<*No one's getting cake till I get cleaned up,*> Sabrina spoke up before Nance could launch a salvo back at Misha. <*I'm covered in cargo netting, and my hull is red. **Red**.*>

"It's not your first time being red," Cheeky offered in an attempt to mollify the ship's AI.

<*I hated it last time, too.*>

"That was ages ago," the captain countered.

<*You swore never to do it again.*>

Cheeky placed a hand on her chest. "*I* didn't swear." She jerked a thumb at Fina. "She's the one who went and made poorly considered promises."

"That wasn't me." The blue-haired woman shrugged. "I'm just a clone."

<You promised pre-cloning,> Sabrina admonished. <Don't try to pull that with me.>

"Hey, I'm not in charge. I didn't make you paint yourself red."

"No one *made* anyone do it." Cheeky threw her hands in the air in exasperation. "This cargo company paints their ships red, so red we are. We all got into this life willingly, knowing that—Fuck! Look what you've all done to me. I *used* to be the fun one!"

Fina leant against the bulkhead next to the main display. "Sucks to be captain, doesn't it?"

Cheeky let out a gasp. "Never! I love being captain of my dearest *Sabrina*."

"I can't tell if you're referring to the ship or AI," Misha said with a laugh.

"Both."

<Both.>

"I'm glad some things never change." Fina's tone grew melancholy. "No matter what happens out there, inside this hull...somehow, it's just timeless in here. Nothing really changes."

<Sure they do,> Sabrina said. <We have chickens now. That's new.>

"OK, fair point," Fina nodded graciously. "But what changes there are just reinforce how magical it is here."

"No," Cheeky fixed her with a cool look.

"No?"

"Don't get all nostalgic. I did my time in the trenches. *I'm* captain now."

Nance snorted. "I don't think any job aboard Sabs gets you out of the trenches."

"You invoking my name?" Sabs asked as she appeared at the bridge's entrance.

"No." Nance shook her head. "I just think I'll hopelessly

mess up your names forever."

"There's an angle," Fina suggested. "Sabs and I could get another ship together."

<*Oh heeeeeeell no,*> Sabrina shouted in their minds while Sabs shook her head vehemently. <*No way are you separating us.*>

"Yeesh," Fina said. "It was just a joke. Honestly, I still have no fucking clue what I'm gonna do after all this shit is over. Sera's gonna run off with Jason and make little pilot kids of her own. Seraphina is running the Hand and loving it, and Krissy is a waaaaaay better president than I could ever be."

<*Somehow, I think there's something in the universe that you might enjoy.*> The former ire in the AI's voice was gone, replaced by sincere compassion.

"Maybe." The clone of *Sabrina*'s former captain straightened and brushed her hair off a shoulder. "I tell you all, though. Don't let anyone clone you. Fucking sucks being a copy of a copy. A third-rate version of a better woman."

"Fina—" Cheeky began, but the blue woman held up a hand, shook her head, and strode off the bridge.

"Fuck," Nance muttered when the door closed. "I guess she wasn't joking around as much as the rest of us."

"I should go talk to her," Cheeky whispered, wondering what she'd say.

Sabs placed a hand on her shoulder. "No, I'll go. You have a station to dock at. Everyone's counting on us."

"Great," the captain said. "No pressure."

<*We've got this. It'll be a cakewalk.*>

"Seriously?" Misha threw his hands in the air. "You just *had* to say that."

<*I feel like we laugh in fate's face so much that if we **don't**, that's when things'll go to shit.*>

"Things go to shit all the time," Nance said as Sabs walked off the bridge.

<Sure, but imagine how much worse it could get if we didn't tempt fate.>

Misha lowered his head into his hands. "That's not how it works, Sabrina."

<Whatever. I don't fear fate.>

"Oh, hey now," Cheeky glanced up at the overhead in alarm. "Let's not get carried away here, girl. Bearding the dragon in its lair is one thing. Walking up and bitch-slapping it is another altogether."

<I eat dragons for lunch.>

"Stars, we need to stop encouraging her," Nance muttered. "Look, we're almost docked, let's focus on that."

"Yes," Cheeky nodded as she powered down the fusion drives and flipped over to the grav drive. "Not as though this whole offensive fails if we don't do our jobs or anything."

* * * * *

Fina slammed a magazine into her favorite slug thrower and then checked the weapon's action and battery charge. Satisfied it was ready to kick Sirian ass, she moved on to her sidearms.

"I'd go easy on that," Sabs suggested as she walked into the ship's hidden armory. "You need it to hold up in combat, you know."

"I think it can take a rough reload," Fina replied, glancing at the weapon to double-check. "I might not know much, but I do know my own strength."

Sabs walked around the far side of the prep table. "What are you talking about, Fina? You're one of the most competent people I know."

Fina set the pistol she was holding on the table, and looked up at the AI. "You sure about that? Everyone treats me like I'm just some sort of comedic extra."

"Well, in their defense, you sort of put on that air. Like nothing matters and everything's a joke."

"That's because *nothing* matters. I'm not special or unique, I'm the leftover one who has no purpose. Tanis and Angela go missing, and no one even thinks to ask me to help look for them. Nope, Sera is the clear choice." Her voice cracked, and she looked down at the table, her hands balling into fists. "I love Tanis and Angela too. Just as much as *she* does."

"Tanis and Angela, or Jason?" Sabs asked in a soft voice.

"Both!" Fina shouted before turning away, her shoulders drooping. "All of them."

"I think I understand," Sabs said, nodding slowly.

"Oh?" Fina glanced over her shoulder at the AI. "How so?"

"Don't forget, I'm a clone as well. Not a child of an AI merge, but a straight-up clone of Sabrina. I know exactly what it feels like to be a stranger in your own home."

Fina nodded, feeling like an ass for treating Sabs differently than she would have treated Sabrina. "I guess we all have trouble knowing where to fit in sometimes, don't we?"

"Cheeky does, too. She's finally got the opportunity to step up and really take the reins, but now you're back, she wonders if maybe she *shouldn't* be captain with you here."

"Fuck." Fina hung her head. "After this job, I'll transfer away. I don't want to ruin things for her."

Sabs shook her head and reached out for Fina's hand. "That's not what I meant, I just wanted to remind you that this has always been a ship of misfits. We recently had four family members leave, and that's upset our flow. Just give things some time, and maybe have a chat with Cheeky to encourage her. Think of it, you could mentor her, help her feel more secure and empowered. I don't know what the future holds for you, but maybe that could be what you do right now."

Fina looked up, and her gaze met Sabs's very human eyes. She nodded. "When did you get so wise? I remember rescuing you from a junkyard, where you were not in a great place—mentally or physically."

A wry smile formed on the AI's lips. "There was this woman who believed in me and supported me."

"Jessica?" Fina asked with a caustic laugh.

Sabs crossed her arms. "Would you let anyone else get away with that self-deprecating shit? No, you would not."

Fina rolled her shoulders and sighed. "You know what, you're right. I wouldn't. Somehow, in my mind, I'd convinced myself that I'm not 'me', that I don't have permission to live as Sera, but instead only be a shadow of what I once was...lingering on when I should have faded away. Getting my ask kicked on Airtha had a bit to do with that, I think."

"Whew!" Sabs laughed. "You were getting downright poetic there. Glad you added some cursing."

Fina winked. "Well, if I'm gonna be me, we need to have some fuckin' shit going down around here."

"That's more like it. So, are you going to lead the infiltration?"

"Should I? Or does Cheeky like to do that sort of thing?"

"Depends on the day. I think here, she might like to stay close to the captain's chair—something you were never good at."

"I know," Fina laughed. "That's why I hired her."

Half an hour later, the ship was docked at the station, and the main bay was open. Nance and Cheeky stood at the entrance, reviewing the shipping manifest with the dockmaster, while a pair of loader drones hovered nearby, ready to begin unloading the cargo.

While the two women enjoyed a riveting conversation about the freshness of some special fruit that only grew properly on Incandus, Fina led Sabs and Misha onto the station, their ISF stealth gear letting them traipse right past the dockworkers and security.

One of these days, this is going to get old. Fina laughed to herself. *But not today.*

The station's bay wasn't much larger than *Sabrina's*, though large doors on either end likely led to more storage areas, while a smaller door in the center of the far wall would be the route deeper into the station.

It was currently closed, so the trio stacked up on one side, waiting for an opening.

They didn't have to wait long. Once the dockmaster counted himself satisfied with the manifest, Cheeky made a request to refuel.

"What are you talking about?" the man's tone was more than a little derisive. "We don't fuel up transport hulls. You're supposed to have enough for a round trip."

"Yeah, I know," Cheeky said with a nod, sounding genuinely remorseful. "Problem is, our regular stop had quotas in place and we couldn't top off. You know how it is, everything is going to prepping the defense fleet."

"Idiots," the dockmaster shook his head. "We're the first line of defense out here. They should know we can't be a fuel dump for every supply ship that stops by."

Cheeky lifted her hands. "Hey, I hear you. I don't know what this place is, but the scope up my ass to make sure all our shit was lined up clued me in that it's a big deal. Either way, we just need…" she glanced at Nance.

"Fifty tons of D2."

"What?!" the dockmaster coughed out the word. "*Fifty?*"

"You're out in the ass-end of nowhere." Cheeky waved a hand at the overhead as though that would somehow prove her point. "It's gonna take that much to get back to Incandus."

The man shook his head. "I can spot you twenty, that'll get you to a dozen different stations where you can top off. Not my job to send you on the way to wherever you want to go."

Cheeky let out a protracted sigh, and Nance shrugged.

"OK, fine," the captain finally agreed. "We'll take it. I assume you'll just bill it to the company?"

"Sure, yeah." He nodded to a control room situated halfway up the bay's interior bulkhead. "Grab and stash, Jonesy. Then hook these ladies up with twenty tons of D2."

Fina couldn't see the response, but the dockmaster seemed satisfied as he walked to the exit and waved the door open. With an invisible salute to Cheeky and Nance, who were now supervising the unloading, she followed the man out into the corridor.

She released a nanocloud and hopped the signal across the bots to communicate with the team.

<*OK, Misha. You know what to do?*>

<*You bet, one level down, sabotage the pumps to buy us more time. No problem.*>

<*Good luck, then,*> Fina replied. <*I think Sabs and I will only need about twenty minutes. Sirian tech is good, but we're better.*>

<*Damn right we are,*> Sabs added.

The group split up, the women going right while Misha went left. The facility was only lightly crewed—at least, it seemed that way, as they only encountered a handful of people in the passages, none of whom noticed the two stealthed infiltrators sneaking past.

Before long, they stood at the doors to the control room, where the control systems for the interdiction web were located.

<*Well, now we know where everyone is,*> Fina commented.

<*That place is **packed**,*> Sabs added. <*I count thirty people, and they don't seem to know how to sit still.*>

Fina gave a silent sigh. <*We should go with plan B.*>

<*Tell me that's not 'kill them all'.*>

<*Course not. We need them to think the network is still working. I was thinking we just set off an alarm or something.*>

The AI laughed. <*The ol' fire alarm drill? Like we did that one time down on Trio?>*

<You got it, Sabs.>

<Give me a moment,> she said as she eased down the passage and proceeded to tap into a network line. *<Wisely, fire alarm triggers are only on their wired network.>*

<Damn paranoid Sirians,> Fina muttered as she took a position directly across from the room's entrance.

<OK, in ten,> Sabs said, and moved into position beside Fina.

At the prescribed time, the alarm went off, a loud whooping siren blaring through the passage, causing Fina to wince as she watched the people in the control room perk up and look around.

For a long ten seconds, no one moved, but then a dozen people closest to the door rose and strode out into the corridor.

"This a test, you think?" one man asked.

"Beats me," another said. "Fire location is just down a level, though. I'll get eyes on, you prep the secondary control center."

"You got it."

<Secondary?> Fina asked as she slipped between the last two people to exit the room, tapping a hand on the sensor to keep the portal open long enough for Sabs to follow after.

<Sure, there's always a secondary system. We just have to plant our breach kit before they toggle control over there.>

The consoles inside the smallish room were arrayed in a tight semi-circle, and Fina sat in one while Sabs took another. The majority of the stations were still occupied with people who were alternatingly looking around in annoyance, or frowning as they continued their work.

<You manage the changes we need to make to their update code, I'll insert the worm,> Sabs directed.

<Look at you,> Fina replied, an invisible smile forming on her lips. *<All in control and everything.>*

<Was bound to happen eventually.>

The former captain shook her head while setting to her task. The thing with any massive networked installation, like the interdiction web around Sirius, was that it was set up with redundant update systems that rolled out code updates in a distributed fashion.

That meant Sabs's changes to the system would be overwritten in short order as the field emitters refreshed their codebases and applied patches and updates. Fina's job was to alter the deployment patterns to conveniently skip a segment of the web, but to report them as properly upgraded.

It took only a few small changes to effect, but she had to make them in a dozen places to ensure that no updates to the deployment system would overwrite her changes. The tricky thing was there was no way to test the changes, but based on the test rig they'd run trials on, it *should* all work.

<OK,> she said after a minute. *<I think I'm good to go.>*

<I'm going to need just a few more—>

"Hey, everyone," one of the men who had been first out of the room said from the entrance. "We've found the fault in the fire suppression system, but we have to trigger a response for it to reset."

"A response?" a woman sitting at the console next to Fina asked, an eyebrow cocked.

"Yeah, a suppression response."

"Seriously?" another man asked from closer to the center of the room. "That's gonna dump that powder shit everywhere."

The man at the entrance sighed loudly. "Yeah, it's a bitch. Let's just do it and get the wailing to stop. Then we can brush it all off and carry on."

"What a pain," the first woman muttered while another laughed.

"Worried about your pretty uniform?"

"Shut up."

"Look," the man at the entrance sounded annoyed. "We can do the staggered move to the secondary, then move back, or we can just dump some dust and deal with it."

A few protests rose from the group, and he coughed loudly. "I wasn't really asking your permission."

"Fuck." The woman next to Fina covered her eyes while working one-handed at her console.

<Where you at, Sabs? We're gonna be outed in a minute.>

<Less than a minute,> the AI replied. <But I'm all set. Let's roll.>

Fina rose just as the woman next to her surged to her feet, muttering something about not wanting to pick crap out of her teeth for the rest of the afternoon. They nearly collided, but Fina managed to stop short, and then follow after to where the man in charge stood blocking the door.

"Get back to your station, Karyn."

"I have an automated process running. I can let it sit for a minute."

"No," he shook his head. "Get back to your station. If you can't handle this inconvenience, I'd hate to think how you deal with a real emergency."

"Kal—"

"Don't 'Kal' me. Sit. The fuck. Down."

Karyn turned and slouched back to her seat, but Kal stood in the doorway, apparently deciding that he needed to block further egress.

<Suggestions?> Sabs asked.

<I'm gonna blow nano in his face, and blind him when the suppression runs.>

<Damn, that's brutal.>

<Open to sug—>

Nozzles popped out of the overhead and blasted a fine powder into the air, covering everything in a dusting of the material. Fina hastily released a nanocloud into Kal's face, and the man jumped back into the passage—probably because her figure was clearly outlined.

"The fuck?" he shouted, then brought his hands up. "I can't see, someone's here! What's going on?"

Fina didn't wait to see if anyone else had spotted them, she simply dashed out of the room with Sabs in tow.

"Hey! Stop!" a voice shouted from behind them.

Seconds later, the fire alarm died out, but a new klaxon began to blare.

<This isn't going so well,> Fina commented as the pair raced down the passage. *<I guess we're onto plan B.>*

<Cheeky,> she called to the ship. *<We're blown. We need plan C.>*

<C?> Cheeky asked with a nervous laugh. *<And that is?>*

<We gotta take the whole damn station—right after we disable their comms so they can't let the friggin' system know we're here.>

<Shit...what happened?> the captain asked.

Fina looked down at her powder-coated arms as she rounded a corner and flattened herself against the bulkhead. *<Don't ask.>*

<OK, I won't. You want us to kill comms?>

<We're closer, and our cover's blown,> Fina replied. *<You two armor up and storm the place. We'll circle back to the ship and get our heavy gear on.>*

Footfalls sounded down the corridor, and Fina got ready to take down the pursuer. It was one of the men who had first left the control room with Kal.

She swung out an arm, the edge of her hand slamming into the man's neck, sending his feet out ahead of his head, and dropping him to the deck like so much meat.

<That way,> Sabs pointed at an adjacent passage, and they dashed toward it, Fina delivering a blow to the man's head on the way.

<What do you think, just destroy comms?>

<We can't, the network updates to the interdiction web pass through the regular tower.>

<Seriously?> Fina shook her head. <Why the hell didn't we just slap a filter on the tower's data stream?>

The AI laughed. <Because we gave them more credit and assumed they'd have multiple transmission systems and parity checking. Looks like this place was rather hastily retrofitted to manage the network, and some corners were cut.>

<I guess we shouldn't complain they were sloppy,> Fina replied. <Makes things easier for us.>

<Does—>

Sabs was interrupted by Fina slamming into a woman striding out of a room and into the hall. Both tumbled to the deck, and the former Hand agent rolled onto her side and swung a boot up into the woman's head as she rose.

The blow caught the Sirian under the chin, slamming her jaw shut and shattering more than a few teeth.

<Huh,> Sabs grunted as she looked through the open doorway. <It's in here.>

<Really?> Fina struggled to her feet and peered inside to see a comm node with a trunk line leading up toward the hull. <Well, lookie there, some luck at last.>

She slapped a passel of nano on the woman's neck, knocking her unconscious, then rose to her feet, dragging the unconscious enemy into the room.

<Give me five,> Sabs said. <This one is going to be tricky.>

<You got it.>

Fina unslung her rifle and closed the door, hoping no one would find reason to check on the node.

* * * * *

<Just like old times!> Cheeky said as she fired on a pair of dockworkers, knocking both to the deck with a wide dispersal

pulse blast.

<*Old times?*> Nance asked, snorting derisively. <*More like 'just like all the time'. I think we've been typecast.*>

<*What are you talking about?*> the captain asked with a laugh as she ambled toward the two downed workers and dropped a lockIt on each. <*We're all the things. Need a station taken down? Send in* Sabrina. *Want to topple an anti-AI regime—or a human-murdering AI? Also* Sabrina. *Need to fly across the galaxy, and eff up everyone in our path?* Sabrina. *Not typecast; ambi-everything.*>

<*That doesn't even make sense,*> Nance said as she leapt up eight meters, her heavy armor easily propelling her to the catwalk that led to the small monitoring room, where a very frightened man huddled behind his console.

There was a brief flurry of activity, and Nance jumped back down just as the bay door opened.

"Shit!" Misha's voice came from the empty entrance as the two women swung railguns toward him. <*I mean…shit.*>

<*You want to stay on the ship for this next part?*> Cheeky asked.

<*Uh…yeah? Police action really isn't my thing. I'll cook a victory roast. How's that sound?*>

Cheeky nodded. <*You got it. Sabrina? Once he's aboard, seal up and deploy crawlers. I don't want anyone cutting their way in.*>

<*You and me both,*> the ship's AI replied. <*Which is why they're already out there.*>

<*OK, good. See you for that roast in a few hours, Misha.*>

<*Gonna need five. It's still frozen.*>

The captain laughed. <*Deal.*>

Nance was already out in the corridor, and Cheeky followed after, neither woman bothering to activate stealth systems. Their goal was to draw focus to them and off Fina and Sabs, and the only thing that mattered was keeping any distress signals from getting out. If the Sirian military learned that one of their control stations was under attack, the segment of the web they controlled would be shifted to another station.

And that would end our little party real fast.

They reached an intersection, and Nance pointed down to their right. *<Lift and ladder shaft there.>*

Cheeky nodded for the engineer to lead the way, then followed after, watching the other passages on her HUD via the nanocloud Fina had released earlier.

No enemies appeared, and the pair reached the lift bank without incident. Cheeky reached out to hit the car-summon control when the indicator showed both lifts descending.

"Over there." Nance gestured to a corner, and Cheeky followed, finally triggering her stealth.

Less than ten seconds later, the lift doors opened, and a dozen soldiers stepped out, clearing the area before moving down the passage. Once they were a few meters along, the two women stepped out of the corner, took aim, and opened fire.

A hail of railfire tore into the Sirian soldiers, cutting down three in the rear before any of them knew what'd happened. Two more went down as the squad turned, and then return fire streamed toward Cheeky and Nance.

The engineer was the first to dive out of the way, and Cheeky trailed behind, *after* she lobbed an EMP grenade into the passage.

<That was bracing,> Nance commented as she activated her stealth and moved toward the ladder shaft.

<Always fun,> Cheeky added as she set a detpack behind a conduit riser. *<Been awhile since I tore a bunch of assholes some new ones.>*

Nance was already up a level, and Cheeky saw that three of the enemy were moving back toward the lifts. She switched her rifle's fire mode and let fly with an electron beam, burning a hole clear through the bulkhead at the corridor's entrance, and sending the Sirians back as bolts of lightning arced through the space.

Satisfied that she'd bought enough time, the captain scampered up the ladder, following Nance up three decks before stepping out of the shaft and triggering the detpack.

A blast of fire burst out of the opening, nipping at the pair's heels as they raced down the passage to where the command room lay.

<*I hope we can get back down to the ship,*> Nance commented.

<*We still have the cargo lifts on the far side of the station. I think we'll be alright.*>

<*You sure about that?*> the engineer asked with a snort. <*Don't forget that Fina and Sabs are still out there. They like to blow things up as much as you do.*>

<*Don't give me that,*> Cheeky scoffed. <*You blow shit up as much as the rest of us.*>

Ahead, a trio of soldiers moved into the passage, weapons sweeping the air ahead of them. Neither of the women even commented on their presence, opening fire and cutting them down without slowing their advance.

<*You'd think they'd have their goons put on something other than some light riot armor,*> Cheeky commented. <*If people are breaching your tin can this far out, they're doing it with some serious gear.*>

<*Well, they didn't expect anyone to send in Sabrina.*>

The captain laughed. <*Now you've got it.*>

Less than a minute—and another half-dozen Sirians—later, they reached the entrance to the station command. The doors were sealed, so Cheeky ambled up to them, looking up at the optical pickup.

"You've got two choices," she called out, disabling her stealth to reveal ISF armor. "You can surrender, and we'll let you live, or we'll blast our way in and just see where the chips fall."

"We can hold out," a voice came through the overhead speakers. "A cruiser is already inbound."

<Is that true?> Cheeky called down to Sabrina.

<Unlikely,> the ship's AI replied. <Closest cruiser was five light minutes out. Sabs and Fina have the comm node locked down, so unless folks on the station called for help the moment their whole fire alarm ploy went sideways, we're A-OK.>

"Calling your bluff." Cheeky tilted her head and gave the optics a saucy grin. They couldn't see it, but it made her feel better. "We have control of your comm systems. You didn't get a mayday out. Now open up. Last warning."

Next to her, Nance pulled a canister of formation material out of her pack, and Cheeky glanced at it, then back up at the optics.

"That is, unless you want to see what it's like to have pico dissolve your body."

A few low curses could be heard before a cough, and then the door unlocked. "Just…don't melt us," the voice said.

<I was just going to melt the door,> Nance commented with a laugh as she put the canister back in her pack and shouldered her weapon.

Cheeky chuckled as she palmed the door control and stepped back, weapon aimed inside.

"I want to see all of you. Come out with your hands up, and lay face down on the deck. Nance here is gonna watch you to make sure you're all good little bitches while I check the room over. If anyone's hiding, you'll all eat beamfire, 'kay?"

<Little bitches?> Nance snickered. <You're getting snarky in your old age.>

<Who you calling old?>

<Aren't you seventy now?>

<Lies,> Cheeky muttered as the door opened and two men stepped into view. She waved them through, nodding to the deck, before adding, <I'm two.>

<Your rebuild doesn't count,> Nance said, stepping to the

side and training her weapon on the men as they laid down.

<Like hell it doesn't. You don't count AIs by their parents' age.>

Nance sighed. *<But you're not—you know, nevermind.>*

"Just two of you schleps?" Cheeky asked. "I have trouble believing that."

"Get your ass out here, Mari," one of the men bellowed. "I'm not eating an e-beam just so you can try to go toe to toe with whoever this is."

"Cheeky," the captain supplied.

"Sorry, what?"

"Cheeky. Like these things." She gave him a light kick in the butt. "Just a lot nicer than yours. *My* ass is precision engineered, not like your randomly assembled, organic shit."

Her attention was caught by a surly looking woman appearing in the doorway, a pulse rifle hanging loosely in her grip.

"Drop it, lady."

The woman looked like she was considering a last stand, but then sighed and let the weapon clatter to the deck before joining the two men.

"Anyone else?" Cheeky asked.

"No." The first man shook his head. "Just us."

"Gonna bet your life on it?" Nance's voice was level and deadly serious.

The woman snorted. "You're gonna kill us anyway."

"Not so." Cheeky crossed her arms. "In a way, this is sort of your salvation. If you were operational in a few days, then yeah, this station might just be blown to pieces by a passing cruiser. Luckily for you, with us here, you're quite safe."

"Oh yay," the man who appeared to be in charge muttered. "I'm so glad."

Nance shook her head. "Could just kill you now…it would save us a lot of trouble."

"*Nance,*" Cheeky gave her engineer an exasperated look.

"Drop the lockIts on 'em, and let's go."

Ten minutes later, after issuing a stand down order from the command center—which some of the crew honored—they reached the comm node to find Fina and Sabs barricaded in behind a heap of fallen enemy soldiers.

"Are you two alright in there?" Cheeky called out. "You said you were secure…but this is not what came to mind."

"Totally," Fina called out. "Just drinking the blood of our enemies and all that."

"Gross!" Nance made a gaging sound.

A laugh came from behind the stack of bodies. "I thought you were over your germaphobia?"

"Fina. Germaphobia and being grossed out by drinking blood are *two entirely different things*."

More laughter came from inside, followed by, "Stand back," from Sabs.

Cheeky and Nance backpedaled as the mountain of bodies toppled over, revealing two grinning women.

Nance scowled at the pair. "Shit…what were you up to in there?"

Fina held up a bottle of whiskey. "We found someone's stash. It's really good stuff."

"Super good." Sabs nodded.

"You're in a synthetic frame," Cheeky joined Nance in frowning at the pair. "You *can't* get drunk."

"I can fake it," the AI replied. "Just have to make a few tweaks to my own brain chemistry."

Fina chuckled as she stepped over the mound. "Don't worry, we can snap out of it when needed. Just trying to have a bit of fun."

"Is it locked down, or do we need to leave someone guarding it?" Cheeky asked, nodding at the comm node.

"Oh, it's toast," Sabs winked. "It looks fine on the outside, but I pretty much melted the node's innards. They'll have to swap it out entirely."

<We only have to hold the station for another two hours,> Sabrina broke into the conversation. <I just got word from Joe. The fleet will be jumping in ninety minutes.>

Fina's expression grew serious. "Good, it's about time someone excised this cancer. Glad it's going to be us."

NEW ORDERS

STELLAR DATE: 05.15.8950 (Adjusted Years)
LOCATION: TSS *Cossack's Sword,* **Outer System**
REGION: Hale's Beacon System, Orion Freedom Alliance

Svetlana drew in a deep breath of relief as she stepped foot on the *Cossack's Sword*'s deck. Even though Caldwell's cruiser was just as safe as hers, there was nothing quite like being home.

The battle to take the Widows' ship had ended not long after her rescue, with only two more of the clones located. Not wanting to leave such advanced tech available to whomever might find it, she ordered the enemy ship be destroyed and for the fleet to reconvene in orbit of an outer-system ice giant.

Caldwell was with her, his eyes still belying worry as he walked at her side toward the briefing room where the captain of the courier ship waited.

"You're sure you're alright?" he asked for what had to be the tenth time.

Deciding that putting his fears to rest was her most immediate concern, Svetlana stopped and turned to face him. "Colonel, your medical staff checked me over, and mine will as soon as we're done with this meeting. I feel fine. The Widows didn't plant a bomb in me or anything, so we're in no imminent danger."

Caldwell had the good grace to appear contrite. "I'm sorry, Admiral. I've just heard a lot about what those Widows are capable of...not to mention seeing them with their helmets off." He gave an involuntary shiver. "They're twisted."

"You're right, there. I suspected they were going to pay me a visit with the sharp-sharp knives before long, but you saved me in time. Now that's one less threat to deal with."

His gaze remained fixed on her eyes, unwavering and unblinking. "You'd tell me, right?"

"I would," she replied. "I promise. There's no reason for any of us to have secrets—especially out here in the PED."

"What do you think they were doing out here?" he asked as they resumed walking.

"Who knows. I've heard that Orion sometimes uses Widows as strike teams in these systems. Part of their whole prohibition against advanced tech."

Caldwell nodded. "Or maybe they were after us."

"You mean as their primary mission?"

"I do."

Svetlana's lips twisted to the side as she considered the possibility. "I suppose. They'd have to know we were going to be here."

"Or they sent Widows out in a broad array ahead of us."

"If they have enough. Based on the data the courier had, a lot of them have died in recent conflicts."

The ISF colonel snorted. "Conflict. That's one way to put it. I can't believe Tangel and Joe let their daughters go on such a crazy mission."

"Or that it worked," Svetlana added.

"A lot of crazy stuff has gone down since we got knocked off the QuanComm network," the colonel said. "It's going to take some time to absorb it all."

"If we ever do."

They walked in silence for half a minute before Caldwell glanced at her and asked, "What do you think the special orders are?"

"Honestly? Could be anything from recall to new targets. We've been out here a bit longer than expected, but it could still go on for a lot longer. I guess it depends on what sort of policing we plan to do with Orion."

Caldwell sighed. "Now *that* is definitely something I didn't sign up for. Last thing on my dance card is playing Good Cop, Bad Cop with a bunch of people who are wishing we'd just leave them alone."

"Sure." Svetlana nodded. "But what do you think is going to happen here in the PED when they learn that New Sol has fallen? This place is going to devolve into war and chaos."

"Maybe, maybe not. Despite the technological restrictions, these folks have lived in peace for centuries. Not only that, they don't really have the capability to make war on one another."

"Not yet. But it doesn't take that long to build up the military strength to strike your neighbor."

With that statement, they reached the briefing room door, and Svetlana palmed it open, entering to see a man and woman sitting at one end of the oval table at the head of the room.

They both rose, and the woman, Captain Allana, took the fore.

"Admiral Svetlana, we're so relieved to see you safe and sound." She offered her hand, and both officers shook it before following suit with the man. "This is my first officer, Lieutenant Quinten."

With the greetings over, they all took seats at the table, and Allana began to speak. "There's so much to share with you, ma'am. We've uploaded a full report of the past eight months' events to your ship's datastores, of course, but you may want to choose what gets disseminated and in what order."

"I've read through some of the highlights, but that sounds dire," Caldwell said.

The courier captain shook her head. "Mostly good, to be honest. I mean, things were touch and go in a few cases, and the war is far from won, but there have been some significant advances. One of which is that Airtha has been re-taken, and Krissy Wrentham is now president of the Transcend."

Svetlana sucked in a sharp breath. "Sera—"

"She's well, as are her sisters. She abdicated the position to her father, who in turn handed it off to Admiral Krissy."

"Wait...what?" Caldwell stammered. "Sera has sisters and a father?"

Allana grinned. "Sorry, sir, ma'am. There's just no simple way to dive into all this. It turns out that Jeffrey Tomlinson had been replaced with a clone some time ago. The original was trapped in stasis in the LMC—"

"The Large Magellanic Cloud?" It was Svetlana's turn to interrupt.

"Yes. It turns out that the Transcend had begun a terraforming and settlement project out there centuries ago. It's all been hush-hush, though."

"And Sera's sisters?" Caldwell prompted.

"Clones."

Svetlana snorted. "The galaxy's gotten weird since we've been tucked away in the PED."

"But there's even better news," Allana seemed to be barely holding in a grin.

"Oh?" Svetlana cocked an eyebrow.

"I imagine you read the report highlighting the fall of New Sol already."

"Top of the heap." Caldwell's tone was sober. "That was a hard-won victory."

Allana nodded. "It was. However, Tanis and Angela survived the destruction of Luxa."

The colonel choked on a breath while Svetlana tilted her head. "Not Tangel?"

"I don't have a lot of details, but it seems that Tangel separated from Tanis and Angela before sacrificing herself. Sera is leading the search for her."

"Search," Caldwell mused. "That's only partially good, I suppose."

"I'm sorry I don't have more," the captain said. "We've been plucking updates from the QC network over the last month, so we don't have full dumps."

"Wait." Svetlana held up a hand. "We've got new orders rolling in."

She glanced at Caldwell, whose lips had drawn into a thin line.

"Looks like I'm headed to the Kap," he said.

"And I've been recalled to Airtha."

The knowledge struck her far more forcefully than she'd expected. After serving for nearly a year together, their time in the PED was over.

Just like that.

"Admiral." Caldwell stood. "It has been an honor to serve with you. When this is all over, come look me up in New Canaan."

Svetlana rose and inclined her head as she shook the colonel's hand. "Little would please me more. The honor has been entirely mine."

* * * * *

An hour later, logistics control had jumped a dozen gates into place around the ice giant, and Caldwell's ships were queueing up to make the leap to Kapteyn's Star.

From what Svetlana had learned, he was set to join a strike force that was assaulting Sirius—the last major hurdle before the Alliance brought the fight to Sol.

Despite the fact that they'd all been neck-deep in the shit for eight months, she was a little jealous. Caldwell and the ISF were getting to push toward the war's conclusion, while she was being pulled back to Airtha, likely spending a few weeks planning and debriefing before anything interesting happened again.

The worry amused the admiral. Before Admiral—er, President—Wrentham had selected her to lead one of the Hoplite forces, Svetlana hadn't seen frontline action in years. Now the prospect of being away from combat for a few weeks had her growing restless.

Still, something inside her was glad for the reprieve. Being responsible for so many lives so far from home was draining. Being back at Airtha—which she was more than glad was back in the right hands—was a welcome thought.

She especially couldn't wait to congratulate Krissy on becoming president. That was an incredible accomplishment, and one that opened up new positions within the TSF's hierarchy.

Play my cards right, and I might be able to get her old job. So long as Rellan or Mardus haven't already homed in on it.

The thought struck her as strange. A moment ago, she'd been eager to get back on the front lines, and now she couldn't stop thinking about joining the general staff back at Airtha.

Rubbing her eyes, she chalked it up to the stress of the past few days.

No need to plan in great detail. We'll just see where things go….

THE STRIKE

STELLAR DATE: 05.15.8950 (Adjusted Years)
LOCATION: ISS *Lantzer*, orbiting Victoria
REGION: Kapteyn's Star System, Alliance Controlled Territory

Jessica heaved a sigh as she reviewed the intel from *Sabrina* one more time. It had revealed that many of the Sirian fleets were spread out across the outer system, beyond Lucent's stellar nebula—the remains of the star's outer layers that had been blown off before it collapsed into a white dwarf.

Usually, those remains would continue to spread out in a wide halo around a star system, but the presence of Sirius A had kept them close, orbiting the binary stars in a hazy smear of dust and gas.

After reviewing their options, Joe had decided to take the I-Class ships to hit one of the outer concentrations of enemy ships, while Jessica's fleet would jump deep into the inner system. She'd determined it was best to send Jaclyn to Incandus, while Boris would be tasked with destroying the shipyards around Radius. That left her with Brilliance.

While the bulk of the Sirian fleets were elsewhere, intel suggested that there were still at least a quarter million ships protecting the heart of the Sirian Hegemony. It was likely that many of those craft were equipped with stasis shields, hard shells that Jessica's fleet would have a difficult time cracking.

But crack them we will.

The fleet was facing a new style of warfare. One where the ships on both sides were almost indestructible, and combat would be waged through the defense and destruction of softer targets.

She had no idea how it would really play out, but it wouldn't be long before they found out.

"The Sirians are lucky we're not assholes like them," Trevor said from Jessica's side, startling her out of her reverie.

The admiral glanced at her husband, and leaned into his side as one of his massive arms encircled her. "Because if we were, we'd just rain starfire down and be done with the place?"

"Either that, or just burn their worlds and leave. We're going to be tactical and spend our lives saving theirs. Hardly seems right."

"There are innocents on their worlds. You know that."

"Yeah." He snorted. "Noctus slaves."

"And children," Iris added. "And probably lots of people who wouldn't be such major assholes if they didn't live in a terrible society."

She sighed and nodded. "I'm glad you're such a nice person, Trevor—because Iris and I are serious bitches."

Iris glanced up from the console she was bent over. "Hey! Okay...you're right."

<We're up in five,> Gil said. *<The gates are primed, just confirming jump trajectory. This star moves too damn fast.>*

"You could register a complaint with it." Iris's tone was laced with droll mirth. "I hear you file those with the corona."

<You can calculate stellar drift across a fleet-wide jump to make sure we all dump out together,> Gil shot back.

Jessica laughed. "Careful, she'll be taking your job before you know it."

"I don't think so," Iris mused. "I'm happy being mobile."

*<You're not mobile. You're stuck inside me. **I'm** mobile.>*

Trevor snorted, and Karma laughed. "He has a point," the big man said. "We don't really get around as much as a ship does."

"Semantics," Iris said with a shrug. "Either way, stellar drift calculations are all you. Just say the word when it's time to jump."

Jessica could tell that Gil wanted to make a comment by a general feeling on the shipnet, and was glad that the AI managed to keep his comments to himself.

"That's right, everyone," the admiral said to her bridge crew. "Let it all out. In just a few minutes, we're gonna be in the shit."

"What else is new?" Karma asked with a laugh. "I think we were born in it."

"Just this, and then Sol," Jessica said. "We're almost done."

"You don't really think that'll be the end of it, do you?" Lucida asked. "Like, the war's still going to take a lot to end."

"Sure." Jessica nodded. "But once we do Sol in, New Canaan's part in this conflict is over, and the TSF can name some other field marshal. We'll have completed what we set out to do...destroy the people who attacked us, and ensure they can't do it again. It's going to be a hell of an object lesson for the ages."

"Kinda wish we didn't have to be the galaxy's teachers," Iris muttered. "Though I suppose it's a bit late now to take that back."

"What about the core AIs?" Trevor asked. "You think they're just going to let this drop? They put a lot of effort into setting us all at one another's throats."

Jessica rocked her head back and forth on his chest before letting out a protracted sigh. "You're really harshing my chill here."

"Harshing?" He snorted. "You been watching vids from that vault again?"

"Maybe."

Lucida cleared her throat. "OK, taking us in."

"First wave is all queued up," Iris reported. "If our jump is good, we'll end up in a convex disk one light second from Brilliance."

<I feel called out,> Gil groused.

"I have full confidence in your abilities," Jessica said.

No one spoke as Lucida eased the *Lantzer* toward its gate, the ship's bow mirror creeping toward the ball of nothing in the gate's center.

For a moment, it all seemed too surreal to Jessica. Here she was, just a girl who grew up on the shores of Lake Athabasca in Canada's north, now casually skirting the edges of black holes to leap across space, and make war on entire star systems.

What has become of us all?

Space disappeared for a fraction of a second; all that it took to travel the ten light years between the Kap and Sirius. The blue-red glow of Kapteyn's Star was replaced with the harsh white glare of Lucent, the white dwarf once known as Sirius B.

Scan updated, and the holotank noted the location of Brilliance Station, high above the world of Incandus, one of the oldest continuously inhabited structures outside the Sol System.

"Initial groupings are in place," Iris reported. "Next wave should be appearing in five seconds."

Though the fleet's target was three hundred thousand kilometers away, the ISF ships were well within the perimeter defenses, and before long, beams were lancing out at the vessels, splashing harmlessly against their stasis shields.

"I count seventy-two rail platforms in range, and ten thousand smaller defense satellites," Karma said. "That's on top of the forty thousand ships in range of us right now."

"You saying we should worry?" Jessica asked with a laugh as she surveyed the sphere of Sirian ships surrounding Incandus and Brilliance Station—a sphere that lay half a light second further from the targets than the ISF fleet, which now numbered one hundred and thirty.

<All ships,> she addressed the captains on the command channel. *<Full spread of high-*v *RMs. Target defensive craft around*

Brilliance—but take care not to damage the station. Not yet, at least.>

"Aye, Admiral." Trevor passed his acknowledgment aloud, while the others responded over the Link.

Within seconds, two thousand relativistic missiles launched from the cruisers, spreading out and firing antimatter-pion drives, thrusting them forward to thirty percent the speed of light. It only took the barrage ten seconds to reach their targets, and over eighty percent survived the journey.

The white glow of Lucent was momentarily eclipsed by the bloom of well over a thousand nuclear explosions.

"Poor bastards weren't even ready," Iris said, a grim smile on her lips. "Looks like we took out...over three hundred destroyers and two repair yards."

Jessica shook her head in surprise. "Did they not have shields up?"

"Looks like a lot didn't," the AI replied. "Cocky bastards."

"Debris is hitting the station," Karma announced. "At least they got *their* shields up in time. Not stasis, though."

The admiral placed her hands on the rim of the holotank. "Good, that means they don't have power sources capable of supplying a stasis shield that large. Going to make our jobs a lot easier. Iris, order the fleet to boost at full power toward Brilliance. Tight burn, I don't want those assholes behind us to get a shot up the engines."

"Aye," Iris replied, and the five hundred ships now in the heart of Sirius leapt forward.

On the main display, light from the far side of Incandus flared, and Karma chuckled. "Looks like Jaclyn is doing her thing."

Jessica nodded silently as she watched segments of the Sirian defense begin to converge on the ISF fleets. The enemy's formation was troubling, and she couldn't help but wonder if they were terrible at tactics, or if they had something up their sleeves.

"You're wondering where the rest of their ships are, aren't you," Iris asked from her side.

"I am. Even if half their fleets are in the outer system, there should be hundreds of thousands more ships here. Did they just not expect us to make it in this far?"

"Maybe…" she mused. "I guess we'll know in half an hour, when we find out how things are going for Joe."

Jessica nodded, looking back down at the display as several flights of enemy ships gained markers indicating that they had stasis shields.

"Ten percent of their fleet so far," Iris commented. "Maintain fire on conventionally shielded ships?"

"Yeah, let's whittle them down. The weapons they're firing are the same either way."

"True that." The AI pointed at a grouping of ships streaming around Incandus. "Looks like they had a bit of a surprise waiting for us. Must have been stealthed."

"Another ten thousand," Jessica sighed. "That's a bit more like it. Being rapid response, at least *those* ones likely have stasis."

"Not sure why you want that," Trevor said. "We're going to be outnumbered no matter what."

"I want them to do things that make sense so I can work up counters," Jessica replied, folding her arms across her chest. "I would have preferred there be three million ships in orbit of Incandus. At least then, we wouldn't have to worry about the rest of their fleet lying in wait somewhere."

<Should we broadcast the announcement for civilians to clear all military facilities?> Gil asked. <I have it queued up.>

"Do it," the admiral said. "It'll take us half an hour to get there, anyway."

"Not all of us," Iris said, giving a long-suffering sigh. She pointed at the holotank, where a small ship was flagged with a blue marker.

Jessica's lips drew into a thin line. "Is that the *Voyager*?"

"Yeah." Iris nodded. "She must have altered her jump to come in a hell of a lot closer, slipping into the shipping lanes amidst the confusion."

"I was going to let her storm Brilliance," Jessica muttered. "I guess this makes sense, get in before they lock down."

"If she can," Trevor commented. "I can't imagine they're letting anyone dock right now."

<*I'd have trouble believing that they're going down there without a plan,*> Gil added.

Jessica resisted the urge to grind her teeth. "Everyone's got plans, but no one's sharing with me. It's pissing me off."

"Well, to be fair," Iris's lips drew up in a smirk. "It's normal for the enemy not to share their plans, you know."

"Speaking of the enemy…." The admiral spun the view on the holotank to show the Sirian ships that were boosting away from the perimeter, many now in range and firing on the ISF fleet. "Doesn't look like their lighter ships have atom beams."

"No, but a few of the cruisers do," Iris said, highlighting a hundred of the six thousand ships that were in pursuit of Jessica's three thousand.

The admiral nodded and looked at the jinking pattern her fleet was employing, satisfied that it was the best they could manage in order to avoid getting shot up the engines, while also staying on course for Brilliance.

After weighing options for a minute more, she glanced at Iris. "Order the fleet to seed missiles, then drop mines ten thousand klicks further in. Let's give them something else to think about."

"You got it, Admiral," the AI replied, and a moment later, markers started to appear as the ISF fleet quietly released ten thousand missiles into the black.

The mines followed shortly after, and then they waited for the pursuing ships to slip into the trap.

As that tactic marinated, fire from the station and the ships defending it intensified, rail shots now striking the ISF ships periodically.

"Those are some lucky shots," Trevor commented as one hit the *Lantzer*, nudging the ship to port with the kinetic force delivered.

"Makes you wonder how many are missing," Jessica said. "Those ships behind us are in a donut formation now."

"Noticed that. Was kinda hoping the Sirians would be dumb enough to shoot at their own people."

Iris laughed. "If only."

"Let's start sending our own rail shots." Jessica crossed her arms, hands gripping her biceps as she looked over Brilliance Station's defensive emplacements.

The station presented no shortage of targets. A two-thousand-kilometer-long arc tethered to Incandus, it was home to over three billion people—at least, that's what the welcome beacon for tourists said. What was of greater interest were the weapons clusters, segments of station where dozens of rail and directed energy weapons bristled on the hull.

Scan had picked up over eighty such locations, and Jessica imagined there were many more. The question was whether or not they could be destroyed without too many civilian casualties.

While it was possible for smaller facilities to evacuate, it would take days for the population of Brilliance to get off-station in any sort of orderly fashion.

"Let's hit the ones on the ends," she said at last. "That way, if we break the station, not too much is going to come free."

Iris chuckled. "You think if we whack it in the middle, Brilliance will break in half or something?"

"Maybe? It's a really old station. One maintained by slave

labor, no less."

"Fair point," the AI nodded. "What do you think about hitting these four?"

Weapons nodes on the station lit up, and Jessica nodded with approval. "You're thinking we can target the nearby reactors once we break through their shields?"

"I am. Oh, look, the missiles are firing up."

Jessica spun the view again, watching as the ten thousand missiles that the fleet had seeded suddenly came to life, streaking toward the pursuing Sirian ships. At the same time, the mines were attaching to at least some of the enemy vessels, their a-grav systems letting the weapons settle against shields without alerting anyone to their presence.

Several flashes of light came from a pair of cruisers, and Jessica watched as their markers changed to indicate stasis shields.

"No mines for them," Iris said.

"Let's hope that doesn't clue them in," Trevor said, looking up from his station.

"A couple of shield flares won't give this away." Jessica spoke with certainty. "I mean…what are they going to do?"

"That." Iris gestured at markers showing dozens of Sirian ships blowing chaff in their wakes, hoping to confuse the pursuing missiles.

They didn't have long to wait. Seconds later, explosions began to bloom around the enemy ships as the missiles caught up. The mines began to detonate as well, weakening shields moments before the warheads struck.

The count of damaged ships in the pursuing fleet climbed rapidly until it was at over seven hundred.

"Four hundred and ninety-three are no longer combat-effective." Iris grinned. "Bet they didn't see that coming."

"I've half a mind to come about and wipe them out," Jessica muttered. "Show them there's really no point in this whole song and dance."

The AI laughed. "You think they'll just say something like 'Oh well, then I guess you can destroy our star system'?"

"No. I suppose not. Though if we wanted to just do that, we could…it would be a lot less work."

"Think we'll need starfire?" Trevor asked. "It was hella handy at the Kap."

"Only an option so long as Cheeky's band can keep the interdiction web down. At some point, someone's going to get a message out to the astrosphere and let them know that there's a big ol' hole in their defense grid."

"I think firing neutronium bullets is going to have to be a last-ditch tactic here," Iris admitted. "I can't see how one can shoot down enemy ships without risking hitting the planet or maybe Lucent."

Their husband sighed. "Fine. It's just so cool, though—especially since their stasis shields can't deflect it."

"Is this a good time to remind you how you wondered if we could blow up Star City when we first found it?" Iris asked him. " 'Because it would look so cool…'?"

Trevor coughed. "Yeah, well, I was young and stupid then."

"It was just twelve years ago," Jessica scowled.

"Yeah, I was only forty years old. Now I'm wise and venerable and all that, and would never suggest something so immature."

Iris cocked a hip and gave him a mischievous look. "What if it was derelict?"

"Don't tempt me, woman!" He gave a mock laugh, then sat up straight. "Whoa…what are those?"

A smear was spreading out from around Brilliance, a haze that was either some sort of atmospheric leak, or—

"That's *a lot* of drones," Lucida whispered. "It has to be millions."

<I think it's closer to billions,> Gil corrected. *<That's gonna be a problem.>*

A HEGEMON'S DESIRE

STELLAR DATE: 05.15.8950 (Adjusted Years)
LOCATION: High Terra, Earth
REGION: Sol System, Hegemony of Worlds

Hegemon Uriel glared at the ten-meter-wide holodisplay that dominated the war room's center. The blue splotch that had once stretched across two hundred light years had contracted just as rapidly as it had grown.

There were still distant systems that were claimed by the Hegemony, and many were cut off, separated from the rest of her empire by the encroaching red area denoting the Scipio Alliance. Tendrils of destruction shredding her burgeoning empire.

Despite their losses, the Hegemony was still a force to be reckoned with, and that was something she needed to make clear to her top admirals.

"We still have major shipyards across our worlds." She gestured at the yellow markers dotting the blue regions of space. "We no longer need to bow to the eco-terrorists who deny our use of resources. The survival of the Hegemony is at stake. We'll harvest whatever we must."

Secretary Saray's lips thinned as he shook his head. "It's a delaying tactic at best. Eventually, they'll wear us down. It's a million star systems against our few hundred."

Both of the man's numbers were exaggerations. The enemy alliance did not draw upon the resources of one million systems, but neither did the Hegemony still encompass hundreds.

She'd counted on her allies to be strong, to shield and supply the Hegemony as they'd struck out against their enemies. For a time, it had worked, but then, one by one, those allies had fallen, toppled by what seemed like an inexorable juggernaut led by Tanis Richards.

Now, word had come that New Sol had fallen. Orion would likely take some time for the Transcend to quell, but it meant no further aid would be forthcoming from that empire.

The latest reports showed the Trisilieds to be on their knees, as was the Southern Cross. Nietzschea was on the run, and a dozen other minor empires had either surrendered, or pulled back from any active support in the war effort.

Despite dire news on every front, there was still reason to hope.

"It's not a delaying tactic with the stasis shield technology," Uriel countered. "Now that I've authorized use of any and all raw resources in the Hegemony, we can out-produce our enemies."

"And control of those fleets?" Saray's brows were knit together. He knew the answer, but didn't like it.

"The SAI arrays can control them. Our new allies have shown us how to ensure they are obedient and effective."

"Ma'am, sir." A commander looked up from her pad, worry writ large on her features. "We've just received word, Sirius is under attack. An ISF fleet has jumped deep into the system, and is attacking Incandus and Brilliance Station."

Uriel shot the admiral a smug look. "We'll soon see how the ISF deals with crushing defeat. They've sent fewer than ten thousand ships into Sirius. It'll be a bloodbath."

Saray gave a slight nod, but didn't appear convinced.

Uriel understood the need for him to be realistic, but more and more, she was starting to think he didn't truly believe victory was possible.

"Very well, Secretary Saray." She turned to face him directly. "What do *you* think we should do?"

The man glanced at her and cleared his throat. "We really only have one option."

"Which is?"

He drew in a deep breath and laid out a plan that surprised even her.

"Will it work?" she asked, unable to keep the hopeful glee from her voice.

"It's our best shot. If we can deal a blow that crushing, they'll have no choice but to pull back and sue for peace."

The hegemon nodded as a smile formed on her lips. *A peace that will buy us time to wipe them out once and for all.*

A NUMBERS GAME

STELLAR DATE: 05.15.8950 (Adjusted Years)
LOCATION: ISS *Carthage*, Outer System
REGION: Sirius System, Hegemony of Worlds

The *Carthage* leapt into Sirius forty-three AU from the system barycenter, almost directly in the midst of an enemy fleet—at least, in the case of stellar distances.

A scant light minute off the ship's port bow lay over six hundred thousand enemy hulls spread across ten light seconds of space.

"Well, they're going to know about us damn fast," Joe said as he frowned at the tactical display. "We're close to a few dwarf planets, but none that will provide any cover against a fleet that large."

<*Our delta-v with the Sirian fleet is only a few kilometers per second,*> Kerr observed.

"Almost like they were able to calculate the vector we'd approach from," Symatra said in her customary dry tones.

<*Are you ever happy?*> the ship's AI asked.

"No."

Joe shot Symatra a mollifying look. She was brilliant at spreading her mind—perhaps one of the best, next to Tanis, but that came at the cost of her putting zero effort into interpersonal relationships.

"Given the enemy fleet's location, let's make for Patterson Point." Joe set a marker on an ore-processing station over two AU spinward in the system. It sat at the outer edge of the binary system's second main dust belt. "That'll set them up for a chase, and we can wear them down on the way."

"Works for me," Symatra said as the four thousand destroyers she commanded began to jump in around the

Carthage.

Last to enter the system was the *Starblade*, also newly equipped with a DMG. No other ships appeared. The entire purpose of the fleet was to serve as a distraction so Jessica's ships could defeat the enemy around the inner worlds.

As the fleet got underway, Scan began to paint a picture of the Sirian defenses around Lucent. Jessica would be vastly outnumbered, but not so much as to cause concern. What *did* cause concern was that Scan could only find a million ships in the system. Based on prior intel, nearly three times that number should be present.

Hiding vessels in a dust-filled binary like Sirius was easy. Moving them, on the other hand, tended to create easily discernable eddies in the stellar medium.

So far, Scan hadn't found any signs of mass fleet movement, excepting what could be accounted for by the vessels they could see.

"Curiouser and curiouser," he murmured.

"The missing ships?" Captain Ophelia said as she rose from her command seat. "Where do you think they are?"

"They could be anywhere," Symatra spoke first, gesturing at the display in contempt. "Though they'd have to be close to be useful."

Joe nodded. "Not on the far side of Sirius, that's for sure. They don't care about the Noctus enough for that. I wonder if Intel overestimated the enemy's presence here."

<The Hand had two agents in Sirius for months,> Kerr said. <I doubt they'd get the fleet size wrong by a factor of three. They had solid evidence.>

"I wouldn't put it past the Sirians to fake their records to appear more formidable than they really are," Ophelia countered.

Symatra nodded. "I'd buy that explanation. What about Sabrina's team? Perhaps they can dig up some more intel on this."

"Worth a shot," Joe replied. "They're still aboard that control station, keeping the hole open. I'll send a message. In the meantime, it's time to make my announcement."

<Ready when you are,> Kerr replied.

Joe squared his shoulders, and turned to face the front of the bridge. "This is Fleet Admiral Joseph Evans of the Intrepid Space Force, acting on behalf of the Scipio Alliance. We demand the complete and unconditional surrender of all stations and worlds in the Sirius System. Civilians aboard military infrastructure, we suggest that you remove yourself from those facilities as soon as possible, as we will be showing as much mercy as your people gave to the people of Kapteyn's Star a few days ago."

He drew a deep breath, blinking slowly before continuing. "Patterson Point is our first target. You have three hours to abandon that facility prior to its destruction. There will be no negotiation. That is all."

Ophelia's lips were pursed into a thin line; next to her, Symatra nodded.

"Succinct, I like it," the AI said. "They need to understand how this will go—though, announcing the timetable makes our actions easier to predict."

Joe shrugged. "We don't have to attack *right* at the three-hour mark."

"What if civilian ships are still pulling out?" Ophelia asked. "That's a really big station to clear out in three hours."

"I'm not a monster," he replied. "Besides, we're probably going to be tangling with the defenders for some time, anyway."

<They're already matching our v,> Kerr commented. <Vectors will intercept in two hours.>

"I assume we're going to target ships without stasis shields first?" the *Carthage*'s captain asked.

Joe reached out to the *Starblade,* and a moment later, a holographic image of Captain Peabody appeared next to a pillar of light that was the other I-Class ship's AI, Turk.

"OK, folks," he said to the group. "It's our four thousand ships versus their six hundred thousand."

"Just a hundred and fifty to one," Peabody said with a laugh. "What could go wrong?"

<The excessive quantum energy draw that will result from defending against that many ships could very well cause a rupture in spacetime that would destabilize this entire system,> Kerr replied.

"This far from the primaries?" the *Starblade*'s captain asked. "I thought that any problems with destabilization would be highly localized so long as we're far enough out of large gravity wells."

"That's the theory," Symatra said. "But we've not really tested how much the fabric of the universe can be ripped before things get *really bad,* so it's hard to say where the limit is."

"I can't imagine that, across the entire universe, no one has ever done this before," Peabody countered. "I'm not saying we should do it, I'm just saying that it might be self-repairing."

<Or we could now know what causes many of the mysterious dark spots and attractors in space,> Turk said, a note of humor in his voice. *<Either way, I'd prefer not to die fighting the Sirians.>*

Peabody nodded in Turk's direction. "Fair enough."

"I don't want to screw around with them any more than we have to." Joe took the reins once more. "We know that Exaldi can't penetrate stasis shields in normal space, but what if we dump the enemy fleet into the dark layer? I know that *some* research has been done on that front."

<They don't have CriEns, so either way, they won't survive for long,> Kerr said.

"Can we open a dark layer rift and push other ships through?" Ophelia asked. "I was of the understanding that it only worked to pull Exaldi out and send them back in because they lack their own mechanism to transition."

"Shit." Peabody shook his head. "Now that's the stuff of nightmares. Self-transitioning Exaldi."

"Just be glad the core AIs didn't see fit to wipe us all out ages ago. That would have been the end of us."

<Of them, too, I'd suspect,> Kerr said. <Either way, if we create a rift like we did over Carthage two years ago, juxtaposing six dimensions of space in the same physical place, we can probably hold it open with the ships sitting right on the edge of the rift—so to speak. The Exaldi can have at them, but if we close the rift, space will separate again, and unless any of the things are currently inside Sirian ships at the time, then they'll end up back in the dark layer.>

"And if some are inside, we'll know soon enough, and can push those ships back in," Joe said.

"This is…brutal," Ophelia said in the extended silence that followed. "Are we really committing to this? I get why we did it at Carthage. There, it was an act of desperation. Here…well, we're the aggressors."

Joe turned to face the ship's captain. "I'm always open to suggestions. Just remember, we're trying to protect all the systems we've liberated that can't stand up against an enemy like this. Also, it's paramount that we don't let stasis tech get out of Sirius. If it starts to spread all over the Inner Stars, this war is never going to end—not until everything worth fighting over is destroyed."

"He's right," Symatra added. "We can't police everyone everywhere forever. Our only hope is to show them that when the hammer falls, it's so terrible that no one would ever risk it."

The *Carthage*'s captain nodded. "I get it. I just hate it."

"OK." Joe held up a fist. "We have three options…well, four, if you count firing neutronium in from Star City, which isn't something I'm willing to entertain. First is we just slug it out with them for a few days till they're worn down—or we are. Next up is picobombs, but we have to get past stasis shielding for those to work. Third we have the Exaldi."

As he listed the options, he extended a finger for each, the command team sharing a few looks as he did so.

"OK," Ophelia said when he was done. "I'm on board with the Exaldi option. How are we gonna pull it off?"

"Not with my destroyers," Symatra replied. "I don't have enough, and they don't have the shielding to get in position even if I did."

<It's going to have to be our drones,> Kerr said to Turk. <We'll have to upgrade their a-grav systems, though.>

"How long will you need?" Joe asked. "Is this a before or after we destroy Patterson Point scenario?"

There was a brief pause, and then Turk spoke. <If we use the ARC-9 engine spec in the pilotless drones, we can pull it off in two hours.>

"Well, that's fine," Peabody glanced at Ophelia. "Especially since we only have twenty-seven pilots between our ships."

Symatra shook her head. "You humans really need a better way to breed. When the Intrepid reached New Canaan, there were far more humans than AIs, but now we outnumber you five to one."

Ophelia cocked a hip as she turned to the admiral. "Have you looked at the galaxy? Are you really sure we need humans to breed faster?"

<Not so much the breeding, but perhaps the raising. Your problem is that you take too long to mature. Maybe once this is over, we can spend some time really digging into how we can encode knowledge into your DNA so that you know things when you're born.>

Joe shuddered, wondering what something like that would do to human individuality.

"Let's get back to the topic at hand," he said. "We're going to retrofit the drone fighters with ARC-9 grav engines, then we'll spread them around the enemy fleet, and open a rift into the dark layer. Enemy ships and Exaldi have fun fun times, and then we get on our merry way."

<One thing to keep in mind,> Turk said. <We're going to need to be **close** to hold the rift open for any measurable amount of time.>

"How close?" Joe asked.

<No more than half a light second,> the AI replied. <Beyond that, we won't be able to manage fluctuations in the field.>

The fleet admiral drew himself up. "OK, then. It's gonna get hairy. The goal is not to have to sacrifice our lives, though. Keeping our two ships safe is paramount."

Turk made a snorting sound. <Glad you feel that way.>

Joe shrugged. "What can I say? I care."

A BILLIONTY BILLION

STELLAR DATE: 05.15.8950 (Adjusted Years)
LOCATION: *Voyager*, **Approaching Brilliance Station**
REGION: Sirius System, Hegemony of Worlds

"Uh...what the hell?" Carl coughed out the question while stabbing a finger at the scan return. "Are those drones?"

<Seems like it,> Troy replied. *<Just a big whack of drones.>*

"Shit," Katrina shook her head as she watched the number of unique returns keep counting up beyond all reason. "I guess they've been preparing for this."

"I don't know all the ins and outs of how stasis shields work." Carl plugged some numbers into a program on his console. "But I don't know that Jessica's ships can withstand that kind of abuse. At the very least, it's going to keep their shields on full bubble, creating a hell of a heat problem for the ship inside."

<I think Jessica has come to the same conclusion,> Troy said with a wry laugh. *<She's sending us a message over the QC.>*

Katrina put it up on the forward display, revealing a rather concise set of orders.

[Unsure what you planned to do, but now you have a mission. Find their drone control. Destroy it.]

Kirb snorted from where he stood at the back of the bridge. "Mayhem was our plan. Now we can do that, and hit 'em where it hurts."

"It works for me," Camille added. "It's gonna involve killing a lot of Lumin asshats, though, right?"

Katrina nodded. "Of course it is."

<So long as we get past them to dock,> Troy said. *<I assume we're going to do the highborn thing again?>*

"As much as I hate it, *being* a highborn Lumin has its

benefits. Let me go get geared up."

"You have ten minutes," Carl called over his shoulder as Katrina walked out of the cockpit and slid down the *Voyager*'s central ladder shaft to the crew deck.

Once in her quarters, she pulled out a multicolored skinsheath from a drawer and quickly slid into it. The one-piece outfit covered her body like a second skin, its silvery surface shifting through a series of rainbow patterns, flooding her cabin with light.

Satisfied that it would pass well enough for Brilliance Station, she set a series of studs in place from her hairline to the bridge of her nose, then two on each cheekbone—a recent addition since she'd last been in any Luminescent-controlled system.

Stepping into a pair of a-grav boots that held her feet nearly en pointe while holding her a dozen centimeters off the ground, she exited her quarters and floated up the ladder shaft and back to the bridge.

"Just in time," Carl said as she entered. "We're being hailed by Brilliance's STC. They're telling us that we're denied access to their nearspace, and that we should land on Incandus."

"Lucent's fires we are," Katrina said in her most imperious tone, causing Camille to chuckle, and Kirb to squirm uncomfortably.

"You're far too good at that," he said.

"Lots of practice," the former Lumin spy replied before walking to the front of the cockpit to stand before the main display. "Put this worm on."

"Worm going live," Carl said, chuckling quietly. "This'll be good."

A woman appeared on the display, only three studs on her nose and none on her cheeks. Her eyes widened when she saw Katrina's display, and she ducked her head. "Mistress."

"Why are you denying our approach," Katrina demanded,

not bothering to pass any sort of greeting.

The persona she was using was a cover she'd established years back, a diplomat from Bollam's World who had a habit of ending the careers—and sometimes lives—of lesser people who displeased or obstructed her.

"I'm sorry, Mistress. I'm under orders to deny any and all craft. You can divert to—"

"If I *wanted* to divert, I would. I'm talking to you because— Fuck. I don't know *why* I'm talking to you. You're useless. Put your superior on."

The woman looked like she wasn't sure who she was more afraid of, but nodded rapidly before disappearing from the display. Half a minute later—during which time, the *Voyager* continued on toward the expanding drone cloud around Brilliance—a new woman appeared.

"I am so sorry, Mistress Katrina." The new woman had two more studs than the first, hers making it up to her eyebrows. "I really do wish that I could allow you to dock, but—"

"Is Brilliance Station at risk of falling?" Katrina interrupted. "Are your masters so derelict in their duties that they would allow the spark of the ages to be destroyed?"

The woman bristled visibly. "Of course not! Brilliance shall shine forever! The enemy has but a few thousand ships. In half an hour, their fleet will be gone."

"So then, what is the concern? I have business on the station, and that is where I am docking."

Mouth working soundlessly, the other woman appeared to consider her options, and then sighed, nodding slowly. "I can grant you priority clearance—but I'm not sure what reason to give."

"Critical intelligence," Katrina replied.

"Oh! Why didn't you say so?" The woman appeared reassured that there was something plausible from a higher caste member to give as a reason. "I'll get you VIP docking."

"I'm relieved that you've come to your senses. Now, if you wouldn't mind, I have things to do."

The woman ducked her head. "Yes, of course. I'm sorry, Mistress Katrina."

The woman disappeared, and Carl chuckled. "Look at that. I have a vector and a bay."

"Smooth like butter," Kirb added.

<Well, we did spend three weeks building the cover last time we were here,> Troy added. *<Glad it paid off a bit.>*

"A bit?" Katrina asked. "We're going to get to play a pivotal role in taking down Brilliance and all of Luminescent Society in Sirius. That seems like it paid off more than 'a bit'."

<Let's not count our empires before they're destroyed.>

Other than passing through a swarm of drones so dense that it completely occluded the ship's sensors, nothing of note happened for the next ten minutes. The bay they'd been assigned was on an upper deck, in the region of Brilliance reserved for corporate heads and visiting dignitaries.

Lesser people could be found in the station's upper reaches, as well, but their presence was to serve, not to enjoy the largess of their civilization.

"You'd all best get ready," Katrina directed. "Camille and Malorie, you're backup this time. Stay with Troy, but remember that we could be boarded at any time, so keep your uniform on—well, Camille. Malorie, do your disappearing act if you get boarded."

The crew nodded, filtering off the bridge while Katrina passed the controls to Troy, trusting the AI to pilot the *Voyager* better than any human could manage.

<So, how do you plan to find where the drone control is?> he asked privately.

<Easy. I'm going to hunt down the SVP of station defense, and torture him till he spills.>

<Really?> Troy made a sound somewhere between a throat

clear and a lion's cough. <*You think that'll work?*>

<*Well, I could just take his mind.*>

<*You swore never to do that again.*>

Katrina sighed and lay her head back against the seat. <*This is different. These are the people who taught me how to do that. I figure, what comes around goes around.*>

<*Exactly.*>

Neither spoke for a minute, then Katrina took a deep breath. <*Well, what do **you** suggest?*>

<*Find the AIs. I'll free them.*>

<*You think they're using AIs? You know how they feel about them here.*>

Troy made his strangled cough again. <*Do you really think they could run more than a billion drones with NSAI? They'll have banks of non-sentients managing the minutia, but trust me, sentient minds are at the helm of this swarm.*>

A grin formed on Katrina's lips. <*So it's a rescue op. I like that even more.*>

* * * * *

Up close, Brilliance looked the same as it always had. Ostentatious. It was also much larger than when she'd grown up in its hallowed halls—something that had only further added to the overwrought opulence of the place.

"I swear," she muttered as the *Voyager* settled down on a cradle that appeared to be made of gleaming topaz. "These people never met something sparkly that they didn't fully embrace."

"If they could figure out how to breathe glitter, you know they'd swim in pools of it," Kirb said with a derisive laugh.

"Don't give them any ideas," Carl warned.

"Won't matter after today." Katrina couldn't help a toothy grin. "This is the end for them. This time, the ISF isn't leaving.

We're staying till the fight is done."

<Technically, that's what happened last time too,> Troy said.

"Seriously, Troy," she admonished. "Don't correct me in my moment of triumph."

<'Triumph' seems a little premature.>

Katrina only groaned as the interior of the ship completed pressure matching with Brilliance's bay, and the airlock opened.

Instead of a regular ramp, a platform with golden railings waited, and once the trio stepped on it, the structure descended to the deck, depositing them in front of a man with a wide face and disconcertingly small mouth.

His lips were pinched into a smile barely the size of Katrina's last thumb segment, and his eyes were so narrowed, she wondered if they were closed and he was looking at her through some sort of remote optics.

"Mistress Katrina." He intoned the words as though uttering them was somehow both a great imposition and an honor. "I greet you on behalf of Brilliance. I am told you possess critical intelligence and are to be escorted—"

"Nowhere," Katrina replied with a disinterested swipe of her hand. "My destination is my business. The last thing I need is the likes of you slowing me down."

The man looked confused. "But I am from the Intelligence Directorate. SVP Hammish sent me to escort you to him."

<Shit,> Katrina said on the team's channel. <I guess this cover's a bit **too** credible.>

"Well, then." She snapped her fingers. "Why are you standing here? Let's go."

As the man ducked his head and led them across the bay to where a station car sat, Kirb couldn't help a small laugh. <So now what are we going to do?>

<Well, no one better to tell us where the drone AIs are holed up than the SVP of the Intelligence Directorate. Once we shake him

down, we go stealth, and boom. No one to stop us.>

<ISF flow armor makes so many formerly impossible things a snap,> Carl feigned a yawn as he looked around the bay. *<I kinda miss the good ol' days where we just had proper dockside shootouts.>*

Katrina glanced over her shoulder at the man. *<You're not serious, are you?>*

<Of course not.> He snorted. *<I've had more than my fill of that shit. Totally ready to squash some low-tech normies for a bit.>*

<Last I checked, there are people with stealth as good as ours,> Kirb said. *<Let's not get too cocky.>*

They settled into the car's interior, more like a mobile sitting parlor than a dock transport. Crystal decanters sat on a diamond-sheathed table in the middle of the vehicle, and all Katrina could think of was what a deathtrap it would be if they got into an accident.

Could come in handy later.

"So," she asked the man whose name she'd found to be Argin. "You don't seem particularly concerned about the New Canaanites attacking us right now."

"Not especially, no," Argin replied. "You saw our drone fleet. Not even Sol would dare attack us here. While the rest of the galaxy has frittered away their resources, we've remained strong and prepared."

Katrina's eyes narrowed. "It sounds more like you didn't help where you could."

Her cover was from Bollam's World, and while it had not yet fallen, the Allied forces were closing in on it day by day as the League of Sentients pushed into Hegemony space.

Argin gave a deferential nod. "I am merely supporting the decisions of my overseers, Mistress Katrina. I hope you understand that. A lowly servant such as I am is not privy to the council that makes such determinations."

<The guy has top marks in groveling,> Kirb observed.

Katrina sent a feeling of agreement. <*Survival trait here.*>

"You must admit, Mistress," Argin continued. "It is some feat to deter an ISF fleet. Already, they are breaking off their assault on Brilliance, circling around Incandus, no doubt to hide behind the planet and lick their wounds—not that it will help."

It was a bold statement to make, and she inclined her head. "How so?"

"Once we show that overwhelming numbers of drones can defeat the enemy, the rest of the Hegemony can shift production from capital ships to cheap, disposable fighters."

"What of control?" Katrina quirked an eyebrow as she asked the question. "Humans and NSAI can't manage that many drones—not in such numbers, and not against enemies as powerful as the ISF. What if they bring one of their I-Class ships to Sirius?"

Argin's expression grew sly. "We have developed specialized NSAI for the task. It will make for a great licensing opportunity when this war is complete. But you can rest assured that even the much-vaunted *I2* will not stand against our drones. I'm sure that once you meet with SVP Hammish, he will discuss an opportunity for Bollam's World to contract with us for a defense swarm of your own."

"I look forward to that conversation," Katrina replied.

<*Hey,*> Carl said. <*Since we're actually going to go through with meeting this Hammish guy, what sort of intel are you planning on sharing with him?*>

<*I've been pondering that,*> Katrina said. <*I have a few ideas. One would be to tell him that this is a feint, and that the real attack is coming on Sol soon, but I don't know that the Sirians would care.*>

<*We could tell them that there is another fleet moving in to liberate all the Noctus platforms around Sirius,*> Kirb suggested. <*Get them to move resources out there.*>

<*Not sure they'd do it,*> she replied. <*I think they'd just blow*

the platforms, if they were near uprising. What we need is intel that will be mutually beneficial to Sirius and Bollam's World, but that will also give them an edge over Sol. That sort of thing is the way to get them to pay attention.>

<Right.> Carl nodded. *<The best way to get a scoundrel to believe you're being honest is to appear selfish.>*

Katrina laughed aloud. *<Bingo.>*

Argin looked as though he wanted to ask what they were discussing, but he held his silence—apparently smart enough to know not to question his betters.

A few minutes later, the groundcar turned off the major concourse they'd been traveling along, and into a narrower corridor that was lined with cat-like mechs, slowly prowling along the bulkheads.

<Those'll be fun to fight,> Carl commented. *<And by 'fun', I mean let's not do that, 'kay?>*

<Troy,> Katrina called back to the ship over an encrypted channel. *<Have you made any headway on their network?>*

<Not a lot. Brilliance is locked down tight right now. All non-essential routes and access points are offline. Can't even get in through waste processing systems.>

<OK, keep trying. I have a feeling we might need to effect a multipronged attack.>

<'Effect a multipronged attack'?> Troy chuckled in her mind. *<Adopt cover as a Lumin, and the corporate-speak just flows from you.>*

<I'm a spy,> she groused. *<I get in character. Do you need an assist from us?>*

<I wouldn't argue against a bridge between the public network and a secure wired net in the intel area,> the AI said.

<Kirb, Carl, that's on you. I suspect that Hammish won't want to talk to my escorts, so you'll be on your own for a bit.>

<Easy,> Carl replied. *<Not my first time patching into a system on Brilliance.>*

<We know,> Kirb said in a droll monotone. *<We were there.>*

<Were you? I seem to remember you holed up with some girl who had…what was it?>

<The most amaaaaaazing diamond breasts,> Katrina supplied, feigning mock excitement. *<And a sapphire vulva, if I recall.>*

Carl shivered. *<Sounds sharp.>*

<Just need the right gear,> Kirb replied with a toothy grin.

<OK, guys…let's not go any further with this.>

Carl shot her a judging look. *<You were the one who supplied the details.>*

<You asked!>

Kirb chuckled. *<I have vid, if you're interested.>*

<Gawd no.> Katrina shook her head. *<I saw enough gemstone pussy in my younger years.>*

<Not too young, I hope,> Carl said with a laugh—which abruptly cut off when she gave him a dark look. *<Oh…shit. As if I didn't already have enough reasons to hate Luminescent Society.>*

Kirb sighed. *<Annnnd that fantasy is ruined. Hold on while I delete those vids and then pour bleach in my eyes.>*

The car slowed, ending the increasingly disturbing conversation, and Katrina looked out the window to see a pair of massive doors standing at the far side of a lavish garden. The doors appeared to be freestanding, a clever holo illusion that was more subtle than she was used to seeing on Brilliance.

I guess that fits, for their spy agency.

Argin got out, and the others followed, weaving through the garden to the pair of doors. Nothing was visible beyond the portal, only a blinding light that Katrina's enhanced vision couldn't penetrate.

Their escort didn't slow, walking across the threshold and disappearing into the glow.

Katrina glanced at her two crewmen, shrugged, and followed. Once through, she found herself standing in a mirror image of the garden, but here, the plants were all made of light, casting multi-hued patterns across the ground.

"I'm impressed," she said aloud, noting that the placement of everything exactly matched what had been visible on either side of the doors. "Excellent attention to detail."

Argin flashed a smug smile. "SVP Hammish is very particular about precision."

"As I would expect." Katrina gestured for the man to lead on.

He crossed the remainder of the park, following a path that caused Katrina to wonder exactly how much on each side of the doors was real and how much was a holoprojection. The illusion was so well done that if she believed in teleportation, she would have thought they'd been transported elsewhere.

Granted, Tangel can—could—do it....

Despite the show, Katrina knew that even if teleportation technology did exist, there was no way people as paranoid as those in the Sirian Intelligence Directorate would avail themselves of it.

At the far side of the park, a series of corridors led deeper into the sector, and here they finally saw a few people moving purposefully about their work.

Katrina still hadn't figured out exactly what she would tell SVP Hammish, then an idea came to mind, and she laughed at the simplicity of it.

Argin glanced back at her, but she just gave the man a sickly sweet smile and didn't explain her outburst. If he didn't have studs up to his brows, she would have reprimanded him for even daring to look at her so casually, but his stature was enough that he could get away with it.

Once.

After a few minutes of walking, they reached a set of doors that were surprisingly plain. Thick oak, and carved with a diorama of the stars and worlds of the Sirius System. Katrina had to admit that the art was impressive—something she herself would have appreciated.

If it were depicting a different system.

A waiting room was set off to one side, and the two men settled on a couch while Argin led Katrina to the doors, pausing briefly before they swung open of their own accord.

"The SVP will see you," Argin said, gesturing for her to enter.

She didn't give him any acknowledgment, sweeping past into the room, taking in the rather demure appearance of what could have been an upper management office anywhere else in the galaxy. A slate-grey floor was surrounded by white marble walls, decorative pillars evenly spaced along their length. Two black couches sat facing one another on either side of the path that led to a large black desk that could have been a block of obsidian. Behind the desk was a wall-to-wall holodisplay showing a view of space, with Lucent in one corner and Incandus filling the lower third.

In addition to the desk and couches, the room was decorated only with a dozen light fixtures, and a small sidebar with several decanters sitting atop its ebony surface.

Behind the desk was a black, high-backed chair. It was facing away from her, its occupant presumably watching the holodisplay.

Not caring to wait on Hammish's pleasure, Katrina walked to the sidebar and selected one of the decanters, pouring its contents into a wine glass she found on a shelf below.

"Rather presumptuous of you, Mistress Katrina," the chair's occupant said in a gravelly voice, still obscured by the seatback's wings.

"And a bit rude of you not to greet me," she replied, taking her glass to one of the sofas and settling into its soft cushions. "But I'll take your wine as your act of apology."

The man chuckled, rising from the chair, revealing a figure in a black skinsuit that somehow still glowed and flashed with color.

The Lumins certainly do amazing things with light—their one redeeming attribute.

"It's nice to actually meet you," Katrina murmured as Hammish walked to the sidebar and poured himself his own drink. "Thank you for taking the time to see me. I think it will be mutually beneficial—especially now that you might have something we can trade for."

"Oh?" he asked, turning toward her with his glass in hand. "And what is that?"

Katrina gestured for him to sit across from her, as though he was of lower stature than she, and waited for him to do so. A look of consternation passed over his face before he schooled it away and took a seat.

Once he was settled, Katrina answered, "We have a power source that can make your stasis shields as effective as the ISF's."

"Well now." Hammish looked genuinely interested, his demeanor shifting in an instant. "And by 'we' do you mean the Bollam's World government?"

Katrina's lips twisted into a sneer. "You know that Bollam's World has no government. Uriel turned us into a vassal state. Our government is little more than her appointed flunkies. I'm speaking of the true leadership of Bollam's. If we were to get your drone technology and stasis shields, it would be a simple task to oust the Hegemony and fend off the League of Sentients when they reach our system."

Hammish cocked a brow. "You understand that Sirius is a member of the Hegemony. Some would consider your words to be treasonous."

"Oh?" Katrina cocked an eyebrow. "Did I come to the wrong place? I suspect there are other directorates I could go to, other SVPs who would love to see their position elevated."

"Don't be coy with me," Hammish retorted. "I'm merely

gauging your commitment. Would Bollam's World really throw off the Hegemony's yoke while also facing down the League?"

She snorted. "The Hegemony will abandon us soon enough. Bollam's is no core world, and will not be protected as such when the enemies close in. We need to look to ourselves for safety. That is why we've focused on energy. Utilizing wreckage from the battle in our system over twenty years ago, we've replicated the enemy's vacuum energy devices."

Hammish sat forward. "What they call their CriEn modules?"

"The same," Katrina replied. "Near limitless power, enough to hold stasis shields up against nearly any onslaught."

"Nearly?"

"Well, heat from the consumption of energy is still a problem."

<How're you guys doing with the network bridge out there?> Katrina asked the two men. <I've got him hooked now. I can have him taking me to their drone control in one minute or five, what do you need?>

<Three, if you can swing it,> Carl replied. <Kirb is bugging Argin while I set up the data route on a holotable someone connected to the secure network.>

<That someone you?> Katrina asked with a mental laugh.

<Surprisingly, no. Someone here actually did that.>

Her jaw tightened as she considered the implications. <Careful, it could be a honeypot or the work of a rival agency. Don't get caught.>

Carl gave a confident chuckle. <Hey. It's me.>

<That's what I'm worried about.>

Hammish had been silent while she was talking with the others, probably watching her network traffic, and aware she was talking to the two men.

"I'm going to need proof," he said after another few moments of silence. "Did you bring one with you?"

"Not aboard my ship, no," Katrina shook her head. "But we did bring one to Brilliance. It's tucked away safely until I can be certain that you have something extraordinary with your drones. For all I know, they could be a bluff, something that's deterred the ISF, but wouldn't stand up to their fleets in combat."

"You can't help it, can you?" Hammish asked, a smirk on his lips.

"Help what?"

"Being haughty. You can't just be straight with me, can you?"

It was Katrina's turn to laugh. "Straight? With you? Good luck with that. I know how your directorate operates."

The SVP gave a knowing shrug. "I suppose you would. Very well, I'll show you our drone-control systems. I have to admit, though. I'm surprised you're not interested in our stasis shielding technology—or how we got it."

Katrina winked at the man. "What makes you think we don't already have it?"

This time, an expression of honest surprise flashed across Hammish's face. As before, it disappeared in an instant—this time behind his wine glass, as he downed the rest of the red liquid and rose.

"Come. I'll show you our control center."

"I don't want to see a room with people sitting at consoles," Katrina said as she stood. "I want to see the nodes. The NSAIs you've made that can effectively manage such a large drone fleet in combat. Then I'd like to see you attack the ISF with them. I want to be sure they work."

Hammish laughed. "I can do the first, the second you'll have to wait on—though I imagine it will happen soon enough."

"Fair enough," Katrina replied as she walked to the sidebar to refill her wine. "Lead on."

Hammish gave her a look of slight annoyance, then turned and strode to the doors. In the corridor beyond, Kirb was still talking to Argin, while Carl reclined on a sofa in the adjacent room. Upon spotting the pair exiting, he leapt to his feet while the other two ended their conversation and watched as their superiors walked past.

<*All set?*> she asked Carl.

<*You bet. Troy's already slipping around the edges of their walls.*>

<*That doesn't make sense,*> Troy chimed in. <*I'm going through cracks, not around the edges. Any good wall goes all the way around, so an edge would just lead to more wall.*>

Kirb groaned. <*Troy, ruining metaphors for the last five hundred years.*>

<*Been at it for a lot longer than that,*> the AI replied. <*And I don't ruin good metaphors, just ones that are faulty. If they really were functional, I couldn't tear them down so easily.*>

<*Now that we have that out of the way,*> Katrina kept her tone level to hide any traces of amusement. <*I'm going to focus on our host here. When we get to where we're going, there will probably be security forces and techs to neutralize. Keep your eyes peeled for opportunities.*>

The journey took almost thirty minutes, most of which were spent in uncomfortable silence in the groundcar. Every so often, Hammish would ask a question about the state of things in Bollam's World. Some, Katrina answered...others, she didn't, merely giving him a level stare in repayment for attempting to milk her for intel.

They passed through a civilian district before reaching a military region of Brilliance, an area where the flashy extravagance was diminished—though not entirely gone.

Here, people seemed far more concerned about the state of

things outside Brilliance than in the intelligence sector. Lower ranking personnel were rushing through the passages, and even officers appeared concerned as they hurried along.

The car slowed as it approached a security arch guarded by an entire squad of soldiers and several of the feline mechs. Once they saw who was within, the soldiers stood at attention, and the car passed through.

Katrina wasn't impressed by the behavior; she knew it to be the norm in Sirius, *especially* in places like Brilliance where the highest-ranking officers and SVPs had little patience for anything that impeded their movements.

The passage beyond the security arch was even more utilitarian: white and clean, but otherwise unadorned. After a hundred meters, it widened, and the car pulled onto a platform that began to lower as soon as the vehicle came to a stop.

Katrina estimated that they descended fifty meters before the lift stopped and the doors opened.

"We're here," Hammish said as he exited the car.

Katrina followed him wordlessly and found herself in another nondescript room with a single door leading out. More soldiers stood at attention, and while she didn't *think* the SVP was playing her, what lay beyond could be the facility she wished to see, or an interrogation room filled with all manner of unpleasant implements.

Nothing for it.

"Your escort stays here," Hammish said as Carl and Kirb exited the vehicle.

"Very well." Katrina locked eyes with the man. "Then so does yours."

He looked her up and down, measuring how much of a threat she posed. "Very well."

They passed between the guards and through the door. Beyond lay a passage with plas grating for a deck, and exposed conduit running along the overhead. Judging by the amount of EM in the air, this was far more likely to be the NSAI control center than an interrogation facility, something for which Katrina was rather grateful.

She was relatively certain she could avoid being on the unpleasant end of any probing implements, but running from the authorities would not make for a very expeditious infiltration.

At the end of the corridor, four of the feline mechs stood, their stubby heads watching the two humans approach. They were larger than she'd expected, their heads even with her shoulders. As they passed by, she reached out and patted one, then another.

The machines didn't move, but Hammish snorted. "You've got guts, that's for sure. Could have just as easily lost that."

"I have cat-like reflexes," Katrina replied with a laugh. "Are we finally here?"

"We are."

The SVP palmed a control on the door, which slid open to reveal a small control room with three engineers seated at consoles facing into a larger room, roughly twenty by fifty meters, filled with two-meter-high cylinders.

Awww shit.

"Those are your NSAIs?" she asked, not bothering to hide her skepticism. "Those look like SAI core cylinders to me."

One of the technicians glanced back at her, eyes wide. His gaze slid to Hammish, then he quickly turned back to the task at hand.

"That's our secret," the SVP explained. "They're sentient AIs, but so carefully shackled that they think they're free while being entirely under our control. All the creativity of an SAI, with the reliability and control of an NSAI."

Through the man's explanation, Katrina kept her expression carefully schooled, not revealing the revulsion building within—or the worry. If the SAIs thought they were free, it would be much harder to convince them to change sides.

Looks like we'll have to opt for shutdown.

<Boys, how are things out there?>

<Things are well,> Kirb chuckled. *<And by 'well', I mean that Argin is taking a nap, and the two guards are trapped in a VR sim and think they're still on duty.>*

<Good, I need one of you in here. I can take Hammish, but I need someone to cover the three techs. Troy, any chance you can nix their Link?>

The AI snorted. *<You should be happy I can even talk to you down there. I'm having to route through Argin's Link—luckily, the Directorate puts some dirty backdoor access in their agents' heads, or I'd have lost you at the security arch.>*

<Looks like we'll have to work fast,> Katrina said as she walked toward the closest console and placed a hand on it. *<Give me a hundred seconds, then both come in. We'll have to keep a remote eye on the guards.>*

<You got it,> Carl replied.

Katrina stared through the glass, counting the SAI cylinders, while the nano she'd deposited on the console worked its way to the hard-Link port.

"What is that…seventy?" she asked.

"Seventy-two," Hammish corrected, stepping up next to her. "Impressive, isn't it?"

"How did you get so many that were suitable for a task like this?"

He chuckled. "The progenitor was an AI we snagged from Sol. It was one of their dreadnought's fire control brains. They were retiring the ship and had the AI scheduled for termination. I managed the operation personally to get it 'free'. Once here, we cloned it and reconditioned it. It now believes it's protecting its saviors."

"Wait…" Katrina shook her head in disbelief. "You can't clone an SAI's neural net like that, not straight across. You need to let it regrow from a base state."

Hammish cast her a look of appraisal and she realized that her utterance betrayed a deeper knowledge of AIs than most people possessed.

"We've examined leveraging AIs a few times in Bollam's," she explained. "So how did you manage it?" <Hold on a sec, guys. I want to learn a bit more.>

"If you recall, I used the word 'license'. We're not going to sell the base technology, we'll sell you product. Arrays of AIs ready to control drone fleets guard their masters."

"And does it take all of them to control the drones you've deployed?"

"No." Hammish shook his head. "We have a second wave we can utilize. There are a few backups in there, as well."

Katrina gave an appreciative nod. "So smaller arrays are possible for less significant defensive positions."

"Of course. We have several more here in Sirius, just waiting to draw the ISF in closer."

The nano she'd deposited on the console reached the hard-Link and jacked in. Katrina followed after, tunneling through to the internal systems, and patched Troy through her own Link.

<OK…I've locked them out,> he announced a few seconds later. <You're good to go.>

<Let's do this,> Katrina said to the two men.

The doors slammed open, and Carl bellowed, "Everybody freeeeeeze!"

Before Hammish had a chance to turn, Katrina swung her hand into his neck, fingers held knife-straight, crushing his larynx. He dropped to the floor, hands around his neck, air raking its way down his ruined throat.

Concussive shockwaves rippled through the small room,

and the three techs fell, one landing on the floor, their head making a solid *crack*, while the other two slumped over their consoles.

"Lock 'em down," Katrina said while crouching next to Hammish. She looked into the man's wide, staring eyes and smiled. "After I free these AIs, I'm going to let them decide what justice is for you."

<*That's not really healthy,*> Troy advised privately. <*Given that these are Hegemony AIs, they're too immature to know how to mete out justice.*>

<*Then we'll keep him on ice till they're ready.*>

<*Seems overwrought,*> the AI replied.

Katrina sighed. <*I suppose.*>

Hammish's breathing was improving, the look in his eyes shifting from panic to rage. "I'm..." he wheezed with one breath. "Gonna..."

"Oh stuff it." Katrina pushed him onto his back and drove a knee into his chest. "You're not making it out of this. None of you are."

"Who...?" the man made the sound while sucking in a pained breath.

"I love how you can use your real name with these yahoos, and they don't have a fucking clue," Carl said from behind her.

"Think waaaay back," Katrina whispered. "To the second ship named *Hyperion*, to the first war with Kapteyn's Star. I'm *that* Katrina. I'm the angel of death, and I've come to end your rotten civilization."

Hammish drew a deep breath, and she only had enough time to realize that there was no rasp in his throat before he twisted and swung a leg up into the back of her head. Suddenly, he was astride her, legs wrapped around her torso, a lightwand held to her neck.

"I don't think so," he hissed, then raised his voice. "Either of you two fuckers move, and I'll scrape the inside of this fallen angel's skull."

"Do it!" Katrina shouted, eyes wild as she tilted her head back. "It'll be the last signal your rotten brain ever sends to your arm. Let's roll the dice and see what happens."

Hammish's eyes narrowed, and she saw his bicep tense, readying for the strike.

And then he froze.

"Turn that thing off and get off me." She hissed the order, and the SVP of Sirian Intelligence complied, his expression going blank as his body followed orders his mind had no say in.

"Fuck," Kirb shook his head. "I hate it when you do that, Kat."

<Me too,> Troy chimed in.

"Me three," Katrina muttered as she struggled to her feet. "At this point, with all I've sacrificed, what's a little bit more of my soul to make sure this shithole burns?"

"Your call, boss," Kirb said as he pulled one of the techs from her seat and laid her on the deck. "Just make sure there's enough of you left when this is over."

"I'm pretty sure they have a nano-salve for it on the *I2*," Carl chuckled. "However, we first have to get back there. What's our next move?"

<I'm already working on it,> Troy replied. <Speaking of souls, these poor AIs have been tortured beyond even knowing what theirs are. I'll have their control of the drones down in twenty minutes or so, but it's going to be a rolling shutdown.>

"Which means we're looking at visitors," Katrina said.

"Yeah, lots of visitors," Carl looked down at the pulse rifle he'd stolen from one of the guards. "This isn't going to hold anyone off for long. C'mon, Kirb, let's go turn that dockcar into a fun little bomb."

"Any other ways down here?" Katrina asked Hammish.

"One," he replied woodenly. "At the far end of the chamber."

"Show me." She nodded toward the door next to the glass windows.

He walked toward it, palming it open while she re-routed his Link connection to proxy through her, monitoring his communications, ready to begin deflecting any inquiries as to the state of the drone fleet.

<Hey, Troy, I'm going to tell the military bigwigs that there's a problem down here. Put the drones into a holding pattern so it doesn't look like they're just dead.>

<You got it, I've also reached out to Jessica and let her know that the station is her oyster.>

Katrina nodded, hoping that her team hadn't taken too long in disabling the drones. <How're things out there?>

<Jessica's fleet has combined with Jordyn's. They're hitting orbital targets while contending with the perimeter fleet. Luckily, the generous folks on Brilliance hadn't shared their drone swarm, so they didn't have to contend with it.>

<How much of the perimeter fleet has moved in?>

<All of it. It's a hell of a slugfest. Over half of the Sirian ships have stasis shields.>

"Shit," Katrina muttered aloud as Hammish led her down a raised walkway that ran through the center of the node chamber. <Can we control the drones? Send them at the Sirians?>

<No, I don't have a high enough bandwidth connection to manage that...and these AIs...let's just say that they've seen enough already.>

<What if you were down here,> Katrina asked. <Directly connected.>

There was a long pause before the AI answered. <You know I hate going mobile.>

<Camille could take you. She can go full stealth. Should be easy.>

<Should.> Troy let the word hang. <I'll think about it.>

<Well, think fast, because I'm gonna seal up this back door before too long.>

THE LONG COUNT

STELLAR DATE: 05.15.8950 (Adjusted Years)
LOCATION: Control Station
REGION: Sirius System, Hegemony of Worlds

<*OK, I'm digging,*> Sabrina said after the orders came in from Admiral Evans. <*But so far, I'm not finding anything on where their other ships are.*>

Cheeky flipped through another screen of comm messages in the auxiliary data hub. "Yeah, me either. How do you just up and disappear two million ships?"

"We just have to go back far enough to establish a solid trail." Fina's head remained bent over her console as she spoke. "Learn where they were, see where they aren't now, and wherever is left is—"

"—an unimaginably large volume of space," Nance completed from her console.

Fina lifted her head at that, and fixed the engineer with a level stare. "I might have a bit of experience tracking things across a lot of space. It was sort of my job for some time."

"OK, OK," Cheeky gave both women a quelling look. "So, I have them refitting ships all across the system up until just a few weeks ago. Then they massed three groups. One went to Kapteyn's Star, the other formed up around Incandus, and the third is the one Joe is playing keep-ahead with. There are smaller patrol fleets all around the system, but they are largely on the same routes as before the buildup."

"So let's look at the shipyards doing the refit," Fina said. "Specifically, ones that did not contribute any vessels to the three large fleets we know about."

"She says like it's easy," Nance replied.

<*You could trade with me,*> Sabs said. <*Come watch over a room*

full of prisoners while I surf through records.>

"You're doing that anyway," Nance replied, glancing at the overhead as she spoke.

<Yeah, but then I wouldn't have to watch these moan-y Sirians anymore, and that would be a total win.>

"Shit…I think I have something," Fina whispered.

"You know where the other ships are?" Cheeky peered over her console at the former Hand director…and former dictator.

Stars…it's still hard to reconcile all of that.

"Maybe. There's a rather interesting message from the AST military about adding to Nibiru's defense. They requested two hundred thousand Sirian ships."

"And they sent them?" Nance asked, crossing her arms. "I find that hard to believe. Even though they're a core Hegemony member, we almost never saw their ships or troops in AST fleets."

"There's no record of the transfer, but shortly afterward, a number of ships matching that count no longer show up in the records at Sol-ward stations."

"Why Nibiru's defense, though?" Cheeky asked, looking from Fina to Nance and back. "What could be going on there?"

Fina flipped through a few screens, her eyes widening as she did so. "OK…they don't come right out and say it, but I don't think Sol's interdiction web reaches that far."

A smile formed on Nance's lips. "That certainly doesn't match the official statements."

"Sure doesn't," Fina met the engineer's expression with a grin of her own. "Would explain where they went, as well as present a bit of an opening. Sol wouldn't want a fleet of stasis ships that large at Nibiru unless they were up to something there."

"It's within a dozen AU of Sedna right now, too," Cheeky added. "Wow…that passage only happens once every few million years."

"Well, it's not all the ships," Fina replied. "But it does point to them being pulled away by the Hegemony. Given that they probably got stasis tech from the Heegs, it makes sense that they'd have to offer some in payment."

"But Nibiru?" Nance scowled. "I mean, it's terraformed and all, but it's still kind of a shithole."

"You've been there?" Cheeky asked.

"Virtual tour once in school," the engineer replied. "Heavy g at one-point-five, and constantly needing fuel to run its fusion sun so the place doesn't turn into a snowball. No way to run a world, if you ask me."

Fina straightened, stretching out her back. "It's a lot of mass, though. It has a number of ancient shipyards too. Maybe they figure it's a great place to put together some sort of rogue retaliation fleet."

"I think we should go check it out," Cheeky said. "The *Carthage*'s drones will have taken out the interdictor satellites by now. No need for us to stay on this dump."

<*Oh thank the stars,*> Sabs whispered into their minds. <*These people are such whiners. You'd think someone never made them shit in the corner before.*>

Cheeky snorted. "OK, team, let's make sure this station is locked down solid, and get on our way. Time to make a jump to Sol!"

Neither Fina nor Nance looked enthusiastic, and she cocked an eyebrow. "What?"

Fina shrugged. "It's just…you know…Sol. Shit's really getting real."

"Fighting god-like AIs on Airtha wasn't real?" Nance chuckled as she shut her console down.

"Yeah, but it's not where we all came from," Fina replied. "I mean…my father was born there. I've heard so many stories about it."

Cheeky walked up to her former captain and placed a hand on her shoulder, expression serious. "Something to consider…it's probably changed a bit."

"Gee…thanks for the warning."

The captain chuckled as they walked out of the room. "Glad to be of service. Now, down to the important business. What do you think Misha's prepared tonight?"

"All I know is that it had better be hot," Nance rolled her head side to side. "Another salad, and he's going out the airlock."

Fina laughed. "What about a hot salad?"

"Then I'll revive him and throw him into the black a second time."

HERE KITTY, KITTY

STELLAR DATE: 05.15.8950 (Adjusted Years)
LOCATION: ISS *Lantzer*, Orbiting Incandus
REGION: Sirius System, Hegemony of Worlds

[Drones are offline.]

Troy's simple statement brought cheers to the *Lantzer's* bridge, and Jessica pulled up the scan data to see the swarm still swirling around Brilliance.

[Looks up to me.]

[Faking out the Sirians. Come soon.]

"You heard him." The admiral glanced at Iris, a smile stretching her cheeks. "Let's do this thing."

"Should we keep Jordyn on task, or bring her around to Brilliance with us?" the AI asked.

Jessica gazed down at Incandus's nearspace, considering her options. "Let's leave her out here. Have her keep picking off juicy targets, that'll keep the Sirians divided while we bring the pain down on Brilliance."

"Is there any word on where their president is?"

<*COO,*> Gil corrected.

"Yeah, their coo-coo," she retorted, laughing.

"I think Leory is on Brilliance," Iris mused.

Jessica cocked an eyebrow. "Based on?"

"Network traffic and the fact they haven't brought the drones around while we burn half their space force."

"Not half," Jessica said.

Iris groaned. "OK, Miss Hyperbole. I think I get to drop some exaggeration every now and then."

"Fine, OK then. We're going get up close and personal with Brilliance. I'll take a strike force down, while you manage the fleet up here."

"Hey, whoa!" Iris waved a hand at Jessica. "I passed up a promotion so I could still do fun stuff like storm a station. Now I have to stay up here and manage a fleet while you get to go down there?"

"It has to be me," Jessica replied. "Just in case there are complications only I can deal with."

"What if those complications come up here?" Trevor asked.

The admiral shrugged. "Then Iris will have to deal with them."

"Really?" the AI groaned. "Trevor gets to go too?"

"Yeah, I need him to slam people around before I electrocute them."

"Or after," he added.

"That too."

Ten minutes later, Jessica's fleet had dropped closer to Incandus, circling around the planet to where Brilliance lay, still surrounded by its drone swarm.

"That thing gives me the heebies," Karma said as he stared up at the forward display. "We *sure*-sure that they're disabled?"

"Uh huh," Jessica said with a nod. "That's what Troy said."

"Can we get a confirmation?" The worry in Lucida's tone matched Karma's.

Jessica crossed her arms. "Unfortunately, no. He's left the *Voyager*."

"Say what?" Karma gaped. "I don't like the sounds of that."

<Don't worry.> Gil sounded a little worried. <He's going down to the node chamber where the drone control is so he can manage things directly.>

"Which means?" Karma pressed.

"It means we hope to take control of at least some of the drones," Jessica replied. "And then use them against the Sirians."

"Oh!" Lucida nodded rapidly, a smile forming on her lips. "I like this plan."

"I don't," Iris groused, her silver eyes boring into Jessica's. "You owe me."

"We could clone my body, and then you could have my unique abilities as well," Jessica suggested.

A cough came from Trevor. "Uh…I don't know how I feel about that. Good…I think? How would I tell you two apart?"

"Easy," Jessica winked at Iris. "We'll just tattoo a '2' on her forehead."

The AI rolled her eyes. "You're selling this so well."

Jessica wrapped an arm around her wife. "OK, we're going to gear up. I trust you all can bring us close to the station?"

"Piece of cake," Iris replied. "Just you 'us', or are you going to take down troops from other ships?"

She paused, considering the benefit of a larger force, then shook her head. "No, we're going to go in fast and hard. Find the COO, nab him, and get out."

"Good deal. I'll still keep a fast response force ready just in case."

Jessica placed a hand on her chest. "You don't trust me?"

Silver hands settled on her cheeks, followed by Iris's lips on hers. "I trust you plenty," the AI whispered. "It's all those fuckin' Lumins I'm worried about."

* * * * *

"Well, hey there," Katrina said as Camille and Malorie appeared in the service tunnel that led away from the node chamber. "Fancy seeing a girl and her pet spider in a place like this."

The woman snorted. "Uhh…OK. I have no idea what that means. I'm here because Troy needed a meatsuit to carry him. His words."

<Guilty,> the AI said from the case Camille held in her left hand.

"And I'm here because I'm not getting left alone on the ship," Malorie added. "Plus, I want to get my pew-pew on."

"Did you bring weapons?"

Camille nodded to Malorie, and a large bag appeared on her back. "Sure did. Enough to make some serious booms."

"Those are the best ones," Katrina replied with a laugh.

Camille set the bag down and pulled the stealth wrap off before opening it up and selecting a small pouch. "A few little surprises for our friends."

"You're a woman after my own heart," Katrina said as Camille turned back into the tunnel. "Can you seal the door up after? I'll get Troy hooked in."

"You got it."

Malorie skittered through the node chamber and leapt up into the overhead, only to hang down from a thread a moment later. "This is like a playground!"

<There's a routing node on the left side of the room,> Troy said, ignoring Malorie as he sent Katrina an indicator that appeared on her vision. <Camille brought connectors that should work, so let's get me plugged in so I can deal with this mess.>

"You got it."

She found the hard-Link line in the bag and carried Troy's case over to the routing node and plugged him in.

"Anything else you need?"

<Yeah, don't let me get shot.>

"Umm...I guessssss I can do that. If you insist."

<I do.>

Katrina nodded, trusting that the AI had already tapped into the room's optics. She walked back to the bag and selected a multifunction rifle and several ammo packs.

"Leave me the plasma torch and a gun," Camille called out from where she was tucking explosives behind a conduit.

"Deal," Katrina replied before shouldering the rifle and clipping the spare ammunition to her belt. *<How're you two doing out there?>* she asked Kirb and Carl.

<Great,> Carl said. *<The car's set to blow, and we brought the two guards into the control room and locked them down.>*

<Camille has a plasma torch that she'll bring once she's done setting things up to go boom.>

<Thanks,> her first mate replied. *<I have to say, by the way, that I'm not sure how keen I am on the fact that we're basically sealing ourselves in down here.>*

Katrina felt the same way, though she didn't want to share her concern with the others.

<We'll be alright,> she assured him. *<Jessica will be here soon, and the Sirians will have to surrender.>*

<Sure,> Kirb added. *<Right after Jessica's fleet takes out the defenders…many of which are on this station.>*

Katrina chuckled. *<Well, at least it's safe here. They have these nodes well-shielded.>*

<So it's a tomb?> Carl asked.

<Sure, whatever makes you feel better,> she replied.

<Just in case anyone cares, I'm all linked up,> Troy said. *<I think I can manage a few million drones at once. I have external scan access too. Jessica's fleet is inbound.>*

Right on cue, Hammish's Link picked up calls from the admirals responsible for the station's defense, all of them demanding to know when the drone swarm would be back online.

<Five minutes,> she lied, sending the response as the SVP. *<We're correcting the data routing issue that knocked us offline.>*

<Make it less,> one of the admirals on the other end growled. *<COO Leory is not impressed with this issue. It couldn't have worse timing.>*

<I understand,> she sent back. *<We'll have them fixed before the enemy reaches us.>*

<We just got a report that the STC can't reach the control team. Are they affected by the routing issue?>

<Must be,> Katrina made sure to sound annoyed. <I'm not really focused on who they can chat with. We're working as fast as we can.>

<We'll send down a repair team.>

"Shit," she muttered aloud, knowing that refusal would make her look suspicious. <We've already dispatched one, but feel free to send another if it'll make you feel like you're contributing.>

The response might have been a little strong, but she didn't think that Hammish was the sort to suffer being second-guessed. Either way, no response came, and she set the Intelligence SVP's Link back on standby.

Back inside the control room, she set the bag atop a table next to the window looking out over the nodes, and pulled out two rifles for Kirb and Carl, along with enough ammo to keep them busy for a bit.

<Come and get it,> she announced just as the two men entered the room. "Damn, it's like I summoned you."

"High powered rifles always summon me," Kirb replied. "Especially this ISF gear. Gonna put holes in bad guys."

"I'll admit…" Carl paused as he hefted his rifle. "I have no idea how we survived for so long on the leavin's we were able to scrounge. We're so spoiled now."

Katrina laughed. "Because you had no idea what you were missing out on."

"You did," Kirb said.

"Yeah, and I never told you because I didn't want to make you sad. Aren't I nice?"

The two men glanced at each other, and a wry grin slipped onto Carl's lips. "Is this a trick question?"

"You two are hilarious. How big a boom is the car going to make?"

"If it goes off at this level, it'll blow the doors in the

passage," Kirb said. "Which is why we need to weld them shut."

"Gonna have to fight Camille for the plasma torch," Katrina said with a wink.

<There's another one in the bag,> Troy interjected.

"Really?" She reached inside and felt around, finally locating the second one underneath another detpack satchel. "OK...the thing was sneaky."

<It's inanimate.>

"So are you," Kirb said with a laugh as he took the torch and walked back into the passage.

<Normally, I'm a starship. I'm very animate.>

"So, do we have a plan other than holding off the bad people till Jessica saves us?" Carl asked.

"Why, isn't that enough?"

"Well...depends on what they throw our way. I mean, they could hit us with an unending stream of goons."

Katrina placed a hand on Carl's shoulder. "Our plan is to shoot them. Then shoot them some more."

He snorted a laugh. "You're like the queen of tactics." Turning to the bag, he rummaged through it. "Ohhh, more explosives."

"You know how Camille is...well, and Malorie, too."

"Sure do," he chuckled while piling the detpacks into his arms. "I'll set these up in here and the passage."

Katrina nodded. "Sounds good. I guess we should move the hapless Sirians out of the line of fire."

"You sure?" Carl eyed the technicians and guards. "They'd make a great barricade."

"Sadly, yes."

No sooner had she moved the unconscious techs to the room's far corner than Kirb came rushing back in.

"Lift's going up," he announced. "Means the big boom is coming soon."

"Or so we hope." Carl gave the other man a sidelong look. "It wasn't really our best work."

Katrina shook her head. "I don't believe it for a second. No one cobbles together an explosion like you two."

Her words were punctuated by a muffled *foom*, and a series of tremors beneath their feet.

"See?"

"Oh thank stars," Kirb ran a hand across his brow. "I was really worried about how the accelerometer hookup was going to work."

"Told you it would be fine," Carl said.

<*Wow, that made a mess up there,*> Troy commented. <*Of course, that also means the jig is up. They know things have gone sideways now.*>

Katrina tapped into the feed the AI supplied, and saw that the end of the corridor where the car lift terminated was a mangled ruin. Twisted bulkheads leaned drunkenly from all sides, sections of deck plate smashed into them—with the bodies of what had likely been the repair team mixed in with the destruction.

"OK...yuck." She slid the feed out of her vision, but flagged it to alert her if movement was detected. <*How're you looking back there, Camille?*>

<*Booms are set and doors are welded. I wouldn't mind some company, though. Malorie is...I have no idea what she's doing.*>

"Kirb, why don't you go join Camille," Katrina said. "Carl and I will keep an eye on this end of things."

He nodded and walked to the node chamber's door. "I wonder if she brought any food?"

"Don't count on it," Carl replied. "And if she did, she probably won't share."

"Typical," the other man muttered.

The feed from above lit up, showing a group of soldiers moving through the wreckage, approaching the half-torn-open hole leading down to the drone control center.

Four of the feline mechs slinked along after and, following a short assessment, leapt down into the ruined car lift.

"OK, Carl," Katrina placed a hand on his shoulder. "Here goes."

"Don't worry," he said, flashing an easy smile. "We got this."

* * * * *

The assault shuttle boosted away from the *Lantzer*, dodging defensive fire from Brilliance Station and the Sirian fleet alike. The vessel shook and rattled as a string of railshots hit the stasis shield, shoving them off course before Jessica brought them back around, angling toward the site that would give them the shortest route to the COO's offices.

"Damn, they really don't want us to drop in," Trevor said. "Think we can fake them out well enough?"

"No idea. Depends on what their own stasis power draws are. If they have more efficient systems than we think, then they'll never buy it."

She pushed the ship into a steeper dive, bow pointed directly at the station, beamfire lancing all around, another kinetic shot delivering a glancing blow before they closed further, slipping beneath the railguns' angle of fire.

Beams still tagged the craft, but none of those struck with enough force to drive them off course.

Jessica double-checked the pre-programmed route, then rose from her seat and set her helmet in place. <*OK, everyone. Get ready.*>

She and Trevor walked into the rear of the shuttle, where a squad of Marines was already stacked up at the rear entrance. At a nod from her, the lieutenant opened the hatch, the black expanse of space yawning at them. The shuttle shifted, now running along Brilliance's surface, towers whipping past the craft on either side.

The holoindicator above the exit started a ten-count, and the Marines tensed, ready to dive out into the black. Jessica mouthed the numbers silently as the timer counted down, already running when it hit zero. It only took five seconds for fifteen people to dive out of the shuttle, each one disappearing from view once clear of the craft's engine wash.

They used grav boosters to keep off the enemy's scopes, lancing down toward the station between a pair of crystalline towers. The 'fall' only took half a minute, Marine boots hitting the deck next to the base of one of the towers without any defensive fire coming their way.

<OK, people,> Jessica began, while Trevor and Lieutenant Wes double-checked that everyone had safely completed the drop. <COO's tower is that way.> She pointed to her right. <Our access point is just on the far side of this spire.>

<Ooh-Rah,> the team responded, and followed after the lieutenant, while Jessica and Trevor brought up the rear.

She'd selected this squad for a very specific reason. Not all of them had been in the military during the Sirian assault on the Kap, but they'd all been alive. Every one of these Marines remembered the raw fear when the enemy fleet lined up to churn and burn Victoria.

Every one of them was eager for payback.

Ahead, she could see the shuttle banking around a tower, coming into range of a defense node. Railshots slammed into the craft, which struggled to stay on course. It was tagged by beams, more railfire, and finally, a string of missiles.

The last proved to be the final straw, and the shuttle exploded, raining debris down on Brilliance.

<You were a good little shuttle,> Trevor chuckled. <Served us well.>

<Sentimental over a transport hull?> Jessica asked, shaking

her head. *<I think we'll manage to build a new one.>*

<You're a riot, dear,> he replied. *<I'll have you know I fixed that bird up myself after our incident with the core AIs out in the PED.>*

<Shoot, really? If I'd known, I'd've picked another one.>

<Well, I fixed them all.>

She laughed. *<I should have known this was a trick question.>*

Ahead, the Marines formed up at an airlock, initiating a breach procedure.

<There's another lock a hundred meters down,> Lieutenant Wes said. *<I think we should hit both.>*

<Good call,> Jessica nodded. *<You take a fireteam down there and stage a diversion once inside. We'll go stealth to find the COO.>*

<Yes, ma'am,> the lieutenant replied with a laugh. *<This is going to be fun.>*

She shook her head in amusement as the five Marines moved down the station's hull to the next airlock. They were halfway to it when a pair of cat-like robots came into view, firing at the team. Beamfire streamed out, slicing the mechs to ribbons before the group moved on.

<Diversion started,> the lieutenant sent back. *<Thanks for giving us the fun job.>*

<You're welcome,> Jessica replied before turning to Trevor. *<I kinda thought they'd be upset.>*

<You just told them they have free reign to kick Sirian ass with zero consequences. You could only have upped that by giving each of them their own cruiser.>

Jessica laughed and turned her attention back to the breach team, which now had the outer airlock door open. *<Fair point. I hadn't thought of it that way.>*

The airlock had a safety grav shield, and the team decided not to bother with maintaining an airtight seal, and simply started cutting into the second door. It only took half a minute for the group of determined Marines to breach it, and when the doors blew outward, they stepped into the opening and began firing.

A group of Sirian troops had been waiting, but they were lightly armored, and the Marines had gone straight to railguns and electron beams.

It only took a few seconds for the defenders to break and run, leaving several bodies in their wake. The Marines followed after, advancing slowly down the passage to the first intersection, where they set up barriers.

<More of those cat-things coming in,> the fireteam leader warned.

The second fireteam activated their stealth and leapfrogged the first, moving further down the passage, ready to hit the enemy from the rear if necessary. Jessica and Trevor held back, crouched inside the remains of the airlock.

A few seconds passed, and then two mechs rounded the corner just as another pair seemed to flow right through the walls, landing atop the Marines.

One went down in an instant, his head severed clean off his body, while another took a clawed swipe to the leg that tore off armor and cut deep into muscle.

The other two Marines didn't hesitate to leap at the mechs, lightwands flashing as they did their own cutting and tearing. Behind them, the stealthed fireteam sent a barrage of carefully aimed railfire at the other two bots, taking them down in a matter of seconds.

<Watch out for those cat-things,> Jessica sent to the lieutenant. <They can go through walls.>

<They can **what**?>

<I remember hearing stories about it. It's ancient tech from way back at the outset of the first Sentience Wars.>

The junior officer groaned. <I thought that was just a legend.>

<Guess not. Must be some sort of phased matter system. They can cut right through our armor too.>

<Well, this just got a lot less fun.>

Jessica sent an acknowledgment, and moved forward to the downed Marines. The team leader was putting the decapitated soldier's head into a stasis pouch, while the woman with the lacerated leg was injecting biofoam.

<I'm good, ma'am,> she said. *<Once I get this packed in, I'll put a stealth wrap around it and be good to go.>*

Jessica considered the woman's words, but knew she wouldn't endanger the mission, so she nodded before approaching one of the downed bots.

<These look similar to the ones I remember learning about as a kid. Better power sources, though, I'd imagine.>

<The bastards,> Trevor muttered, then turned and fired a series of shots at a target down one of the side passages. *<We need to get in stealth and get moving. Any longer here, and they'll box us in.>*

Jessica nodded again and glanced at the fireteam that had advanced further down the passage. *<Move on to our first rally point. I want to get to a comm node so we can reach out to Troy. If anyone has a bead on where the COO will be, it's him.>*

<You got it, ma'am,> came the reply, and the Marines moved off while Jessica turned back to the decapitated body.

<We've set a charge on it,> the corporal said. *<Just gotta clear the area.>*

She nodded at the stealth pouch he carried on his back. *<Keep that safe.>*

<Yes, ma'am. With my life.>

A minute later, Private Miranda, the injured woman, was back on her feet, favoring her wounded leg—more to reduce strain than from pain—but otherwise moving without issue.

<Let's take that passage,> Jessica indicated a route that would lead them to the rally point, but in a direction less likely to encounter enemy reinforcements.

The team disappeared from view, moving briskly through the service corridors until they came to a nondescript door.

They didn't have precise plans for Brilliance, but she suspected her team had to be close to public areas at this point.

Threading a nanofilament through the space between the doors, Corporal Arnold put up a view on the combat net. Beyond, the passage continued for a few meters before opening into a broad, multi-level atrium. Fountains in the center sprayed plasma in the air, a spectacle entirely ignored by the dozen civilians she saw hurrying past the opening.

<Looks like we're getting close,> she said. *<There'll have to be increased security soon.>*

The fireteam went first, three Marines easing through the door and out into the space beyond. Once it was flagged as clear, Jessica and Trevor followed and moved toward the fountain, while the fireteam moved around the perimeter.

<We're only one tower from the COO's,> Trevor said when they stopped for a group of civilians rushing past. *<There should be more security.>*

The deck rumbled beneath their feet, and Jessica suppressed a laugh. *<I think our little diversion with the lieutenant's team is doing its part.>*

<I guess, but they can't be that dumb. We breached through two separate airlocks. Shouldn't take an NSAI to figure out that we have multiple teams.>

<A girl can dream.>

An errant air current lit up on Jessica's vision, her armor's sensors flagging it as having no origin.

<Corporal Arnold, we've got stealthed defenders,> she reported.

<Aye, ma'am. I just picked one up as well. Looks like more of those fucking cat-things.>

<Just our luck. I wonder how many of those the Sirians have?>

Trevor passed an update onto the combat net, highlighting twenty more possible stealthed cat-mechs. *<I'm seeing a small EM fluctuation from these locations that match ones coming from the two we've spotted.>*

<Shit,> Jessica muttered. *<I guess the answer is 'a lot'. Where do the Sirians get off having cool tech like this?>*

<We've been spoiled, playing on easy mode,> he replied.

A memory of her harrowing fight with the ascended AIs in the PED came to mind, and she shook her head to clear it away. *<If this has been easy mode, I don't want to imagine what hard would be like.>*

<Me either. So, what do we do? Those things are prowling everywhere.>

The Marines were moving cautiously along the right side of the room, and because Jessica had opted to go straight across—which had seemed like a good idea at the time—she was now looking at a space filled with seven of the cats, each one crossing the area in a highly irregular pattern.

<Oh shit.> Realization dawned, and she bit back further curses. *<They're searching for us.>*

<I think you're right,> Arnold said.

<We're going to have to double back,> Trevor advised.

Jessica shook her head. *<No, that'll take too long. We can't tip-toe our way through Brilliance in search of their COO. I'll tell Hiro to move on to the second rally point. Time to do things the fun way.>*

<Here we go,> her husband muttered.

She ignored his statement. *<I'll draw them out. Everyone else, shoot them before they get me.>*

<Ma'am?> Arnold sounded more than a little alarmed. *<Is that seriously your plan?>*

Jessica stepped away from the fountain and slipped around one of the cats, drawing energy from within herself. Two of the mechs paused, then swung toward her, clearly sensing the EM buildup in the air.

<That's right, kitties, come to momma.>

When they were just a few meters away, she stretched her hands out and released electron streams, bolts of lightning arching from her fingers to the closest cats, hopping to another three nearby while tendrils of light spidered into the floor and a few unfortunate passersby.

The two closest cats—and the humans—fell to the ground, while shots rang out from the Marines as they targeted the other cat-mechs that had been exposed by the burst of energy.

Jessica turned and released another stream of electrons at a cat attempting to sneak up on her, taking it out before the electrons arced to several others. The discharges had filled the atrium's air with static, the invisible shapes of the remaining cats becoming easier to detect with augmented vision.

<Well done,> Trevor said as he fired a stream of rail pellets at one mech, then another.

<Look out!> Miranda shouted, and Jessica spun to see a mech's claws hurtling toward her face with the animal close behind.

Her lightwand was out in an instant, blade severing the creature's right 'paw' as she sidestepped. The thing landed rather gracefully for only having three feet, and Jessica fired another burst of energy at it, dropping the bot to the deck.

More shots rang out, and then Arnold called out, <Clear!>

Trevor echoed the statement, and Jessica took off at a run for the door leading to the next tower, her husband close behind, while the Marines dashed into the open to follow.

Weapons fire came from across the atrium, lancing between the ISF force, and tagging one of the Marines, then Trevor.

"Fuck!" he shouted. "When being massive sucks."

He paused at the exit and unslung his heavy repeater, slamming a magazine of thumb-sized—his, not Jessica's—HE slugs into the weapon.

Via the few drones they'd dispersed, Jessica could see that on the right side of the atrium, a squad of Sirian troops was spreading out, taking shots at the exit.

She was about to offer to cover Trevor when he stepped

out, firing ten HE rounds in rapid succession. Seven hit their intended targets, and five of the enemy were vaporized — the other two likely wishing they had been.

He ducked back into the passage and slapped a detpack on the bulkhead. <*OK, now we can go.*>

The Marines had already ranged down the passage, Arnold stood at a wide staircase that led down toward the COO's tower, visible through a crystalline wall that gave a view of the spires jutting from Brilliance's surface.

Miranda and Lane set up on either side of the passage, covering cross corridors until Jessica and Trevor reached their position.

"Duck," Trevor said, the smile in his voice coming through loud and clear.

Jessica just barely had time to get around the corner as flames burst from the passage.

"Really, sir?" Miranda asked, her limp looking a little more pronounced as she eased out around the corner to look down at the twisted ruin of the hall.

"Sorry," Trevor shook his head. "I didn't think that much of the blast would funnel down this way."

<*Let's move, everyone.*> Jessica made a point of addressing them on the Link. <*It's pretty clear where we're going, and I don't want to give the Sirians more time to get ready.*>

The team nodded their agreement and moved down the stairs, everyone reactivating stealth systems, though a few of them were no longer at peak effectiveness.

<*Next time, don't get covered in soot,*> she admonished Trevor privately.

<*Yeah, that was a bad move. I think that pack was dialed up higher than normal.*>

<*This is why you check them before you set them,*> she said.

<*Noted. It sure did the job, though.*>

Jessica took one look at the destroyed passage before

descending the stairs, and couldn't help but laugh. <*That it did. Just the beginning of a much-needed remodel for this place.*>

The corridor at the base of the stairs intersected with a few others, and then dropped another level before ending in a field of grass, dotted with copses of trees. The land sloped down still further, but she could just make out a glinting ribbon of light.

<*Damn…there's a river down here.*>

<*Wow, that's a great holo,*> Lane murmured, staring up at the overhead. <*My suit's scan can barely tell that it's looking at fake sky.*>

<*Stay frosty,*> Arnold warned. <*It'll be cake to hide more of those fucking cats down here.*>

<*I used to like cats,*> Miranda muttered.

The group moved through the grass, staying to the worn paths, scanning the gently waving stalks for any signs of stealthed enemies. It only took a few minutes to reach the river, which Jessica realized wasn't water, but a strange plasmic state of matter. It *looked* like flowing light, but moved like a liquid.

<*Let's jump it,*> she suggested.

<*I'll go first,*> Trevor said, and took a running jump, his powered armor's a-grav assist sending him across to the far shore.

He moved to a large, ruddy boulder and set up next to it, a trio of microdrones spreading out from his location.

Lane followed, then Arnold.

<*You go next,*> Jessica told Miranda. <*I'll be right behind you.*>

The Marine sent an acknowledgment, grass crushing beneath her feet as she dashed toward the river. Jessica took off after her, jumping just a few seconds later.

She was moving faster than the limping Marine, and caught up to her at the peak of their arcs. They were nearly at the far shore when a beam lanced out from a copse of trees on their right, hitting Miranda in the chest. Her armor's a-grav failed, and she lost height, legs dipping into the river.

Jessica altered her trajectory and grabbed the Marine, heaving her to the shore to reveal thighs burned away to the bone, and nothing at all below her femurs.

"Sweet *fuck!*" the other woman bellowed. "This just isn't my day!"

Trevor was hewing lumber with his heavy repeater, and after knocking down half the trees in the copse where the fire had come from, switched to hitting another nearby stand, decimating it as well.

<Was there another shooter?> Jessica asked.

<No idea. I was just being thorough.>

<I appreciate that,> Miranda said while groaning. *<OK…nerves are being shut off.>* She looked up at Jessica. *<Sorry. I swear I don't get so fucked up normally.>*

The admiral knelt next to her, and placed a hand on the woman's shoulder. *<It's OK, shit happens.>* She looked up at Arnold. *<Corporal Hiro should be at the second rally point by now. We're going to meet up with him, and have them come back to get you to an egress point. Call down for pickup if there's no safe way off this thing.>*

<Ma'am…are you sure?>

<I am. After we meet up with Hiro, we'll sync up with your LT and move on Leory. You just get Miranda and Edge safely back to the Lantzer.*>*

The corporal nodded. *<You can count on us.>*

Using the last of the fireteam's stealth wrap, they got Miranda concealed, and moved the team to a nearby copse of trees, where the Marines hunkered down to wait.

<Stay safe,> Jessica said, clasping Arnold on the shoulder. *<We'll get the job done.>*

<We have no doubt, ma'am.>

Jessica and Trevor moved off, working their way up the

slope to the edge of the park, and down a series of passages that led them to the suspected location of a comm node that would put them in touch with Troy.

As they drew close, a drone's signal hit Jessica's sensors, and she hopped across it, connecting to Corporal Henry.

<How're you holding up, Marine?> she asked.

<A few brushes with those cat-things, but otherwise, we're good. And you, ma'am?>

<Arnold's team took casualties. They're going to meet up with Lieutenant Wes, and get to an exfil point. Did you find a comm node?>

<I did,> the corporal replied, a modicum of worry in his voice. <We haven't breached it yet—didn't want to alert the baddies to our being here.>

<Good, we're two mikes out. See you soon.>

<Yes, ma'am.>

The corporal's tone was deferential, reminding her how young some of the Marines were. Henry had been born during the *Intrepid*'s flight from Bollam's World to New Canaan, and he was one of the oldest members of the platoon.

<They're all just fucking kids,> she said to her husband. <So many fucking kids.>

Trevor sent a warm feeling as he trailed after. <I know. I keep seeing our kids' faces when I look at them. All of us tearing at one another just because some AIs want to keep humanity in check....>

<Generally, that's true, but Sirius was a festering pile of trash from day one. No AIs to blame this one on. Just good ol' human asshattery.>

<Never a shortage of that shit.>

The pair fell silent until they turned down a nondescript corridor that led to a service passage. Within waited Henry's fireteam, the corporal and private Naomi at the near end, and privates Esla and Unger at the far side.

<Any Sirians down here?> Jessica asked.

<Not that we've seen. Most civilians have moved deeper into the station, and we've only seen a few soldiers on this side of the river.>

Jessica pursed her lips, afraid of what that meant. *<OK, let's breach this node and see if Troy knows where the COO is—because it doesn't seem like he's anywhere near here now.>*

<And if he doesn't know?> Trevor asked.

<Then we'll have to find a VP somewhere and work our way up the chain.>

Disabling her stealth now that the team's nanocloud had scoured the entire passage, she nodded to Henry. *<OK, let's go take a look at this node.>*

The door to the comm node was midway down the passage, and after a minute's work with a hackIt, they had it open, and Jessica jacked into the control console's hard-Link.

The first thing she found were messages on the military channels directing reserve forces to the drone control center. So far, the facility hadn't been breached, which was good news, but she felt a spike of worry for the small team she'd sent down there.

I hope they've disabled the system and gotten out by now.

She picked up ISF breadcrumbs in the comm network, and followed the route, making a connection with the AI in a minute.

<Troy. Are you cleared out of drone control yet? Half the Sirian military is on its way.>

<Oh yeah? They can join the half that's already banging down our door.>

<Are you trapped? Do you need exfil?>

<By choice, yes, and that would be nice.>

Jessica did her best not to groan. *<Why are you making me drag things out of you?>*

<Sorry, busy. Passing you to Katrina.>

"Shit..." she muttered aloud, wondering what was taxing the AI so strongly.

The contact shifted, and she felt a familiar mind. <*Katrina?*>

<*Jessica! Can't tell you how good it is to hear your voice! Say, can you get us the fuck out of here? That'd be swell.*>

<*Troy said something about you being trapped there by choice....*>

<*Yeah,*> the other woman paused for a moment. <*The drone control system? It's AIs. A lot of them. More than we can carry.*>

<*OK.*> Jessica pulled up a station plan on the console. <*We're on our way.*>

A TRUER TALE

STELLAR DATE: 05.15.8950 (Adjusted Years)
LOCATION: Drone Control Center, Brilliance Station
REGION: Sirius System, Hegemony of Worlds

Katrina leant against the wall and drew in a deep breath, doing her best to calm her pounding pulse.

"Bracing, eh?" Carl said, laughing as he grabbed an enemy's rifle and pulled out the power cell, checking its contacts before sliding it into his rifle. "Good thing Troy figured out how to take control of those mech cats, or we'd be chew toys by now."

<Just the nine hundred and twenty-seventh time I've saved your asses,> the AI said. *<You know, not counting the times I do it back to back to back.>*

"All hail Troy, the victorious AI," Katrina muttered as she straightened and checked her rifle over before pulling up feeds from the few remaining optics in the car lift and tunnel above. "Shit…there's a fresh platoon moving in. Don't these goons all realize they're marching to their deaths?"

"Guess they don't care," Carl replied as he checked over the two last cat-mechs. "Too bad the stealth ones are all dead."

<They have two of them at the rear door,> Troy said.

<Hey, Kirb,> Carl called back. *<You holding out on us with the stealth kitties?>*

<Not me,> Kirb replied. *<Malorie and Camille keep riding them into battle like they're fricking war steeds. They're currently rampaging through the service corridors, mowing down Sirians.>*

Katrina bit her lip. *<Malorie, Camille. Don't range too far. We can't have Kirb getting overrun.>*

<Don't worry, mom,> Malorie groused. *<I can see him from where I am. Besides, overrun by who? We've easily killed an entire*

company. The Sirians are running scared, crying about invisible monsters. It's great.>

Katrina decided to let the others do what they thought was best. *After all, this isn't even their first time riding war cats into battle.*

Carl sighed and stacked another enemy's body atop the makeshift barricade. "I take it you're not going to make them share."

"You try to tell Malorie she can't ride her invisible cat. Let me know how that works out."

He snorted a laugh. "I'll take my chances with the Sirians."

A trio of rounds tore through the passage, slamming into the node chamber's window, adding to a long crack that was growing in the thick, transparent carbon.

Carl returned fire, and they were rewarded with a muffled cry. No sooner had the sound faded than more shots rang out.

Katrina had leant out and added her own rounds to the fray, when Troy's voice came into her mind.

<Jessica just contacted me.>

<Patch her through!> she all but shouted, laughing when the admiral spoke.

<Katrina?>

<Jessica! Can't tell you how good it is to hear your voice! Say, can you get us the fuck out of here? That'd be swell.>

<Troy said something about you being trapped there by choice….>

<Yeah.> Katrina glanced over her shoulder at the AI cores. *<The drone control system? It's AIs. A lot of them. More than we can carry.>*

<OK.> Jessica paused, likely accessing plans. *<We're on our way.>*

<Better hurry,> Troy interjected, passing the two women a feed.

It showed a ship in a docking bay, a luminous figure

already moving across the deck.

<Hard to be sure where it's going, but that core AI is moving in your general direction.>

<Shit!> Katrina exclaimed. *<How far?>*

<Twenty klicks, but it's moving fast.>

<I'm going to have Iris drop a platoon,> Jessica said. *<Not sure how long it'll take.>*

<Hopefully less time than it takes that thing to get here…if this is where it's going,> Katrina replied, turning her attention back to the attacking Sirians. *<Though, even without that bastard, things are kinda dire down here.>*

<We're already moving,> Jessica sent. *<We're not far. Be there in a few minutes.>*

"What's up?" Carl asked during a brief reprieve. "You looked relieved, then a bit scared."

"Order?"

"Bad then good."

"An ascended AI is on its way here…probably."

Carl coughed and then muttered a string of curses. "And the good?"

"Jessica might just get here first."

"Is she bringing an army?"

Katrina considered the question for a moment. "Well, she did say 'we', so she's not alone, at least. Not that she needs anyone else. The woman can single-handedly kill those things."

He nodded before firing another stream of shots down the passage. "Yeah, I know that, but I'd like to have her *and* an army. I assume our goal at some point is to get the fuck outta here with these cores?"

"Yeah, once Troy says they're ready."

<They're ready.>

"That was fast. How long have they been all set?"

<A bit. But you've been busy, and it's going to take some doing to

get them out of their towers. There really wasn't a way to do it and hold off the barbarian hordes.>

"Fair enough," Katrina replied, then reached out to the others. *<Hey, folks. Looks like an ascended AI is coming to say hi, but so is Jessica.>*

<Seriously?> Malorie asked with a gleeful laugh. *<I hope we get to see her suck the life out of that thing. That'll be the balls.>*

<The balls?>

<Sure. It's a saying.>

Kirb chuckled. *<I guess everything's a saying somewhere. Even weird-ass stupid ones.>*

<Hey, Kirb.> Malorie's amused tone came over the Link a moment later.

<What?>

<There's a fireteam coming your way. You got 'em?>

The man coughed. *<That's a friggin' squad. Care to lend a hand?>*

<No, my pride and feelings are both too hurt. I need time to heal.>

<Malorie…> Katrina warned while quickly swapping mags before firing on a pair of heavily armored Sirians crouched in the mangled ruin of the car lift.

<Fiiiine.>

Katrina kept a portion of her attention on the fighting at the rear entrance, and another piece of it on nearby optical pickups, keeping an eye out for the nimbus shape of the ascended AI. She still remembered her encounter with Xavia—something she'd thought of as a positive experience until the being's 'memory' tried to compel her to kill Tanis.

She was still conflicted over the encounter. Xavia had saved her life, and by extension, many others. Though she'd done some questionable things over the years, Katrina considered herself to be a force for good.

I mean…look what I'm doing now.

Still, it was impossible to put aside the worry that being the pawn of an ascended AI had tipped the scales against her.

Another Sirian came into her sights, and she targeted the woman's neck, firing an electron beam and rail combo that tore the enemy's head off.

Redemption, one Sirian corpse at a time.

The thought didn't offer nearly as much comfort as she might have hoped.

The battle droned on for another few minutes, the Sirians launching new waves while the defenders scavenged weapons and ammunition off the corpses.

During a lull, Carl leant against the bulkhead, chest heaving.

"This is getting ridiculous. Why do they keep coming? A smarter person would just cut through the walls and surround us."

"They're probably doing that," Katrina replied. "Just keeping us busy with expendable lives in the meantime."

"Damn." Carl pointed at the carbon window that separated the control room from the node chamber. "When did that happen?

Katrina glanced back to see a meter-wide hole blown in one of the panes, and shook her head. "I have no idea. Jessica had better get here soon."

She was still looking back at the node chamber when something began to take shape in the room, a nimbus glow amongst the conduit in the overhead.

"Awww fuck," Carl muttered. <*Hey, you two,*> he called out to Camille and Malorie. <*Next time, bring Shadowtrons, 'kay?*>

"Hold the Sirians." Katrina struggled to her feet. "I'll deal with that thing."

"How?" his eyes grew wide.

"Dunno, I just need to buy time."

She half-ran, half-stumbled toward the door into the node chamber, leaning on the first AI cylinder. A stabbing pain ran through her side, and she looked down to see blood on her armor.

When the hell did that happen?

She focused on the section of her HUD that showed an injury map, and realized that a stray shot had hit her just seconds ago.

Damn...I need a coffee.

"Stay where you are!" Troy's voice boomed through the node chamber, and Katrina wondered if he was talking to her or to the being that had settled amongst the cylinders. "Make another move, and we'll tear you apart."

~And how do you plan do to that?~

The being's words seeped into Katrina's mind, and she shook her head at the sludge-like malaise that came along with them.

"We have more tools at our disposal than you think."

~I don't see any slepton emitters, not that it would help, anyway. You're entirely at my mercy, Troy. And you, Katrina. Xavia had such high hopes for you—though I knew her plans would never come to fruition. You're a weak vessel.~

"Ouch," Katrina muttered as she stumbled to the next AI cylinder, followed by the next. "Words hurt, you know."

~Everything hurts fragile things like you. It is no matter. This diversion served us well enough. Now your fleets are within the drone swarm.~

"Fuck," Katrina whispered, wondering if this had been the being's plan all along, or if it was just taking credit for lucky circumstance. "Well, you'll have to get through me first."

She was within a few dozen meters of the creature now, thinking about anything she could besides Jessica, knowing that the ascended AI could plumb her thoughts, should it choose to.

It seemed to sense her reticence, and turned—or appeared to turn—toward her.

~Clouding your thoughts won't work, woman. Not for long.~

Katrina gritted her teeth as luminescent tendrils stretched out toward her. "I don't need it to work for long."

~No? Curious.~

Then the thing was inside her mind, tearing it apart.

UPPING THE ANTE

STELLAR DATE: 05.16.8950 (Adjusted Years)
LOCATION: ISS *Carthage*, Outer System
REGION: Sirius System, Hegemony of Worlds

"Let's fire a shot across their bows," Joe said as the ISF and Sirian fleets closed within a quarter million kilometers of one another.

<*DMG?*> Kerr asked, and the admiral nodded.

"Yes. Coordinate fire with Turk, pick something large."

"They can do math," Symatra said. "With our DMGs, it'll take a week to destroy all their ships, and they'll know it."

He glanced at the AI's holoimage and nodded. "I'm aware, but it's very possible that their rank and file do not know about our new weaponry. We've built up quite the reputation, and I want them to wonder how safe they are, even behind their stasis shields."

"Fair enough."

<*We've picked a pair of dreadnoughts on either end of their formation,*> Kerr said after a moment. <*We think it'll make for shock and awe.*>

"Works for me," Joe replied. "Fire when ready."

Deep within the ship, matter was fed into the small black hole, the energy spewing out through its relative jets and harnessed into the DMG beam, which hit the targeted Sirian capital ships in a brilliant flash of light.

It took several seconds for the hot plasma and debris to clear, but once they had, all that remained of the enemy craft were several large segments of hull.

"Hit two other ships on the far side, too," Symatra observed with a chuckle. "Nice shooting."

<*Thanks.*>

"OK, time to hail them." Joe glanced to the officer heading the comm section. "Put me on."

The man nodded, and Joe stretched his shoulders back, adopting a stern expression. Normally, he hated posturing and bluster, but despite what he'd said earlier about utterly destroying the system, he'd begun to reconsider. There was enough on his conscience already.

"Sirian captains and crew. This is Fleet Admiral Joseph Evans. As you can see, defeating your vessels, even with stasis shielding, is not impossible for us. You know that we have other weapons in our arsenal that are equally destructive, and you do not possess the ability to breach our shields.

"I'm giving you this one chance to stand down and surrender to the Alliance. By using stasis shielding of your own, you will force us to strike your vessels with more destructive weaponry, and when we do, there will be no time or opportunity to reach escape pods."

The words felt leaden as they left Joe's mouth. Back at the Kap, the anger at how the war had taken so much from him had burned in his mind, and he'd been prepared to do anything to end it.

Now, he just felt tired.

"We have a response," the comm officer said.

Joe nodded. "Put it up."

A man of middling height, slim and fit-looking in his gleaming white uniform, appeared on the forward display.

"Admiral Evans." His expression was neutral, but a haughty tone came through with the two words. "By order of COO Leory, you are to cease all operation in the Sirius System, or be destroyed."

"How do you expect to do that?" Joe asked, not bothering with any formalities. "We can destroy your ships with impunity, but there is nothing you can do to ours."

"With how long it will take you to work your way through

our fleet, I think we'll have time to try a few things. Given the nature of our new allies, you might be surprised by what we have up our sleeves."

"Same goes for us," Joe replied. "Look at the force disparity. Would we be here if we didn't think we could win?"

The Sirian chuckled. "I think you're so used to winning that you don't know defeat when it's staring you in the face. It's going to feel unimaginably good to destroy you on the field of battle."

Joe gave his own laugh, no small amount of derision added to the sound. "A Sirian fleet defeating an ISF one? That would be a first. I hope your crews know what they're getting into."

The man on the display gave a slight grimace, his eyes sliding to the side. It was clear that crew loyalty in the face of an enemy fleet so small—yet entirely undaunted—had to be his primary concern.

"You're just banking on past success," the enemy commander replied. "It's not going to work this time. Your campaign of destruction ends here."

"OK." Joe gave a heartfelt sigh. "Just remember when this thing kicks off in earnest, there might not be a chance to surrender again."

The other man snorted. "We'll offer you the same lack of courtesy."

He disappeared from the display a moment later.

Symatra caught Joe's eye, apparently sensing his mood. "Well, you tried to do the right thing."

"Yeah." His lips thinned for a moment. "Captain Ophelia, bring us into position for the drone launch."

DO YOUR WORST

STELLAR DATE: 05.16.8950 (Adjusted Years)
LOCATION: Brilliance Station
REGION: Sirius System, Hegemony of Worlds

Jessica and the Marines raced through Brilliance, barely slowing as they crossed wide concourses and atriums. Troy had provided the most direct route to the node chamber's rear entrance, but it wasn't necessarily the easiest.

Twice, they got bogged down fighting Sirian troops that were dug into their positions, but each time, the group managed to disengage and find a new route. Even though they were stealthed, Jessica imagined there had to be hundreds of enemy soldiers following behind.

At present, Corporal Henry was in the lead by a hundred meters, ensuring there was nothing that would slow the team down, and directing them to alternate routes if there were too many Sirian forces in their way.

<At the access point,> he reported a few seconds later. *<Got a lot of Sirians here.>*

<How many?> Jessica asked as she rounded a corner, still a ways from the lead Marine.

<A dozen. They seem to be scared to go in. Something about a spider monster in the tunnels.>

Trevor snorted. *<One guess who that is.>*

<Wait on us. We'll take them out the old-fashioned way.>

<Understood, ma'am,> Henry sent. *<Question, though. What way is that?>*

<Lightwands. We'll do it close and quick. Then I'm first in.>

A single click came back in acknowledgment, and half a minute later, Jessica, Trevor, and the rest of the fireteam were standing around the milling enemy soldiers.

Everyone selected targets, waited for a five-count, and then electron blades ignited, slicing into the Sirians with frightening efficiency.

A few of the defenders got shots off, some even hitting the stealthed opponents, but none did more than expose portions of matte black armor before the shooter died.

<Let's go,> Jessica said once the bloody work was done.

They raced down the service tunnel, following a trail of bodies while searching for Katrina's team's signal.

"Malorie!" she shouted after she'd still not picked up a sign of their allies, but knew she had to be getting close. "Don't shoot, it's us."

"I know," a voice said from right next to her, and Jessica jumped to the side, rifle swinging toward the spider-woman, who appeared to be hovering in midair. "That ascended thing is almost here. Take my cat."

Jessica nearly jumped again as one of the feline mechs appeared beneath Malorie.

"You domesticated them already?" Trevor asked from behind Jessica. "I'm impressed."

"Troy did," Malorie explained as she skittered off the creature to hang from the overhead. "Hop on, it's contact Linked."

Jessica nodded wordlessly and leapt astride the creature. The moment she placed her hands on its neck, a Link connection appeared, and she accepted it, seeing the simple interface for controlling the cat appear on her HUD.

Seconds later, she was barreling through the passages. Another connection touched her mind, and she allowed it in.

<Troy?>

<It's here, hurry!>

That was all she needed to push the cat forward, pouring on every bit of speed the creature could manage. Ahead, a point of light appeared in the dim passage, and she gritted her teeth as it grew larger. She burst into the node chamber a second later to see the ascended AI, long strands stretched out, penetrating Katrina's body.

"Get away from her, you *bitch!*" she screamed, leaping off the cat and sailing through the air to collide with the luminous being.

~*Fool,*~ it murmured as Jessica fell through its tentacles to land on the deck. ~*You think you can*—~

The thing's words cut off as Jessica managed to grab ahold of a thick section of the being, grimacing as the once-AI's energy began to flow into her body.

"I can, and I *will.*"

The AI lashed out at her, gossamer tendrils of light whipping at the admiral's armor, shredding it from her body until she stood in the tattered remains of her base layer, body glowing like a lavender star.

~*I'll kill her,*~ the being hissed. ~*Let me go, you can have Sirius.*~

Jessica glanced back at Katrina and the one thick shaft of light still inside the woman's body.

"No." She reached out and grabbed the AI's limb, ripping it free from her friend, hoping she hadn't done more harm than good. "You fuckers could have made that choice ages ago. But you decided to play at being gods. Now you reap what you've sown."

~*We are gods,*~ the ascended AI screeched into her mind. ~*You live at our sufferance!*~

Jessica continued to draw in more and more of the being's life force, draining its energy away, recharging her cells with the raw power.

"If you're a god, what does that make me?"

The creature's glow had begun to diminish, more and more of its limbs withering away, even as it continued to futilely slash her.

Then it was little more than an egg-like blob on the deck. Jessica sucked in a deep breath and drew the last joules of energy from the being, looking on in surprise as the final remains dissolved into a carbon-like ash.

A figure raced past her, and Jessica turned to see Camille crouched beside Katrina, cradling the woman's head in her arms.

"Is she…?" Jessica whispered the words, afraid to hear the answer.

"She's alive." Camille nodded. "But—"

"A little help?" Carl's voice carried from the room's main entrance, and Jessica looked up to see him falling back from the control room as Sirian troops flooded in.

Rising up to her full height, Jessica strode through the maze of AI cylinders until she reached the raised walkway and the clear line of fire it offered.

"Die, fuckers!" she screamed.

Stretching out her hands, she let the energy she'd absorbed from the core AI blast out, shattering the carbon window and burning the soldiers beyond to husks. The bulkhead and stacks of bodies were next, melting away under her rage-driven surge.

By the time she'd released the overabundance of raw power, half a kilometer of station on the far side of the control room was burned away, and smoke and ash filled the air.

She felt something warm around her ankles, and looked down to see that the raised walkway had melted, her feet sinking into the red-hot deck.

"Jessica!" Trevor's voice came from behind her, and she looked over her shoulder to give him a tired smile.

"Can you lift me out of this before it hardens?

Her husband laughed, and his massive hands slid beneath her arms, pulling her free and cradling her gently. "Woman…you sure don't do things by half, do you?"

She laid her head against his shoulder and drew a deep breath. "I wouldn't even know what that looks like."

THE CRUSH

STELLAR DATE: 05.16.8950 (Adjusted Years)
LOCATION: ISS *Carthage*, Outer System
REGION: Sirius System, Hegemony of Worlds

"They're really a bunch of stubborn bastards," Symatra muttered as a fourth wave of Sirian destroyers swept toward the ISF ships.

"Nice and steady," Joe replied, watching the *Starblade* move away from the *Carthage* on the holotank, both ships easing into positions where their AIs could control the most drones.

The AI shot him a sour look. "That's what I'm doing. I've already lost seventeen ships, though. Looks like it's just too much draw on these destroyers to run the CriEns at max in order to feed the accelerators and shields."

"Shit," Joe muttered. "Gotta keep up the pretense that we think we can win this by some sort of conventional means."

<*Firing,*> Kerr announced, and the *Carthage*'s DMG unleashed another torrent of energy, wiping out the eleventh enemy dreadnought.

"Wish we knew which one of these things their leadership was on," Ophelia said. "There's just too much inter-ship traffic to pinpoint the command vessels."

A marker on the holotank showed the *Starblade* firing down the center of the enemy formation, hitting one dreadnought and two corvettes.

<*Just two minutes until we're in position,*> the ship's AI announced.

"Time till the drones are ready to open it up after that?" the fleet admiral asked.

<*Symatra, Turk, and I think that it would be best if they operate as an attack swarm, breaking apart as they delve deeper into the*

Sirian formation. Too soon, and they'll figure out what we're up to.>

"And if they do?" Joe asked. "We can release millions of drones. With stasis shields, there's no way they can wear them down."

"I just don't want to telegraph," Symatra said. "No reason to, at least."

Joe nodded, gnawing on his lip.

The Sirians seemed too cocky—even with their new shields. He just wanted to end the conflict, deal with the system, and get ready for the final push into Sol.

Maybe by the time Sera finds Tanis and Angela, we'll have this whole thing wrapped up.

A small doubt wormed its way forward from the back of his mind, a worry that maybe Sera *wouldn't* find them in time. He quashed the negativity as quickly as it had appeared, refusing to give it an audience.

He said nothing further until the prescribed time for the drone release, watching as the slow war of attrition took place between the Sirian ships and Symatra's destroyers. The enemy was losing ships far more quickly than the ISF, but even so, the disparity ratio was swinging further in favor of the enemy.

"Release the drones," Ophelia ordered when the ship was finally in position.

Joe couldn't help his feral smile as the robotic warriors, under the control of Kerr and Turk, poured out of the I-Class ships. They immediately branched off into multiple swarms, sweeping amongst the enemy, laying into the Sirian hulls with millions of beams.

The enemy seemed to understand that the control systems for the swarms were aboard the *Carthage* and *Starblade,* as all fire was suddenly directed toward those two vessels.

The massive carriers shrugged off the assault, their shields releasing so much energy as they annihilated incoming particles that several nearby enemy ships—and one of

Symatra's destroyers—were vaporized.

No one spoke on the bridge as the drones split into smaller and smaller groups, working their way to the perimeter of the enemy fleet until the Sirian vessels were surrounded. With so many targets to choose from, the enemy couldn't concentrate fire on the flitting robotic warriors enough to take many down, and by the time the everything was in position, only one percent were gone.

Joe was about to issue the command, when he realized he'd been holding his breath. He did his best to mask a ragged gasp before uttering, "Do it."

The view on the main display grew clouded by the waves of gravitons pouring out of the drones. Then it was occluded by something else.

At first, the Exaldi were nothing more than indistinct shapes, blobs of nothing in the black. Then they began to shift and morph, gaining edges, long tentacles stretching toward spacecraft. A cruiser gouted plasma as one of the monsters began to sink through its hull, feeding on the ship's engines. Seconds later, a massive explosion bloomed elsewhere in the Sirian fleet, taking out half a dozen carriers.

"What the hell was that?" Joe asked, focusing the display on that region of space.

<Chunk of dark matter collided with a destroyer,> Kerr supplied.

"Almost looked like antimatter annihilation," Symatra commented. "Note to self: avoid dark matter."

"That's not a chunk," Joe said, gesturing at the outline of an obstructed area. "It's eight hundred kilometers across."

"What's that thing's *v*?!" Ophelia demanded. "We can't have it leave the rift."

<It will exit the envelope in ten minutes,> Kerr advised. <We will need to transition everything inside back into the dark layer before then.>

Joe set his jaw. If they closed the rift too soon, functional enemy ships would simply transition out, and they'd all be back where they started.

"OK, now what's *that*?" Ophelia gestured at the display, where the outlines of several dreadnoughts became cloudy and indistinct.

<*I think those are drones,*> Kerr said. <*Jessica did send an update over the QC about the Sirians having a billion drones down at Lucent, but I thought she was exaggerating.*>

"But they hate AIs here," Symatra scowled at the display. "And they couldn't control this many drones without them. If they think they can best us with NSAI-controlled drones, they're sorely mistaken."

<*Those things aren't moving like NSAIs are at the helm,*> Turk said, joining in on the *Carthage* bridge's conversation. <*Oh, and they're headed straight for our drones.*>

Joe nodded silently as he watched the enemy swarms move through the melee, threading the masses of Exaldi and their own ships like drunken sailors, weaving erratically toward the edges of the combat.

"Space must not be consistent in there," he said. "looks like they're having to swap between grav and conventional thrusters."

"Agreed," Symatra said. "I'm moving my rail ships around to defend the perimeter. If they take out more than half our field generators, we won't be able to push the Exaldi back into the DL."

"Fuck," Joe muttered. "I hate rooting for those *things*, but c'mon, you big bastards, tear those Lumins apart."

All throughout the rift, enemy ships flared brightly as the mass-seeking creatures smashed themselves against stasis shields, wearing down power reserves and pelting the surrounding ships with relativistic debris and radiation. Over ten percent of the enemy fleet was already gone, the survivors boosting out on direct vectors, frantic to exit the bubble created by the ISF drones.

It made them easy targets for Symatra's rail ships, as well as the two I-Class carriers' weapons. Space was far from 'straight' in the rift, but Kerr and the weapons teams were compensating for the bends, and as the Sirian vessels drew closer to the edges, it became easy to hit them.

Unfortunately, it also became easier for their drones to engage the ISF field emitters. Though the ISF craft and their ARC-9 defenders possessed their own stasis shields, they were not able to withstand concentrated fire from thousands of enemy beams, and swaths of them began to fall under the barrage.

"There have to be control ships," Joe said as he tagged the vessels that had initially disgorged the drones. "Hit these with DMGs."

The I-Class vessels pivoted, laying down short bursts from their main gun, the blasts shredding Exaldi and ship alike. It took several rounds to finally hit the dreadnoughts, and by then, over a third of the ISF's drones had been destroyed.

"Shit," Joe cursed. "Comm, scan, they have to be controlling them from somewhere. Can you find the EM sources?"

"I'm sorry, sir," the lead scan officer looked up from his console. "It's just such a mess."

"We have to close it up, sir," Ophelia urged. "Another minute, and we'll lose the ability."

"Kerr, do it at the last possible moment," the fleet admiral ordered. "The Sirian fleet is still half-operational."

Symatra nodded, her expression grim. "Though they all have to be straining energy reserves. It evens the odds a lot."

<*Twenty-five seconds to rift closure,*> Kerr announced, placing a counter on the forward display.

On the holotank, the activity inside the rift was barely

discernable. Ships were swarmed by Exaldi, smaller bits of dark matter were careening off shields and hulls, and the drone war at the perimeter added a haze of confusion over it all.

No one spoke as the countdown continued and damage estimates updated so fast that Joe could barely read them. Then the number hit zero, and Kerr's voice came into their minds.

<It's done.>

The hazy nothing of the dark layer disappeared, along with the Exaldi and many of the Sirian ships. A few popped back into normal space seconds later, and Scan began the work of determining how many enemy vessels still posed a threat.

"The drone fleet didn't even miss a beat," Symatra murmured. "I think whatever is controlling them was outside the rift all along. I'm leveraging my destroyers' sensors to hunt them down."

"I might have something!" Scan said a moment later.

The AI approached the scan team's consoles while Joe frowned at the holotank.

"Shit...there are Exaldi in a lot of those ships," he murmured.

<I'd noticed that as well,> Kerr said. *<Turk and I are rapid-building new drones. We'll have enough to do this again in thirty minutes.>*

"The Sirians are running," Ophelia gestured at the enemy ships, the bulk of which were moving toward the inner system.

"Shedding Exaldi as they go," Joe muttered, lifting a hand to his face. "I should have closed it sooner...."

"Should we pursue?" the captain asked. "Or do we clean up this battlespace first?" She gestured at the tank, which showed hundreds of thousands of hulls still being devoured by the things that had escaped being sent back into the void.

"Open a channel," Joe ordered Comm.

The officer nodded a moment later, and he drew a deep breath.

"To whomever is commanding the Sirian drone fleet. If you destroy more of our field emitters, we won't be able to clean up the remaining Exaldi. Left to their own devices, they will eventually consume this entire system. Our estimates show that after an hour, it will be impossible to contain them, and they'll spread throughout Sirius. The preservation of your system is now up to you."

He cut the message, and caught Ophelia giving him a curious look.

"What is it, Captain?" he asked.

"Just wondering where you got that timetable from."

"My ass," Joe gave a caustic laugh. "But the time really doesn't matter. If they keep shooting down our drones, it's going to happen either way."

Ophelia gave an understanding nod. "Maybe we should offer them quarter. I'm not sure if Sirians will sacrifice themselves to save their system."

"Found them!" Symatra called out from the comm station. "Bastards are just fifty thousand klicks above us. A group of five or six cruisers, from the looks of it."

"Direct all weapons to that location!" Joe shouted.

Both I-Class cruisers and the three thousand remaining rail destroyers opened fire on a seemingly empty stretch of space. The initial volley caught the enemy ships before they raised shields, and two explosions blossomed in the dark. The subsequent fire struck stasis shields, matter annihilation flaring brightly.

"Drone control died!" Scan shouted. "Looks like they can't keep enough of their shields open to maintain signal."

"Keep up the pressure, Kerr. Get the main gun on those ships," Ophelia ordered.

<On it,> the AI replied.

Joe widened the view of the battlespace, noting that the ISF drones were shredding the enemy bots now, though their automated evasive maneuvers meant it would still take several minutes to make a sizable dent in their numbers.

Scan had identified three hundred Exaldi, mostly smaller creatures, still scavenging amongst the disabled ships in the Sirian fleet. Thus far, they hadn't moved beyond where the rift had existed. The operational enemy ships were spread out across half a cubic light second of space, trailing freshly disabled hulls that the dark layer creatures still fed on.

"I kinda feel like my hour estimate was rather generous," he frowned. "We need to deal with that other fleet."

<I have a solution,> Turk said. *<But you're not going to like it.>*

"I rarely expect to, in situations like this," Joe replied. "Lay it on me."

<Turk, no,> Kerr's voice implored. *<You can't.>*

<Kerr, we have to,> the *Starblade's* AI said before pausing a moment. *<Admiral Evans. If we bring the* Starblade *into the middle of the enemy fleet, I can emit a gravitational field large enough to transition them all into the dark layer, and hold them there long enough to be sure the Sirian ships can't get back out.>*

"Turk." Joe shook his head. "You will have to have them all within your shield bubble to do that. You'll be completely exposed."

<It's the only way,> Captain Peabody joined in the conversation. *<I'm right up there with the people who hate the Sirians most, after losing so much at the Kap. But I don't want the destruction of this system on my conscience.>*

Joe felt a lump form in his throat, and he nodded silently until he found his voice. "OK, Captain. But I want you to get all non-essential personnel off the ship. And don't be martyrs. If you can get back out, you do it."

<I'm not suicidal,> Turk replied with a self-deprecating

laugh.

<Don't worry,> Peabody added. <This is a volunteer op. Nonessentials are being directed to shuttles. Be prepared to pick them up.>

"Of course," Joe replied.

"Drone control ships are destroyed," Symatra announced a few seconds later. "Pretty sure that cowardly enemy fleet commander was up there too."

Joe gave her a satisfied nod. "Good. Now to remove their drones and re-transition this batch."

He looked down at the holotank, resisting the urge to call the *Starblade* back as it boosted toward the fleeing Sirian ships.

Peabody had been a brother in arms for nearly a century, a fellow pilot who'd worked his way up through the ISF, and became one of the heroes of the Battle for Victoria.

Now, of all things, he was sacrificing himself for Sirians.

The bridge fell silent once more, as Symatra aided in destroying the remaining enemy drones while Kerr deployed the fresh field emitters.

Five minutes later, they had enough to re-open the rift with the destroyers' aid. Like clockwork, the dark layer yawned, and then the enemy ships and Exaldi were pushed within, the drones transitioning with them to ensure all the enemy ships remained inside the DL until they were consumed by the Exaldi.

"Well, that's done," Joe said, noting a few escape pods that had managed to get outside the envelope. "We'll need to watch those."

"They're on our radar, Admiral." Ophelia's voice was nearly toneless, and he looked over his shoulder at the captain to see her staring listlessly at the forward display, which showed the *Starblade* approaching the fleeing enemy ships.

A stream of dark layer creatures trailed in its wake, drawn away from the Sirian hulls they'd been consuming by the larger mass moving past.

The great ship, a legend after less than a year in service, slowed to allow the things to catch up, the monsters annihilating themselves against the massive ship's stasis shields. As it approached the Sirian vessels, a few fired on the ISF ship, but their shots barely registered on the ship's shielding.

It took a few more minutes for the *Starblade* to reach the center of the fleeing enemies. Its presence seemed to confuse the other ships, as it wasn't firing on them. A few drew close, and Joe wondered if it was to gain protection, or perhaps in hopes that the Exaldi devouring their vessels would be attracted by the I-Class ship's larger mass.

<*He's about to do it,*> Kerr said. <*Three shuttles are on their way to us.*>

"OK."

Joe tried not to let the sorrow into his voice, wondering all the while if he could have done something differently, or if Tanis would have come up with a better strategy.

I need you back. Where the hell are you?

Forcing himself to watch the display, he pursed his lips as the *Starblade* and the fleeing Sirians disappeared. Only a smattering of enemy ships was left on the far edges of the battlespace.

"Symatra." His voice was hoarse. "Take out any stragglers. Ophelia. Pick up those shuttles while we clean up our wreckage."

Both women acknowledged Joe's orders, but he didn't hear their words or any other bridge activity as he stared out at the empty patch of space where the *Starblade* had been minutes before.

REMOVED FROM OFFICE

STELLAR DATE: 05.16.8950 (Adjusted Years)
LOCATION: Brilliance Station
REGION: Sirius System, Hegemony of Worlds

<*I want to go up with her,*> Troy said to Jessica. <*Please.*>

"Up where?" Jessica asked as she leant against one of the AI cylinders. "Oh, right. Yes, backup should be here soon, and they can take you up to the *Lantzer* with Katrina."

As she spoke, the admiral's eyes settled on the temporary stasis bag that held Katrina. Not knowing what the core AI had done to her, it had seemed best to stop any further damage as quickly as possible.

"I don't know if our medics will be able to do much. This seems like it might be a job for Earnest and Finaeus."

What she didn't share with the AI was the news that the two scientists had disappeared not long ago. They'd left a message in Star City to keep their 'special mission' under wraps, but hadn't shared any more information than that.

<*If they're not available, Bob will know what to do.*> There was a note of desperation in the AI's mental tone, and Jessica nodded wearily before replying.

"Perhaps, yes. I'll try to find out if the First Fleet is remaining in New Sol for long. We'll figure out the best way to get her to him."

<*Perhaps we should take her to the* Voyager. *I could jump her directly to New Sol and the I2.*>

"Shit. That does make more sense." She struggled to her feet. "I really need to get out of this hole and get some light on my skin."

Trevor appeared at her elbow a moment later. "Easy now. Usef will be here soon. Then we can gather these AIs and get out of here."

"Usef?" Jessica cocked an eyebrow. "I thought he'd been delayed."

"And miss the sort of mayhem you kick up?" Usef's voice boomed across the node chamber, and Jessica turned to see the huge Marine ambling toward them, a whole platoon flowing into the chamber behind him.

"I suppose I am a hell of a draw," she gave him a weak smile. "When did you get here?"

"Not long ago at all," the colonel replied. "We ended up doing a rapid hop out to Star City, then due to some gate alignment issue, skipped through Aldebaran, then the Kap, and finally here. Honestly, my head's still spinning from it."

Jessica laughed, then held her own head. "Ow...mine too, but not from your trip. Remind me again never to absorb an entire core AI's energy."

Usef's mouth fell open, and he glanced at Trevor, who nodded.

"Yeah, she sucked it dry," her husband confirmed. "Thing looked like a balloon with a hole in it...without the part where it whips around like crazy. You know, it was more like a time lapse of a grape withering in the sun."

"Shit." The colonel shook his head in amazement. "Next time, wait for me so I can see that."

"I'd really like there not to be a next time," Jessica said, feeling worse at just the thought. "I'm never going anywhere without a shadowtron again."

"Seems logical." Usef glanced over his shoulder and nodded to a Marine. "Get the admiral a shadowtron."

"I'll take one too," Trevor chimed in.

"What?" Usef elbowed him in the side. "You guys don't have them on the *Lantzer*?"

Jessica rolled her eyes. "Cut it out, Usef. You know we do, we were just in a rush."

He gave a derisive laugh. "You heard the part about how we hopped across half the galaxy to get here, right?"

She couldn't hold back the smile any longer. "I want your company stationed aboard the *Lantzer* from here on out. It's been too long since we've worked together."

"Months." He nodded. "Miss the girls on *Sabrina*, too."

"What about Misha?" Trevor asked.

"Pretty sure he's one of the girls now," the Marine replied.

A lieutenant approached with two shadowtrons, and Usef nodded to Trevor and Jessica.

"Ma'am, sir," he said deferentially as he handed them over.

Jessica checked the weapon before she slung it across her back. "Thanks, Marine." She looked back up at Usef. "*Sabrina's* insystem. Maybe we can get together with them for some drinks."

"Think so?" he replied, looking from her to Trevor. "I heard that Joe wanted to burn this whole system down."

"That got out, did it?" she asked, to which the colonel nodded soberly.

"Unfortunate," Trevor added.

Jessica gave a heartfelt sigh. "Joe's in a bit of a bad place. He loses his daughters for half a year, then gets them back only to learn Tangel's dead. Then it turns out Tanis and Angela are alive, but Sera's gone after them, though it's been days...."

"Yeah," the huge Marine grunted. "I'd say he shouldn't be in the field right now, but no way can I tell the old man what to do. Maybe you—"

"Oh fuck no." Jessica shook her head vehemently, instantly wishing she hadn't. "There's no way I'm doing that."

Trevor placed a hand on her shoulder. "But maybe you should."

<We've collected the cores,> Troy interjected. <Any time you all want to stop yammering, we should get them out of here, and take

Katrina back to the Voyager.>

Jessica glanced at the stasis bag, and Usef followed her gaze.

"Shit...I was wondering where she was. What—"

"Ascended AI had its grubby hands inside her head," Jessica said. "Troy and her crew are going to get her back to their ship, and then to Bob. Can—"

"Say no more," the colonel interrupted. "Lieutenant Wes will escort them back to their ship. Would you mind getting the cores up to the *Lantzer* on the way, Troy?"

<To be honest, if we're going to Bob, wouldn't it be ideal to get the cores to him? They'd recover best in his expanse.>

"Works for me," Jessica said. "Safer, too, since we're likely to be in the thick of it for some time."

"Excellent." Usef paused for a moment, passing orders over the Link. "Now, I hear there's some dick COO here that needs his ass kicked."

Jessica nodded. "That would be nice. Maybe we can force a surrender and nip this whole thing in the bud."

The colonel winked. "Well, you're in luck, because we scraped up some intel on the way in that he's holed up in a bunker deep in the station's core."

"Shit, Usef!" Jessica threw her hands in the air. "Why didn't you lead with that?"

The Marine smirked. "You didn't see yourself when I came in. Looked like you needed a few more minutes."

"He's got a point." Trevor chuckled and wrapped an arm around her shoulders. "You looked like shit."

"And now?" she asked, brow cocked as she looked between the two men.

"What would you say?" Usef asked, turning to Trevor. "Warmed-over shit?"

Jessica's husband laughed. "Oh, you'll not catch me so easily. C'mon, let's go bag us some corporate bigwig with delusions of grandeur."

"You're a wise man," she said. "And yeah, let's go find that asswipe. At the very least, he's earned a bit of a beatdown."

"I might just know a Marine willing to do that," Usef mused.

The admiral snorted. "Get in line, boyo."

STARBLADE

STELLAR DATE: 05.16.8950 (Adjusted Years)
LOCATION: ISS *Carthage*, Outer System
REGION: Sirius System, Hegemony of Worlds

<*They're away,*> Kerr announced as a hundred of the ship's probes disappeared into the dark layer, searching for the *Starblade*.

"It might take a bit to find it," Symatra warned, her holographic form drifting closer to Joe. "There's going to be a ton of Exaldi activity."

"I know that," the fleet admiral said. "Still, we have to look. I'm not leaving them behind."

The bridge fell silent at his words, and Joe could tell that his mood was starting to affect morale.

He'd always prided himself on being a more or less pleasant person to be around, while still ensuring the ships under his command were well disciplined — or, he used to be.

Maybe I should return to New Canaan. Spend some time with the girls. Symatra, Peabody, or Ophelia could have run this just as well without me.

"The gate components have arrived," Ophelia spoke up after a few minutes of silence. "Should I have them begin assembly?"

"Yes." Joe uttered the single word, eyes glued to the holodisplay, waiting for some report from the probes that the *Starblade* had somehow survived.

Granted, it had been ten minutes. It was unlikely in the extreme that even an I-Class vessel could weather Exaldi for that long.

"I..." He wanted to apologize to Ophelia, but couldn't think of what to say.

Suddenly, she was at his side. "It's OK. I understand."

<*Probes are returning,*> Kerr announced. <*There's...no sign of the* Starblade. *Analyzing data.*>

"That doesn't look like enough wreckage or Exaldi activity for so much mass, either," Symatra said a moment later.

<*Don't jump the gun,*> Kerr admonished. <*There's a lot of wreckage, and it's hard to tell what's what.*>

"There!" One of chiefs in the scan department jumped up and pointed at the main display. "Something's coming out!"

Twenty thousand kilometers away from where the *Starblade* entered the dark layer, a shimmering occlusion blocked Sirius's light.

<*It's them!*> Kerr cried out as the *Starblade*'s shape grew more distinct. <*Shit...what a mess.*>

Joe nodded silently, his eyes roving over the other ship's hull. Holes—some kilometers across—gaped in multiple locations, and the sections that were more intact were bleeding atmosphere into space, some mixed with plasma and explosions.

"Get us over there," he ordered.

It was like a scene from a nightmare, such a great ship laid low by a feral enemy, mindless killing machines capable of devouring something so powerful.

Nothing we've built compares to the raw hunger of those monsters.

"I have a faint signal," Comm announced. "Trying to clean it up."

Joe nodded fervently. "We'll grab hold of them, and get them through the gate to New Canaan."

"I'll have the engineers build the gate closer to the *Starblade*," Ophelia said.

Peabody's voice suddenly came over the bridge's audible systems. "So...uh...mayday?"

"Jorje!" Joe rasped. "What's your status?"

The other ship's captain laughed weakly. "Well, we're gonna need a real big vacuum. Took a bit to get away from the things, once the enemy ships were torn up enough to not transition back. Turk and I didn't want to bring them back out with us again. We had to dump a shit-ton of probes singing a siren call to pull them out of our hull."

"And Turk?" Joe asked.

"He's gone silent on me, but I know most of his nodes survived. I think he's just working on healing. We lost…quite a few other people, though."

"I'm sorry," the admiral sighed. "I really am, Jorje."

"Me too. We're just going to put out fires till you get here, OK?"

"We'll be just a few minutes, Captain," Ophelia said. "Get any wounded ready, and we'll have shuttles in your bays to grab them. You did amazing work. Saved a star system."

The *Starblade*'s captain gave a derisive laugh. "Yay. Go us. Next time, can we save a star system worth saving?"

Joe clenched his jaw, the words cutting him like a knife. He knew that the captain hadn't meant it as an insult, but he couldn't help but think about how Admiral Krissy had advised against attacking Sirius.

With so many people in the ISF having an irrational— though well-earned—hatred of the system's Lumin rulers, it was clear to see why they were not the best suited for the mission.

Hindsight….

[Jessica.] He reached out to the woman he felt was in a much better mental state to continue the mission. *[The* Starblade *has suffered critical damage. I'm going to transfer to it and take it back to New Canaan. I'm placing Symatra's fleet and the* Carthage *under your command for now. Your current orders are to finish removing Sirius's military capability, then we'll assess whether forming up there, or back at the Kap is best.]*

He didn't bother shortening the message, as there was a direct QC connection between the *Carthage* and *Lantzer*. He also didn't have the energy to consider how to make the message concise and legible.

[Iris here, Joe. Jessica's currently comms-silent down on Brilliance. She and Usef are closing in on Leory, so we should have things well in hand soon. She also took out an ascended AI that had given the enemy their mass drone control capability. I'll pass on the orders to her, though. Are you OK?]

Joe chuckled, unsurprised that Iris had read between the lines. Having spent most of her life on a ship filled with as much personality as *Sabrina*, she was a good judge of mood and character.

[Not really, no. I need to go see my girls. I should never have left them.]

[Smartest thing you've said in a week, sir. Safe travels. I'll convey these orders to Jessica when she's back in contact. I'd suggest once you have things shored up out there, instruct Symatra and Ophelia to move insystem. They have gates here that we can use to transfer out if needed, and we can assess whether or not we need to move on to the installations around Sirius.]

[Understood,] Joe replied. *[And good luck.]*

A KING'S KNEE

STELLAR DATE: 05.16.8950 (Adjusted Years)
LOCATION: ISS *Andromeda*, Amora
REGION: Cal Amor System, Trisilieds Kingdom

Corsia stepped out of the pinnace, walking down the ramp and onto the palace grounds, where an emissary stood, flanked by ceremonial guards.

Above, the *Andromeda* hovered, casting a shadow over the palace's kilometer-high spires, the threat of destruction clearly spelled out by the primed railguns aimed at the world below.

"King Somer awaits you," the emissary said, eyes narrowing as he looked back at the pinnace.

"Were you expecting someone else?" Corsia asked.

The man frowned. "Do you not have an escort?"

The admiral couldn't help but smirk. "They're already here." She nodded to his right, and an ISF Marine materialized. "Now, I believe that I expected to meet with your king."

"Yes," the man nodded, quickly regaining the stoic calm of someone used to dealing with uncertainty. "If you will follow me."

"No." Corsia shook her head. "I do not attend your king, he attends me."

The emissary's mask cracked again for an instant, but he nodded, lips thinning. "I'll tell him, but I believe he wishes to meet in private first."

The admiral raised a hand, and the crack of a railgun thundered. Across the plaza, a decorative fountain exploded, and debris rained down around them as Corsia crossed her arms.

"I'm not prepared to be overly patient."

<You really hate this, don't you?> Jim asked from within the pinnace where he waited.

<I do,> Corsia replied. *<Politicking is the worst. I feel bad for Tanis, being stuck doing this all the time.>*

<That's for sure. I can't wait till this is over with.>

"He's agreed," the emissary said a moment later. "If you'd agree to your Marines—"

"No." Corsia's flat tone sliced through the air. "Your king needs to understand what's happening here."

"Which is?" the man asked, an air of nervousness leaking out with his question.

The admiral stared at him with her cold, blue eyes. "Your unconditional surrender."

Swallowing, the Trissie ducked his head and didn't speak further until a man in flowing purple robes trimmed with silver and gold emerged from the palace, striding across the grounds toward the pinnace with a small retinue following after.

It was easy to see the glower on his face even without magnifying her vision.

Here is a man entirely unused to being summoned.

Before he reached Corsia and the emissary, he was already yelling.

"What is the meaning of this? Is this how you show yourselves to be civilized? Your warships looming overhead, taking potshots at our ancestral art? Have you no respect? No couth?!"

The admiral didn't respond, her arms still folded across her chest as the sovereign came to a halt a meter away.

For nearly a minute, they stared at one another, neither speaking, or even blinking. Finally, the king threw his hands in the air.

"I thought you wanted to speak?"

"I do," Corsia said with a slow nod. "Are you ready to do

that, or are you going to squawk for a little while longer?"

The king opened his mouth to respond, but then snapped his jaw shut, shooting daggers at her with his eyes.

"Good," Corsia replied. "King Somer, by order of Field Marshal Tanis Richards of the Transcend Interstellar Alliance, The Nations of the Scipio Alliance, and—most importantly— the governor of New Canaan, I'm placing you under arrest for your unprovoked attack on New Canaan on four-one adjusted year 8948. All rights and privileges you may have held as king of the Trisilieds are hereby stripped and revoked, and you will be placed in my brig for transport back to New Canaan, where you will be tried and sentenced for your crimes."

As Corsia had spoken, the king's face had reddened, and then whitened. When the words 'transport back' were uttered, he began to sputter, and when she finished, he shook his head in defiance.

"You're out of your mind, woman. I'll not be taken to your kangaroo court to be tried by your AIs. I am king of a thousand star systems! Somer is lord here, not you, Admiral."

At his words, the honor guard drew their weapons, aiming them at Corsia. She gave a small nod, and lightwands flashed, held by stealthed Marines, who cut off the guards' hands, sending twenty rifles falling to the ground as cries of pain surrounded them.

Two Marines materialized, nodding to the Trisilieds guards, motioning for them to move away and treat one another's injuries.

The admiral took a step closer to the king, her eyes centimeters from his. "Do you know how many of my friends died that day you attacked Carthage? Do you know how many have died since, as we brought about our recompense? You had your chance for peaceful surrender. That time has passed. There is no negotiation. You are utterly defeated."

The king's mouth worked silently, and he turned to his

emissary and the men and women who had accompanied him. None spoke, each one glancing nervously at the others, wondering where the remainder of the Marines were.

"Take him aboard," Corsia said.

At her words, a pair of Marines materialized next to Somer, clamping their hands around his arms before marching him onto the pinnace.

She half expected him to rail at her, but the king had found his composure, and walked up with some measure of dignity.

A woman stepped forward, Somer's wife, Queen Judina. "Please," she said, eyes wide. "Let me accompany him."

Corsia nodded silently, and the queen raced up the ramp after her disgraced husband.

"Prince Remal," she called out, gaze sweeping across those accompanying the king until they landed on him. "Step forward. By your people's laws, you are their ruler now."

A young man with dark locks of hair sweeping across his brow stepped forward, hands twisting nervously. "Admiral," he said, ducking his head quickly.

"Come," Corsia invited as the pinnace lifted off behind her. "Let's talk about the details of your surrender in more comfortable surroundings."

* * * * *

"So, King Somer'll be going off to the farm, I suppose," Jim said later that day as he and Corsia lay in bed together.

"Maybe," she replied. "There might be a death sentence for him."

"Really?" her husband propped himself up on an elbow. "I thought we weren't going to do that."

She shrugged. "There might be an exception made for top leadership. Depends a bit on what President Wrentham does with Kirkland."

"And perhaps Hegemon Uriel?"

"If she survives. The battle for Sol isn't going to be like this triumphant flight we've had, coasting into the Pleione System. You know the Jovians. They'll fight till the bitter end."

"And we won't be able to use picobombs on High Terra," Jim added. "At least, I sure hope we don't. I wouldn't mind walking it again."

"Stars," Corsia shook her head. "Sol is going to be so hard. I honestly don't know how Jessica is dealing with being back in the Kap. That place must hold a lot of feelings for her."

"For us too," Jim said.

"Good feelings, though." Corsia rolled over to face her husband, pulling him close. "Can you imagine? We spent decades together there, and never did this."

She wrapped an arm around him, and his lips found hers, warm bodies pressed against one another, legs entwining.

Even though Corsia's body wasn't fully organic, the sensations of another person pressing against her, pushing into her, was unlike anything else she'd felt in her long centuries. It was pleasure, pain, blessed release, and re-energization all at once.

No wonder the humans love to do it so much.

Still, as she lost herself in the throes of lovemaking, a part of her mind couldn't stop thinking about what she'd seen through the rifts, between the cracks in reality where another universe lay....

*Now what would **that** feel like?*

SOLBOUND

STELLAR DATE: 05.16.8950 (Adjusted Years)
LOCATION: *Sabrina*, Outer System
REGION: Sirius System, Hegemony of Worlds

"Well *that's* weird." Cheeky tilted her head, a frown creasing her brow. "I sent a message to Joe on the QC network about our intel, asking him to approve a jump to Sol, and it got rerouted from the *Carthage* back to New Canaan, then to Jessica's ship."

Misha turned from where he was cleaning up the counter after the second-watch meal. "Like a freakin' pinball machine."

Fina, who sat across the table from Cheeky, leant forward. "Is Joe alright? Has something happened to the *Carthage*?"

"I don't know," the captain replied. "Though I plan to find out. Either way, I didn't get a response from Jessica…Iris was the one who replied. She sent coordinates to the *Carthage*'s current location in Sirius, and told us to await orders once there."

Nance rose and grabbed her coffee cup, stretching languidly. "Always taking orders from Jessica and Iris. It's our lot in life."

<*I like orders from Jessica,*> Sabrina said. <*You know she cares for us.*>

"What about my orders?" Cheeky asked, feigning indignance.

<*I like yours even more, but you're not your own CO.*>

The captain laughed, then gestured to Nance. "Hey, while you're up, grab me a fizzy water."

"Girl." Nance gave her a deadpan stare. "You're literally five steps from the chiller."

Cheeky turned and looked at the appliance. "Yeah...but you're closer."

"I'm not, actually." Nance crossed her arms.

"Standing counts as at least five or six steps. Plus, I know you're going to get cream for your coffee."

The engineer set her jaw. "I drink it black now."

"Liar."

Nance threw her hands in the air and stalked to the chiller. "Fine." She grabbed the first fizzy water she saw, and tossed it at Cheeky.

"Strawberry! My favorite."

"Still the best thing to come from the *Intrepid*," Misha said, reaching over to the small hydroponics garden on the counter, where he plucked one of the red fruits from a plant and popped it in his mouth. "Almost better than bacon."

"Whoa now," Cheeky said after a sip of her water. "Don't go getting all carried away. You don't want to invoke the spirit of Tangel."

The room fell silent, and she heaved a breath.

"Sorry...too soon. I meant to just say 'invoke Tangel', but then...well...."

"Sera will find Tanis and Angela," Fina said with a confident nod. "Who knows, maybe they are still Tangel. Maybe Bob was wrong."

No one responded, though a number of somber looks were exchanged.

<*I've laid in a course,*> Sabrina said after a few moments. <*The* Carthage *is ten AU anti-spinward of us. We'll be there in under a day.*>

"OK," Cheeky said, rising from her seat. "Once we have updates on how the battles went, I'll reach out to Jessica for clarification. Not really excited about just waiting in the middle of Sirius for further orders."

Nance nodded. "Me either. Although, we'll be with the

Carthage, so that's something."

"Hey," Misha frowned and cocked his head to the side. "Did Iris mention the *Starblade*?"

Cheeky pulled the message back up, reading over it on her HUD. "Hmm...no. That's odd. It was supposed to jump in with the *Carthage*."

"Ominous," the cook commented.

"Probably just because it's the command ship," Cheeky said. "They didn't mention Symatra's fleet, either."

"Good point." Misha turned back to the counter. "Everything's probably fine."

Nance nearly spat out the sip of coffee she'd just taken. "Dude! Seriously? Why would you *say* something like that?"

A CAPITAL CAPTURE

STELLAR DATE: 05.17.8950 (Adjusted Years)
LOCATION: Brilliance Station
REGION: Sirius System, Hegemony of Worlds

<Do you mind if I lead, Admiral?> Usef asked Jessica as they approached the bunker deep within Brilliance.

<Don't trust me to keep my head on my shoulders?> she asked, then remembered the Marine that had been decapitated by the cat-mech, and grimaced. *<Nevermind, yeah, I'm OK with that.>*

Usef chuckled. *<I just went from feeling valued to expendable...and I did it to myself.>*

Jessica laughed with him, shaking her head at the huge Marine. *<I've missed working with you, Colonel.>*

<And I, you. Just think, we're so close to Sol. Maybe once we put that mess to bed, we can go on a vacation to Tyre.>

<That the place where you always wear the tiny swimsuit?> Trevor asked with a mischievous wink.

The Marine gave him a light punch on the shoulder. *<Why, you want to know where to get one?>*

Jessica turned to give her husband an appraising look. *<I'm in.>*

<And I suppose I am, too,> he replied, then gave Usef a light punch of his own. *<You gonna do that whole take-the-lead thing you were talking about?>*

The combat net updated, and Jessica saw that an entire platoon of stealthed Marines had moved past them, keeping to the edges of the wide concourse that the force was moving down.

Trevor snorted. *<Showoff.>*

A hundred meters ahead, the concourse ended in a cylindrical grouping of lift shafts. The data they had indicated that a hidden lift was situated in their center, this one going down, while the others only traveled to decks above.

<Automated defenses ahead,> Usef announced, slowing to a halt.

<Let's wait till the platoon at the lower entrance gets in place, then,> Jessica said. <I don't want these rats fleeing their sinking ship.>

Usef nodded. <We'll slip a squad past and get them into the shaft. Should be easy to fool their scan.>

The admiral wasn't quite so sure, but she had learned to trust the colonel's instincts. He rarely made mistakes, and never overestimated his abilities.

<I'll run advanced recon while they deal with the sensors,> she said.

<You got it, Admiral.>

She moved toward one of the decorative pillars that ran down the side of the corridor, and hunkered down behind it. Trevor joined her and took up a defensive position in a nearby alcove. Once her body was safe, she pulled up feeds from the nanocloud that was spreading through the passage and into the lift shafts. She directed a streamer of nano into the hidden lift and down its long shaft, curious what would be revealed below.

A little under a hundred meters later, the nanoprobes reached the bottom of the shaft and slipped around the cracks in the heavily reinforced door.

Inside was a rather bland-looking corridor that ended in an equally uninspired foyer. That space contained a dozen guards, as well as active EM dampening that threatened to sever her connection to the drones.

Wishing she had Iris along to help with this sort of work, Jessica guided the nano to a small control panel, and slipped it inside. A passing familiarity with Sirian tech made it easy to spot the network data connection, and she set the nanoscopic bots to building a rudimentary interface.

Once connected to the segregated network in the COO's bunker, she explored the space, identifying different systems until she'd found the optic feeds.

What she saw caused her to nearly choke in horror.

<Well, fuck,> was all she managed to say on the command net. *<No rush getting down there. Leory isn't going anywhere.>*

<Why's that?> Trevor asked.

Jessica passed him the visual, and heard a shocked gasp come from his direction. *<I think he'll need limbs…and a body.>*

<Plus, that hole in his head will make it hard to use his thinking thing,> he added. *<Like…everyone in that room is torn to shreds. What did that?>*

A quick tap of more feeds got Jessica her answer. Positioned in dark alcoves were a dozen of the mech cats, each one covered with blood. *<I guess they had a technical problem.>*

<Who do you think did it?> Usef asked.

<My money is on the ascended AI,> Jessica replied. *<I bet our friend Leory and his admirals knew something they don't want us to find out.>*

Trevor gave a grunt indicating reluctant belief. *<I wonder if that's why it came to Brilliance. It was cleaning up a mess, not stopping us.>*

<It seemed rather intent on stopping us,> Jessica said. *<And I don't know that these things are suicidal.>*

<Maybe…> Usef paused a moment. *<Maybe they can be compelled.>*

She supposed it was possible—and also not something that made her feel any better about killing the thing. *<Usef…can you take care of this whole mess? Document the shit out of everything. I think I need…I dunno. A moment or something.>*

<You got it, Admiral,> the colonel's response oozed confidence. *<Nothing we can't handle. Once we have this place locked down, we'll move on to station command. My other*

companies will have it cordoned off shortly.>

<Excellent.> Jessica rose, glad for the stabilization her armor provided. Trevor was at her side in an instant.

<Let's get you back to the Lantzer,*>* he placed an arm around her. *<I think that fight took more out of you than you expected.>*

<Yeah,> she gave a weak smile. *<Once I get some light, I'll be fine.>*

The fireteam of Marines from the *Lantzer* was still present, and she was going to use them for protection on the way back to the docks, but Usef wouldn't hear of it, detaching a platoon of his own to do the job.

Ten minutes later, they were aboard a convoy of groundcars, taking a longer but less dangerous path to Usef's assault shuttles.

Partway along the route, a connection came in from the *Lantzer*, and Iris's voice came into her mind.

<How're things down there, Jess?>

<A fucking mess, Iris. Did you get an update from Troy?>

<I did. The Voyager *just disembarked. He said you looked pretty worn from taking down that core AI.>*

Jessica sighed, nodding to herself and wishing she wasn't in armor. The car they'd commandeered had what looked like very comfortable seats, but with all her gear, they just kept her hunched forward, half-twisted to fit in the space.

<It took a lot out of me, yeah,> she replied after trying to shift into a better position. *<We also found that Leory and his senior VPs and admirals were all dead.>*

<Wait…were? As in they aren't anymore?>

<Uh…oooops.> Jessica laughed. *<I meant are. No zombie-Lumin leadership to battle today.>*

The AI snorted. *<Pity. Things have been interesting up here as well.>*

<Uh oh.> Jessica knew what 'interesting' implied. *<Lay it on me.>*

<We mopped up the Lumin defenders pretty nicely—thanks to Troy getting control of their drones. Once he sussed out the command protocols, we took direct control from the ships, and can now thank the Sirians for nine hundred thousand little pew-pew machines.>

<OK, that sounds like good news. What's the bad?>

<Joe had a harder time of it where he jumped in. There were well over half a million ships waiting for him. They pulled a 'Defense of Carthage' move and unleashed Exaldi on the Sirians. Unfortunately, the Sirians had another bot swarm and made a mess of the emitters. Exaldi got out, and…well…. It sounds like things got dire.>

Memories of her recent battle with ascended AIs, and the partially successful attempt to use Exaldi to defeat the enemy, flooded Jessica's mind. She'd made a tactical error that could have seen the entire Theban System destroyed. The fact that Joe had opted to use the dark layer creatures offensively surprised her.

<It seems the Starblade used a rather gutsy maneuver to suck the Sirian ships and escaped Exaldi back into the DL.>

Jessica's mouth fell open as she considered what that must have involved. <But—>

<Yeah, the ship is trashed. Joe's taking it back to New Canaan for repair.>

The implications of that hit Jessica like an asteroid. <He's saddling me with this mess?>

<Well, he's leaving Ophelia and Symatra under your command. So…in a nutshell, yeah.>

If there was one person—excepting Tanis—who she thought would soldier through no matter the situation, it was Joe. The fact that he'd made such a major tactical error, and then decided to remove himself from the field, spoke volumes about his emotional state.

<Well. Let them know that once they've scoured the area for stray Exaldi, they're to move insystem to back us up. I'll be up there

shortly.>

<*Good,*> Iris replied, the relief in her mental tone palpable. <*Because there's more that we need to discuss in person.*>

<*Fuck, Iris,*> Jessica groaned. <*Why would you say that? I don't need to hear that!*>

<*Burden of rank. I'll see you soon.*>

* * * * *

Jessica updated Trevor with the highlights of her conversation with Iris, and he did his best to distract her until they reached the *Lantzer*. Once there, she made a beeline for the dorsal observation deck and disabled all shielding while shedding every scrap of clothing she wore.

"Oh sweet fucking stars," she moaned as Lucent's light bathed her. "Why can't all stars feel like this?"

Trevor, who stood a few meters behind her, chuckled and shook his head. "You need a lesson in stellar life cycles?"

She turned to face him, moaning again as the blue-white light bathed her back. "You wanna give me one? Things might get a bit tingly here before long."

Her husband smirked, appearing to consider the option. "I won't lie, getting frisky while you're recharging is always a thrill, but I think this time, you need to recover solo. Who knows what Iris is about to throw at us."

"Figured you two would be hiding here," Iris said as she entered the lounge.

"Figured, or just tracked us on the ship's sensors?" Jessica smirked at her wife as the AI sidled up to Trevor and wrapped an arm around him.

"Oh, I could have traced you, sure. But trust me, I didn't need to. The moment Gil told me you docked, I was on my way."

Jessica laughed, spinning in a slow circle with her arms

stretched overhead, letting the light bathe every square centimeter of her skin. "I have to admit, I was kinda worried I'd damaged my cellular structure by sucking in that whole ascended AI, but I think I'll be OK."

"That's good," Iris said, "because I need you to be ready for that other bit of news."

"Which is?"

"Well, with Joe on temporary leave, and Tanis still missing, Governor Andrews wants to put you in command of the ISF."

Jessica had been drawing in a deep breath, but she choked on it when Iris completed her sentence.

"They want to *what*?" she asked once the power of reason had returned. "I can't command the ISF! I'm not senior. Not by a long shot!"

"You're forgetting Tangel made your promotion to admiral retroactive," Iris said. "One could argue that Carson or Corsia outrank you, but there are other considerations that make you the best fit."

"Which are?" Jessica demanded through gritted teeth.

"Your work with the League of Sentients and Scipio. Not to mention our ties to Star City. People will follow you."

"Follow—wait. *What*?!"

A smile crept across Iris's face. "You know…there's that whole clause in the Scipio Alliance's fine print that says the alliance is commanded by the field marshal."

"Fuck," Jessica muttered, all thought of the sunlight striking her forgotten. "And that means me."

"Shit." Trevor's mouth hung open. "Doesn't that make you the leader of pretty much everyone who isn't a core AI?"

She fixed her husband with a penetrating stare. "Shut up before I show you just how tingly I can be right now."

"Easy," Iris gave her a mollifying look. "Trust me, I know better than anyone how little you want a position like this. If I could think of a better candidate, I would put their name in the hat, but...."

"Yeah," Jessica sighed. "I can't think of anyone, either. I mean, Carson would hate it more than me. He'd probably resign to avoid it. Corsia...well, I love her like a mother, but she can be a bit...."

"Prickly?" Iris suggested.

"Yeah, that's a nice way to put it." Jessica chuckled before squaring her shoulders and going through a mental list. "Sanderson kinda fits that same mold as well. If it wasn't for the fact that Sera was missing, I'd say we should make her do it."

"Doesn't the person have to be from New Canaan?" Trevor asked.

Jessica nodded. "Yeah, but Sera is a citizen of New Canaan. Something Tanis did for her back when her father got killed. Well, her clone father."

"What about Fina?" Trevor suggested. "She's in the system, even."

"Oh!" Iris gasped. "I can't believe I forgot that!"

Jessica's eyes narrowed. "You forgot she's in Sirius?"

"Pfft." The AI waved a hand. "I knew that. But I forgot what she found."

"Still have trouble believing you forgot *anything*," Trevor said.

Jessica nodded in agreement. "However, we're all ears."

Iris proceeded to explain what Cheeky's team had discovered about the spotty coverage of Sol's outer interdiction net, as well as the movement of Sirian ships to Nibiru.

"Nibiru," the admiral muttered, shaking her head slowly. "I wonder if they're going to pull a Mercury on it."

"A what?" Trevor asked, an eyebrow raised.

"Mercury...the original innermost planet in the Sol System?" Jessica prompted. "Named after the messenger god?"

He shrugged. "Not ringing any bells. I'm not super up on shit in the Sol System, though. Place is like a shell game with planets. You can never tell which ones still exist."

"Just Mer—" Jessica stopped herself. "OK, I guess they took Oranos apart, too. And Pluto got moved to Jupiter."

"See?" Trevor chuckled. "Planet shell game."

"Seems like there could be a better metaphor," Iris said. "Either way, I get your drift, Jessica. They mined Mercury away back in the third millennia to make the system's major orbital structures. I imagine they could do the same with Nibiru, if Uriel could get public backing."

Jessica nodded, realizing that the ISF closing in on Sol was probably just the sort of thing that would get the Hegemony the leverage she needed to co-opt just about any resource for military purposes.

"Perfect place to build a fleet, as well," Trevor said. "Looks like it's over a thousand AU from Sol. No one's going to pay it much heed."

"Here's the thing, though," Jessica said, unable to stop a smile from tugging at the corners of her mouth. "It's so far out that you can use dark layer FTL to arrive right on its doorstep. That's one of the reasons most systems don't do much with their outer dwarf planets. Too hard to protect from marauders."

"Marauders like *Sabrina*?" Trevor asked with a laugh.

"Just like *Sabrina*," Jessica replied. "Though she's gonna need a new paint job and cover."

Iris tapped a long, silver finger against her chin. "What about a Sirian courier?"

"Perfect!" Jessica snapped her fingers. "Now to convince Sabrina to let us give her another makeover."

"What about the other thing?" Trevor prompted.

"The thing where I'm the supreme commander of all the

things?" Jessica asked, feeling weariness crash back down on her again. "First, I should double-check with Jason that this is really what he wants. I guess then the next step will be to confer with Krissy and Diana. We're on Sol's doorstep…it's time to plan our final assault."

HEGEMON'S FOLLY

STELLAR DATE: 05.17.8950 (Adjusted Years)
LOCATION: High Terra, Earth
REGION: Sol System, Hegemony of Worlds

Uriel strode into the secluded chamber at the base of the tower housing her offices and the war room.

"Loaris! You said those SAI arrays would work," she bellowed the moment her long strides carried her across the threshold. "You promised that the drone fleets could defeat the ISF ships."

~*They can,*~ the nimbus being floating in the center of the room replied. ~*The Sirians, in all their hubris, simply failed to protect the control room properly.*~

"How do you know that?" Uriel demanded.

~*You can see it plainly in the scan data. The drone swarm went inactive. It wasn't destroyed. Even the ISF recognized that they wouldn't survive a head to head encounter.*~

"Still, this means Sirius will fall."

Uriel felt somewhat better, knowing that the drones would still be effective, but didn't feel generous enough to give the being a free pass.

"With the enemy holding both Kapteyn's Star and Sirius, they can mass their forces right at our doorstep."

~*And what of Secretary Saray's plan?*~

Uriel began to pace back and forth across the front of the room, her eyes darting to the creature at each turn. "We're proceeding apace. It's going to take some time to assemble everything we need, we don't have the resources to do it quickly. If you—"

~*Do not ask for more resources from us,*~ Loaris thundered, limbs stretching out to touch the sides of the chamber. ~*We have our own concerns. Your troubles are not ours.~*

The hegemon drew up short, not wanting to get too close to the creature's light-tentacles. "I would have pressed for peace ages ago if not for your encouragement—stars, I *tried*. Now look at us! We're making one last desperate—"

Uriel's mouth snapped shut as one of Loaris's limbs whipped toward her, stopping centimeters from her nose.

~I think I've had enough of you. The task at hand clearly exceeds your capabilities.~

"If you gave us the same level of technology that—"

The hegemon's words were cut off again, this time by the pulsing strand of light wrapping around her neck.

*~It was your greed that got you into this mess. I'm just taking advantage of it. Do you really think I want the Hegemony to **win**?~*

Uriel gave a strangled gasp, unable to fathom why the core AIs would provide her with stasis shield technology if not to help her defeat the Alliance.

~It doesn't matter,~ Loaris said, another strand of light brushing against Uriel's head. *~I'll take more direct control from here.~*

PART 3 - SOL

NIBIRU PORTAGE

STELLAR DATE: 05.25.8950 (Adjusted Years)
LOCATION: *Sabrina,* **Approaching Nibiru**
REGION: Sol System, Hegemony of Worlds

"And there it is," Fina said from where she stood at the front of the bridge. "The home star."

"I mean...we could see it from Sirius," Cheeky said. "No biggie. Not a lot brighter from here."

Misha shook his head. "I don't know, Cheeks. We're *in* the Sol System. Like, where our entire species is from. All of us. Everyone. Sol, it's where it's all going on."

"Milking it a bit much there." Nance gave a dry laugh. "Still, I have to agree. This is kinda cool. Too bad it's full of Terrans and shit."

Cheeky nodded in agreement. "Yeah, I'm not so keen on people from these parts, either. Still, that doesn't diminish the significance."

" 'Keen on people from these parts'?" Sabs laughed. "You're pining for Finaeus, aren't you?"

The captain shrugged. "Maybe a bit. Jerk just disappears on some super-secret mission with Earnest, and doesn't even leave his wife a special letter?"

Fina's lips twisted. "Yeah, sorry about that. Uncle Fin has always been a bit myopic."

Cheeky matched the other woman's expression. "Trust me, I've been with him for over a decade. This is something I've learned."

<As much as I love chatting about Finaeus, what do we think of the scan data?>

"You mean the data showing half a friggin' million ships at Nibiru?" the captain asked. "If you must know, I hate it. I hate it a lot."

"I second that," Nance chimed in. "And wow...did Nibiru used to have a ring?"

"Small one," Fina said. "Just to manage climate."

Cheeky gestured at the screen, where a second ring sat above the planet, bristling with ships. "That definitely looks like more than just a small one." She focused the ship's sensors in on the best-lit side. "Yeah, so that thing is a shipyard. They *are* mining Nibiru to build a new fleet."

"We need more intel," Fina said. "But I don't know if starting at Nibiru is the right option. That place is going to be locked down tighter than Bob's ass—"

Her statement was interrupted by a snort from Sabs.

Fina rolled her eyes and continued. "We should go there, instead," she gestured at a barely discernable point of light, which gained the label 'Sedna'.

"Right." Cheeky inclined her head. "The rare meetup between Sedna and Nibiru. Must be weird to have another world so close out here."

"Via dark layer, it's only thirty minutes—even at this low *v*," Sabs informed them.

"OK, sounds like a deal." Cheeky lowered herself into the captain's seat. "Plotting a course."

Fina nodded and settled behind her console. "OK, I'm updating our data payload to make it look like we were bound for Sedna all along."

A few minutes later, the ship slipped into the dark layer, traversing the ninety light minutes of space in a third of the time light required, snapping back into space above the small, idyllic world of Sedna.

"Here we are," Cheeky announced. "Sedna, sweet...wait, what the heck?"

She waved her hand, and a message appeared on the forward display, broadcast from the world below.

"Interdicted?" Nance scowled at the words scrolling before them. "A nanophage? Since when does Sol have things like nanophages?"

"Pretty much never," Fina replied, her brow furrowed. "They happen out in the fringes from time to time, but not in the Hegemony...they have the tech to lick any of them."

<We're being pinged by an AST cruiser,> Sabrina spoke up. <They're informing us that this is an interdicted zone, and we have to turn back.>

The crew all glanced at one another, each coming to the conclusion that, despite the apparent buildup at Nibiru, Sedna being so close *and* being interdicted due to a mysterious phage made it the more interesting destination.

"Yeah, we're going to need to land there," Cheeky announced. "Stall them for a minute, Sabrina. We need to come up with a plan."

FEAST OF CHAMPIONS

STELLAR DATE: 05.25.8950 (Adjusted Years)
LOCATION: ISS *Carthage*, Incandus
REGION: Sirius System, Allied Occupied Space

Caldwell stepped off the shuttle and into the *Carthage*'s cavernous A1 docking bay. He'd never set foot aboard the ship, but its similarities to the *I2* made him feel right at home.

He connected to the shipnet and found that even it felt the same, the comforting presence of a multinodal AI settling on the edge of his consciousness like a familiar friend.

A brief query informed him that the meeting was being held in the ship's port-side habitation cylinder, at a restaurant named 'Kerr's Pier'.

He already knew that Kerr was the name of the ship's AI, and wondered why an eatery bore the same name. The thought slipped from his mind as he approached the maglev station to find none other than Colonel Usef waiting for the next car.

"Colonel," he said by way of greeting, keeping his voice dry and formal.

Usef snorted without turning. "Like I didn't know it was you getting off that shuttle, Caldwell."

The big man turned and held out a hand. Palms met, and the two men pulled close for a heartfelt embrace before separating again.

"Been too long," Caldwell said, eyeing his long-time friend up and down. "Looks like all the cushy assignments in the Inner Stars have been good to you."

"Cushy?" Usef chuckled and shook his head. "Says the guy who got to freewheel and rampage across the PED. Pretty much war against people in the stone ages if you ask me."

A laugh slipped past Caldwell's lips as a maglev car arrived. "Yeah, well, you know how it is. Little destruction here, little pillaging there."

"Really?" Usef cocked an eyebrow.

"Stars no. I mean, yeah, some systems were a piece of cake to deal with. Show up, blow some shipyards, knock down some Orion patrol boats, hop out. We ran into some shit here and there, though. Heck, at the very end, Admiral Svetlana got captured by Widows. We had to breach their ship and rescue her."

"A Widow ship?" Usef asked as he settled into a seat, the plas groaning beneath him. "I wouldn't expect them to be operating in the PED right now. Not with Orion falling apart around them—plus, Cary summoned all the Widows to her."

Caldwell sat across from Usef, nodding as he settled into his own seat. "Yeah, I heard about that...let me just say, that was all friggin' nuts. Maybe our Widows didn't get the message or something. Either way, we took them out."

"And the admiral?"

"Checked out by both ISF and TSF doctors. She's right as rain."

"Good to hear."

The pair lapsed into silence for a minute, then Caldwell asked the question desperate to claw its way free. "But what about Admiral Evans? I hear he had a breakdown."

"You know better than to listen to scuttlebutt." Usef swiped a hand through the air as he spoke. "The admiral's just been through the shit. First his daughters were missing, then his wife—again. He's not catching a lot of breaks lately. To be honest, he gets my respect for knowing when he needs to take a back seat."

"And Admiral Keller?" Caldwell figured he may as well milk Usef for everything the Marine knew while they were alone.

"No one better to be our pro-tem leader," Usef replied. "I've known her for ages. Solid as a rock."

"Pro-tem?" he ventured. "So you think Tanis will be back."

"Dude." Usef leant back in his seat, delivering a measuring stare. "You don't? This is Tanis-Fucking-Richards. She'll be back."

"You're not worried about the core AIs? Isn't a trip to the core what turned Sera's mother into Airtha?"

"Tanis isn't Airtha. Besides, she has people who really believe in her, not some narcissistic whackjob of a husband. We also have Bob, Earnest, and Finaeus. There's nothing they can't fix."

Caldwell gave a reluctant nod. Usef had been around a lot more mental surgery than he had. The idea of someone reconstructing his mind gave him chills.

"Either way, Jessica will do well in the position, no matter how long her pro-tem status remains. She's crazy smart and a lot...wilier—is that a word?—than people think."

"I remember her surviving that battle with the Sirian scout ships outside the Kap," he replied. "That was something."

"Yeah, I was just a cadet," Usef said. "But she was a legend even then."

The maglev car passed outside the ship, arcing along a grav rail to shoot through an opening in the rotating cylinder.

"I was just a kid then..." Caldwell shook his head. "But I guess you know that."

Usef chuckled. "Sure do. You were an asset to my 'toon, though. Kicked a lot of ass in the Defense of Victoria."

"Can you believe that *those* were the simple times we'd kill to go back to?" Caldwell asked, joining in with Usef's laughter. "Still, we're almost through all this, right?"

He hadn't meant there to be as much pleading or near-desperation in his voice, but he supposed there was no reason to hide it. His stream of questions had likely conveyed his state of mind to the other man.

"Sure hope so," Usef replied with his trademark calm. "I promised Trevor I'd show him where to buy the best skimpy swimwear on Tyre."

"Oh stars…" Caldwell covered his face as the train pulled into a maglev station next to a broad lake inside the cylinder. "What an image to put in my mind right before we eat."

Usef winked as he rose from his seat, the plas sighing in relief as he did. "What can I say? I'm here to help."

"For some definition of 'help'."

The two men walked down the platform and onto an empty street, where overhanging trees created a shady bower. The restaurant was a kilometer down the road, and while Caldwell considered summoning a groundcar, it was probable that they could walk the distance before one arrived.

"Wouldn't it be nice to see these ships properly crewed someday?" he asked after a minute. "Transcend ships are bustling with activity, people everywhere. ISF ones…well, they all feel like ghost towns."

"I'll trade you," Usef replied with a wry smirk. "I've had an entire battalion crammed into a few cruisers and transports for the last few months. We're cheek by jowl most days."

"Oh yeah?" Caldwell laughed. "Which cheeks?"

Usef barked a laugh. "More importantly, which jowl?"

"OK…I think one of us doesn't know what that word means."

The other man continued chuckling for a minute, then inclined his head. "Maybe. Either way, I get your sentiment. Most of the time, our ships are pretty lonely places. Coming back to the ISF after my stint on *Sabrina* was pretty jarring."

"Now *that* must have been an adventure."

Usef nodded vigorously. "Oh, you have no idea. If Tanis hadn't served on that ship, she would never have believed half my reports."

Ahead, the restaurant came into view, nestled among the trees, backing out onto the lake. The sounds of conversation reached their ears, and the pair picked up their pace.

As they approached the front doors, a car pulled up, and Captain Ophelia stepped out, smiling in greeting at the two men. "Fashionably late, I see."

"Lots to do," Usef replied. "Had to make sure a bunch of sparkly crybabies didn't riot."

"I heard the Noctus are the ones more likely to riot," Ophelia said. "At least in some of the smaller stations."

The colonel nodded. "Yeah, it's a full-time job trying to get their leaders to keep their people in line. I get that they have about a billion years of anger built up, but slaughtering all the Lumins in some sort of rage-filled bloodbath isn't going to sit as well in their memories as they think."

"Is President Wrentham going to help?" Caldwell asked. "She's got the resources to send in peacekeepers."

"I think so," Ophelia replied. "Going to have to ask Jessica. She's been on the QC with Krissy so much today, we needed fresh blades."

"And this is why I fuck up every so often." Usef gave the other two a wink as he held open the quaint wooden doors. "No way they're making me a general or," the big man shuddered, "an admiral. Can you see *me* commanding fleets?"

"The horror," Caldwell deadpanned.

Ophelia gave him an appraising look. "I don't know...I think you'd actually be good at it. You've a mind made for tactics, and you genuinely care about people."

"Fuck!" Usef bellowed. "You take that back right now. I can't have that shit getting out!"

A look of shock came over the captain, but it left just as quickly, and she burst out laughing. "Shit, Usef. Don't do that. You're fucking terrifying when you want to be."

The Marine adopted a mock sulk. "And don't you forget

it."

A nonplussed servitor greeted them and guided the trio through the empty restaurant and out to the back deck, where Admiral Keller stood talking with a group of people. Caldwell easily picked out Commander Trevor, who looked like a near copy of Usef—except he appeared as outwardly jovial as Usef was on the inside. Next to them was a woman who looked identical to the admiral, except she was silver.

Caldwell activated augmenting overlays, and the data next to her gave the name Iris. He cocked an eyebrow in surprise. He knew who Iris was, but hadn't realized she appeared as a carbon copy to her former pairing partner.

Standing with them was a man who had his back to the colonel. Caldwell's HUD gave no information about the individual. He had lanky, blond hair and broad shoulders. Next to him was a woman also with blonde hair. For a moment, Caldwell thought it was Sera, but the name that appeared above her head read 'Seraphina'.

Shit...it's one of the clones.

She was giving the unnamed man an unreadable look, and Caldwell's curiosity changed to surprise when the mystery man turned, showing himself to be none other than Governor Andrews.

Not knowing who he should address first, Caldwell was saved by Jessica waving the newcomers over, calling out, "No formalities, everyone, we're keeping Jason's presence on the downlow."

"There was just no way I couldn't make the trip out here to gloat over the Sirians' defeat," he said by way of greeting. "This place has been the source of my greatest shame for over a thousand years."

"Sorry?" Seraphina asked. "How's that?"

The governor grimaced. "It was ages ago, back in my Phantom Blade days. We came here to free some AIs, and found the beginnings of this whole filthy Lumin-Noctus caste system they have. We saved the AIs and kicked the Lumins in the balls, but…well…we never came back. Helping the Noctus in the Kap was a bit of a salve, but this is a hell of a lot better. I only wish that core AI hadn't shredded their COO. Would have been nice to see him properly atone for his people's sins."

Usef wore a pained look. "If it's any consolation, I don't think he died slowly."

"Some." The governor's lips twisted into a sour smile.

Beside Jason, Seraphina reached out to touch his arm, but then her hand stopped midway, and she withdrew it, folding both arms across her breasts, her hands gripping her biceps.

"We're just waiting on Symatra and—ah, here he is, Admiral Greer!"

Caldwell found himself wondering if he'd been invited to the wrong party. Greer was one of the TSF's most celebrated leaders, not to mention the man whose cool demeanor had kept things from deteriorating in the Ascella System when the *Intrepid* arrived seeking asylum in the Transcend.

Greer waved as he approached, an easy smile on his lips. "So…you folks do know that you're building warships, not colony ships, right?"

"Gotta bring a little bit of home with us," Jessica replied with a shrug. "Show the enemy how outclassed they are."

The TSF admiral nodded while looking around. "I don't have a lot of firsts anymore, but this is one of them."

"Thanks for the assist, John," Jason said, offering his hand to the admiral.

"Wait." Seraphina's brow lowered. "You have a first name? I can't believe it's not rusty from disuse."

"I oil it regularly," Greer replied. "And I'm more than happy to be here. Sirius has been a sore spot for my family for ages. My great-grandfather led the terraforming here. When it was complete, the GSS made the colonization offer to the ancestors of the Noctus, not the financiers who stole the system from them."

"Damn." Jason shook his head. "Looks like a lot of us have reason to celebrate this victory."

"Well, don't get me wrong, Krissy's not too happy that you 'jumped the gun' and took it."

New Canaan's governor shrugged. "Well, she's not the boss of us."

Greer laughed. "Well, she's the boss of me, though that doesn't mean I agree with her."

"She's the boss of me, too." Seraphina gave a wry smile. "And I'm all for taking down tyrants, but I don't know if this was the ideal system to hit next."

Jason turned toward Seraphina. "Krissy's your boss like I'm Tanis's boss. Which is to say, not at all."

"I'm going to have to get used to thinking of her as Tanis…and Angela as well," Jessica said as she took a step back and gestured at the table. "But before we get into weighty topics, let's settle down and order drinks."

The group filtered around the large, round table, everyone finding seats at random. Caldwell grabbed one in the middle, only to find Jason Andrews on one side and Jessica on the other.

He pulled up the restaurant's drink list over the Link and selected a dry red wine, sending the request to the NSAI responsible for managing the orders. Everyone else remained silent for another minute, waiting for the others to place their orders.

Eyes up and looking around the group was the common signal to let other diners know that one was ready to converse again, and Caldwell did so, noting Usef was smirking.

<What's so funny?>

<You,> the other Marine replied. <You look so uncomfortable.>

<I just want to know what I'm doing here,> Caldwell admitted.

<My fleet didn't do anything to take Sirius, I have no special connection to it. I can't think of why my presence is required.>

<I guess we'll just have to find out,> Usef replied.

"Oh!" Ophelia's eyes widened. "It looks like a delegation from Scipio has made it after all. I wonder if Diana has deigned to favor us with her presence."

Seraphina snorted. "I hope not. That woman can be a major pain in the ass."

Jason shrugged. "Worse than some, better than others. I suppose we should wait to order, then."

"Might be polite." Jessica gave the governor a wink.

"Wow...no one waits for *me*?" another voice said from the restaurant's doorway.

Caldwell twisted in his seat to see someone unmistakable walk onto the deck. "Admiral Symatra," he blurted.

"Colonel," she gave him as warm a smile as ever graced her lips. "I'm very glad to see you. You were missed for the past eight months."

"Is that a body?" Jessica asked. "Like a physical one?"

The AI shrugged. "I'm trying it out. My core's not in it, though, don't worry. I'm not *that* reckless."

"We're just waiting on our Scipian friend," Jessica explained. "Then we'll be ready to discuss what's next."

"No rush, though," Jason said. "In fact, I'm all for enjoying a good meal before we get into what comes next."

"Works for me," Jessica replied, then glanced at Greer. "Unless folks have things they need to rush back to?"

The TSF admiral chuckled. "You know as well as I, Field Marshal, that there are always things to rush back to, but to be honest, a few hours of distraction-free time in the company of friends is worth its weight in neutronium."

Jessica made a face at Greer. "I wish you wouldn't use that title for me."

"Because of the responsibility, or because Tanis will be

back?" Jason asked.

"Both. But…since we're on the topic of Tanis, I'm curious what everyone thinks of sending a rescue mission to the core."

"Are we assuming that Sera failed?" Seraphina cocked an eyebrow. "I for one don't believe that for an instant."

Jason's expression grew serious, and he leant forward. "I only know of two people more qualified to enter the core than the team that already went to rescue Tanis and Angela. That would be you, Jessica, and Cary. But Cary is not yet…ready to go on a mission like that, and you're needed here."

The field marshal opened her mouth to reply, but Kerr's voice filled their minds.

<I've been conversing with Bob regarding this matter. He's insistent that we do not send anyone else to the core.>

" 'Insistent' as in giving a direct order?" Jason's brows were halfway to his hairline. "None of his non-interference nonsense?"

<He was not making a suggestion. I got the impression that he would actively **stop** an attempt to send anyone further to the core.>

"It's been two weeks, though," Jessica said. "If they're not back by now…."

<I'm just relaying his message. He said they'd all make it back.>

"How many people wonder sometimes if Bob's actually been to the future and back?" Jason asked, raising his hand.

Jessica's shot up, as did Usef's. Everyone else looked unsure, or downright perplexed.

Except for Symatra. She just scowled at the group and shook her head. "Everyone knows you can't travel backward in time. If he went to the future, then he wouldn't be here now."

"Well, either way." Jason drew a deep breath before continuing, "If he feels that strongly, then I'm inclined to go along with him on it."

"Speaking of Bob," Jessica said as the servitor set their

drinks down on the table. "Should we recall First Fleet from New Sol? I can't see us assaulting Sol without the *I2*."

"I thought we weren't talking business yet," Usef gave her a languid wink. "At least, not until Petra arrives."

"How do you know it's Petra?" Jason asked. "Did you peek?"

The Marine shook his head. "Nope. She's over there."

He pointed out onto the lake, where a white figure was gliding low over the water, periodically flapping long wings that nearly dipped into the gentle waves below.

"Showoff," Seraphina muttered, a smile on her lips belying her true feelings.

Caldwell had never seen Petra; he'd still been back at New Canaan when the *I2* ventured to Scipio. But he'd heard rumors of the ambassador's epic rows with the empress. Scuttlebutt had it that her wings were some sort of punishment from Diana.

Less than a minute later, Petra swooped up over the railing, wings lifted high overhead, then she settled to the deck gracefully next to the table.

"Your groundcars really don't accommodate wings, Captain Ophelia."

"So I've been told," the *Carthage*'s captain replied as she gestured to the remaining seat. "I'll speak to engineering about it."

"Oh, don't," the woman said dismissively as she folded her wings behind her back and settled into the chair. "Gives me an excuse to fly through your larger passages and scare the shit out of people."

Ophelia laughed, a smile on her lips. "Noted."

"Grab a drink off the menu," Jessica directed the newcomer. "I suppose we could go ahead and get some appetizers while we're at it. Anyone have any preferences?"

A brief discussion ensued where Caldwell voiced his desire

for something with fresh fruit.

"I'd been just about to enjoy a fruit salad on Hale's Beacon when Svetlana got attacked," he explained. "I've been craving some ever since."

"That certainly was crazy." Seraphina shook her head. "Widows in the PED after Cary recalled them all is rather troubling. Makes me wonder if there were splinter groups, or if some are just out of communication. We'll have to make it a priority to try and round them up."

"I'll say," Caldwell replied, nodding vigorously. "They're rather disconcerting, to say the least."

"It's sort of the point, I gather," the Hand's director replied.

"Sounds like business again," Usef said, a smirk flitting across his lips.

Jessica gave him a sour look, and Iris laughed. "Well, what else do we have to talk about? It's not like any of us spend a lot of time on our favorite hobbies lately."

"Speak for yourself." The Marine grinned. "I've been practicing my tsunami-surfing for when this war is over. There's a veteran's competition being set up on Tyre."

"Maybe I'll get in on that," Caldwell said. "I never managed to get in on one of your trips there."

Usef winked. "Just have to make it a priority."

"What about you, Jessica?" Jason asked.

The admiral's expression became clouded for a moment, then she glanced at Iris and Trevor. "Well, I think we'll take a tour around New Canaan. There are about a million people I need to catch up with. I haven't seen half of my friends since we all went into stasis at the Kap. After that, a trip to Star City will be in order."

"I have a feeling that place is going to become quite the popular destination," Seraphina said. "They're going to have to screen candidates for the Dream."

Jessica shrugged. "If they let people go in it at all."

269

"Do you know something we don't?" Jason asked.

"Well, they all live inside the neutron star, right?" She paused, and the others all nodded. "What if that's getting full? Maybe they don't want others there. Heck, how much do we really want every Tom, Dick, and Harry in the galaxy ascending?"

Jason got a far-off look in his eyes, and drew in a deep breath. "I suppose we're going to have to trust Lysander to make the right call on that. Stars...he was the last person I ever expected to see again."

The governor looked around the table. "You know...he's the one that got me into all of this, back on Alpha Centauri, when I was just a short-range pilot, doing hauls between El Dorado and Proxima."

"Like a billion years ago," Iris said with a wink.

"Close," the governor replied.

The servitor appeared with several platters, and Caldwell realized he hadn't placed an order.

"I took the liberty," Ophelia said. "Anyone who wants to order something else is welcome to, though we should have a good selection."

"One thing is for sure," Petra said as she reached for a slice of quesadilla. "I'll be headed back to Alexandria with Diana as soon as we can manage it."

"Time to clean out the viper nest there?" Seraphina asked.

"Nests," the ambassador corrected. "At least three major ones, countless minor. We've had...what, five coup attempts since forming the Alliance? It's like they're on a schedule or something."

"Clockwork coups." Greer chuckled. "So glad I never got assigned to a Watchpoint in Scipio."

Petra frowned at the admiral. "There aren't any TSF Watchpoints in Scipio."

"Not anymore." The man winked before taking a bite of a

spring roll.

"Anyone else have any fun plans after this is all over?" Jason asked.

The group went around the table, talking about the places they wanted to visit and things they wished to do. When his turn came around, Caldwell expressed a desire to return to a few systems in the PED.

"Really?" Seraphina fixed him with one of her frequent scowls. "The PED?"

"Machete for sure," he replied. "You haven't had whiskey till you've had theirs. That shit is the best."

"Long trip for some spirits," Jason said. "But hey, we can do it with the gates…while they're up, at least."

The governor's words caused everyone to fall silent, and he looked around the table, shaking his head.

"What?" he asked. "You all know we can't leave the gate system in place. It's going to be the FTL Wars all over again, except worse. With gates, you can make war on people on the far side of the galaxy in an afternoon. Can you imagine if pirate organizations got their hands on them? After the war's over, we have to disarm the galaxy as much as possible."

"I'll second that," Jessica said. "Slugfests between stasis-shielded ships are insane. It won't take long before people resort to antimatter to overwhelm shields."

Greer grimaced and glanced at Seraphina. "Not the sort of thing we want to have happen. I suppose this is just an extension of our old uplift program…except maybe this time, even we aren't ready for the tech we have."

"That won't be easy," Petra said. "I don't see Diana giving up her gates. They've already become an integral part of how Scipio operates. It's also going to make the coups a lot less common, once travel increases between the quadrants."

Jason shrugged. "Well, it's either that, or we have to carry on being the galaxy's police. Which do you want?"

"I think we can find a door number three," Petra replied. "No need to turn this into a false dichotomy."

"Perhaps," Jason inclined his head. "I don't know what it will be, but maybe there's an option we've not yet considered. Either way, we should discuss what happens next with our campaign against the Hegemony."

"Before the main course?" Jessica asked.

"We're bound to get off track again," the governor replied. "I understand that you've sent *Sabrina* ahead to gather intel?"

The field marshal nodded. "We have. Records show that Sirius sent quite a few ships there. The more we hunt, the more we find. It could be as many as a million."

Jason shook his head. "Have I mentioned that I hate this system?"

"Might have slipped out," Usef said.

"How are they going to infiltrate Sol?" Petra asked. "That place has to be locked down tight."

"It is," Jessica replied. "At the heliopause. However, they didn't go there. Intel shows that the buildup is happening at Nibiru."

"Well, that's odd." Jason slid a hand along his jaw. "It's, what...about a thousand AU from Sol?"

"Give or take a bit," Jessica replied with a nod. "They actually skipped on to Sedna, as Nibiru was a bit too hot. Sedna's just a few minutes away by FTL, so it was a better option. They said the place is under lockdown for a nanophage outbreak, but so far, they think it's a smokescreen."

"A nanophage on Sedna?" Jason paled. "I sure *hope* that's a smokescreen. I don't like the idea of a phage that can best Sol's tech."

"They seemed certain of it," Jessica said. "They're working out a way to land and see what's up. Sabrina has a dose of pico on hand to deal with things if it really is a nanophage."

"Seems unlikely that they'd be blasé about a phage," Petra

commented. "I mean, they have a massive buildup at Nibiru, probably a last stand sort of force at this point. If Sedna was about to grow horns, I could see Uriel just nuking the thing and being done with it."

"Horns?" Seraphina asked with a laugh. "Is that what you think a phage would do to a planet?"

The diplomat gave a shrug, a smile tugging at the corners of her lips. "I mean, it's possible."

"Nightmare-inducing." Jason shook his head. "Either way, whatever intel they gather will shape what we do next. I'm in favor of a finishing blow. We should disable their interdiction web, jump right down to High Terra, smash their defenses, and declare an end to the war."

"Might be presumptive," Greer said, a smile in his eyes. "But I like it."

"Jessica?" Seraphina asked. "You're our leader."

Caldwell turned to the Alliance's head, and watched as a small war of emotions flitted across her lavender visage.

"In principle, I'm a fan of getting in and smashing. Basically what we did here. Jump in and hit the most valuable target with overwhelming force. Problem is, Sol might not have such a lumpy defense distribution."

"Not to mention the Cho," Iris said. "I don't want to think about what would be required to subdue that thing."

"Easier to build a wall around it," Jason muttered, then realized everyone's eyes had fallen to him. "Metaphorically speaking, of course."

"Sure," Jessica laughed. "Though even literally, it's probably not wrong."

"Focusing on High Terra seems like the best play to me," Petra said. "Scipio has wargamed taking Sol for ages, and that's always been their conclusion as well. Capture High Terra, and level guns at the Cho. In all honesty, it's their greatest liability. Seven trillion people on one structure."

"Yeah, we're not gonna do that," Jessica said. "The Alliance doesn't operate like Scipio."

"Didn't say we have to operate that way. But we could make them think we do."

"Kinda already have evidence that wouldn't work," Usef countered.

The winged woman fixed him with a cool look from her pale blue eyes. "Have you seen how the war has gone on our side of the Hegemony? Trust me, they'd believe it if it was Scipian ships parked around their precious habitat."

"Let's do our best to avoid too many war crime tribunals," Greer said. "Though I applaud the sentiment. Besides, in the meantime, the TSF will begin to amass forces here. I have authorization to bring in peacekeeping units to ensure that the Noctus don't do things they'll regret later, as well as a final force to bring into Sol."

"What sort of fleet composition can you bring to bear?" Jessica asked the TSF admiral.

"This is a critical time." Greer pursed his lips for a moment. "If we overextend, then we could see our adversaries take advantage and hit us somewhere we least expect. That being said, now that things on the Orion fronts are winding down, I think we could bring in a few hundred thousand ships at least. Mostly destroyers and light cruisers. We're still dealing with some splinter groups within the former Transcend borders that think asserting their strength against Airtha is the best use of their time."

"That's more than a little annoying," Jessica muttered.

"You're telling me," Seraphina said. "I'm doing my best to get them in check, but the Hand has never focused much internally, and what assets we do have there have been displaced by all the upheaval."

"We will bring our entire mobile offensive force," Petra said. "Currently, it stands at three hundred thousand ships, though that's spread across more than a dozen systems."

Jessica inclined her head in acknowledgment. "We may not want to pool so many resources here. Perhaps some in the Kap, and others in Virginis. Speaking of which, no one from the League of Sentients was able to attend, but they expect to be able to field a hundred thousand ships. Lighter tonnage, but a lot of AI crews."

"This isn't going to be enough," Jason shook his head. "That only puts us at around a million ships. If all of the Sirians' ships are there, they alone will outnumber us."

"We won seriously outnumbered here," Jessica countered. "Granted, that took a lot of luck."

"And recklessness," Seraphina added. "If Sol has a billion drone swarms like they did here, we can't count on finding their control centers—not without solid intel on the ground, at least. We need to find their control stations, and get people in place to disable them."

"You're right," Jessica replied, nodding in agreement. "That means multiple teams with QCs to let us know when it's time to move in."

"Once we get the initial report from Sabrina," Jason said.

"I don't think we should have individual teams running around with QC blades on hand," Usef said. "That's kinda risky. We need a base of operations inside Sol, with a fast response team on hand in case any control centers don't go offline."

Jessica gave him a measuring look. "I get the feeling you have an idea who that should be."

The Marine shrugged. "I don't know what you're talking about, could be anyone."

"Thing is..." the field marshal turned to face Caldwell. "I was planning on bumping Caldwell here up to admiral...and if I send you in, it would be on his ships...so you'd be clearly subordinate to him, but you're senior in both grade and service."

Usef pursed his lips, glaring at Caldwell. "I feel like I've been set up."

Caldwell raised both his hands. "I had nothing to do with this. Don't think I want you answering to me."

"So you'll take the promotion to general?" Jessica didn't bother hiding the smirk that formed on her lips.

Usef opened his mouth to reply, then set his elbows on the table and hid behind his hands. "This is payback for the glitter cannons, isn't it?"

"Glitter cannons?" Jason asked.

"They were spectacular," Trevor replied.

Jessica's smirk shifted to a genuine smile. "Sorry, Usef. As much as I'd like to find some way to give you your comeuppance for the cannons, this is actually a compliment for a job well done."

"Well, shit," the Marine muttered, still hiding behind his hands. "Next time, I'll have to do something even more obnoxious to your command seat."

The field marshal grinned at him. "Do your worst."

Seraphina glanced between the two. "You two all set? Because I might have an agent on High Terra close to Uriel's inner circle already."

"Really?" Jason turned toward her. "Anyone we know?"

The Hand director's lips twisted into a half-smile. "Sort of. You remember Elena?"

"Not personally." A scowl settled on the governor's brow. "If memory serves, she betrayed you at least three times, and tried to kill Tanis twice? Oh, and she murdered the clone version of Jeffrey Tomlinson."

Seraphina nodded. "Yeah, that's her."

"I thought she was in the *I2*'s brig?" Jessica's eyes darted to the side, looking for information on her HUD.

"She was," Seraphina confirmed. "But if you recall, she'd

been mind-altered by Garza and Lisa Wrentham. After her mind had been cleared, she was no guiltier than I was for what Airtha made me do."

She paused, her gaze settling heavily on Jason. "And you are with Sera…preferring the original vintage, I guess. So do I not deserve to be happy?"

Jason had the good grace to look somewhat ashamed, and ducked his head. "Of course you do. We all do. I was just surprised is all."

"Looks like Tangel approved Elena's release," Jessica added.

"I just…" Jason shook his head. "Nevermind. You're right, Sera—Seraphina. I'm sorry."

A silence settled over the group, and Caldwell found himself wondering what it would be like to feel like an extraneous person, a copy that couldn't partake in all the joys and pleasures you had experienced, due to not being the original.

It struck him as a special sort of hell.

"So, what's next?" Symatra asked, finally breaking the silence.

"Seems to me we have a newly conquered system that needs to be brought to order," Greer replied. "That is, if we plan to turn it into something capable of launching the largest assault humanity has ever known."

"Fuck," Jessica muttered. "No pressure."

INSPECTED

STELLAR DATE: 05.25.8950 (Adjusted Years)
LOCATION: *Sabrina*, Approaching Sedna
REGION: Sol System, Hegemony of Worlds

"You sure about this?" Nance gave Cheeky a nervous glance as the pair stood at the starboard airlock's inner door. "That's a squad of AST soldiers out there, and they don't look friendly."

"Sure?" Cheeky gave a quiet laugh. "No, not at all. But there's a pair of inspectors with them, so I think they're on the up and up. Besides, we need to get down there, and getting dirtside requires inspection."

Nance gave her a worried look, "And if there is a phage?"

"Then you can wear one of your old hazsuits. Those things are nano-resistant, right?"

"Nano-resistant, yes. Nano-proof? No."

Cheeky placed a hand on the other woman's shoulder. "Well, either way, it's our job to figure out what's going on and get Jessica the intel she needs."

"Field Marshal Jessica…" Nance spoke the words slowly, as though she was tasting them. "Can you believe it? We flew with her for decades."

"Well, I mean, we flew with Sera for quite a while too, and she turned out to be heir to the Transcend."

<*You two are making me all nostalgic,*> Sabrina interjected. <*I just want to get everyone inside my hull and give them a big hug. Why do they all have to leave?*>

"Fina's back, at least," Cheeky offered.

<*Which is awesome. But where Sera was always grouchy, Fina's kinda sad. I hope she finds her place in the universe again.*>

Cheeky sucked on her bottom lip, teasing it between her

teeth. She suspected that what Fina needed was to sit in the captain's seat in *Sabrina*'s bridge.

But that's what I need too.

The airlock's light turned green, and she palmed the control, opening the inner door. Inside stood the two Hegemony inspectors and three soldiers in light powered armor.

For their part, Cheeky and Nance wore shipsuits emblazoned with the Sirian transport company's logo, though beneath, their flowarmor-enhanced skin provided nearly as much protection as the enemy's gear.

"Welcome aboard the *Cauldron of Light*," Cheeky said, stretching out her hand. "I'm Captain Charlene, and this is my engineer and first mate, Bella."

<I hate that name,> Nance groused.

<You're extra punchy lately. Not like this is our first undercover job…. What's got your girls in a knot?>

<Honestly? I really don't know. I guess it's that half the people we care about are missing…. Tanis, Angela, Sera. Heck, I even miss Finaeus. It's been wearing on me more than I'd like to admit.>

While the two women were speaking, the lead inspector, a narrow-faced woman named Arquette, introduced herself as well as her aide, Morales.

"Inspector Morales will verify that your antimatter bottle is in good standing, with all the proper logs. In the meantime, I would like to take a look at your cargo, then tour your ship."

"Of course," Cheeky ducked her head. "And your escorts?"

"They'll all come aboard, too."

Struggling to hide a grimace, the captain nodded.

"And can you confirm the names and locations of the remainder of your crew?" Arquette asked.

"Our hand, Fina, is on the bridge. Misha, our cook, is in the galley."

Morales chuckled. "A cook? On a ship this small?"

Cheeky shrugged. "Technically, he's a deckhand as well, but given his skills in the galley, and propensity to drive a loader into the bulkhead, this is a much better use of his skills."

<*I heard that,*> Misha muttered over the shipnet.

<*You did hit the bulkhead three times in your first year aboard,*> Sabrina said, still sounding a little put-out over the incidents.

<*How many times since?*>

<*Uhhh…do you really want to know?*> she asked.

<*Yeah, I—*>

<*Wait,*> Sabrina interrupted. <*They're trying to breach our network.*>

Fina joined a second later. <*Nice work on setting up a sandboxed outer network, Sabrina.*>

<*Learned a bit over the years. Iris really knew her shit.*>

While the conversation carried on over the Link, Arquette kept up a steady stream of chatter, telling Cheeky and Nance about the host of Hegemony regulations that they would be expected to adhere to when landing, how Nunataq was the only safe region on the dwarf planet, and how the supplies they were carrying needed to be delivered on time and without damage.

She kept it up until all twelve AST soldiers were aboard the ship. Two remained at the airlock, while another pair went to stand guard outside the galley and bridge. The remaining eight split between Arquette and Morales, trailing behind the inspectors on the way to their disparate destinations.

Sabrina maintained a feed of both groups' progress on the secured shipnet, and Cheeky kept a view of Nance and her group occupying a segment of her consciousness while keeping up idle banter with Arquette.

Inspectors tended to come in one of two flavors. The first was the dour individual who loved to inflict misery on unsuspecting ship captains—they were the easiest to deal with, due to general predictability, as there were only so many things someone could do to mess with a ship and its crew.

The second was, to Cheeky's mind, the convivial inspector. Nine times out of ten, their amicable nature was merely a smokescreen to put their prey at ease, only to pull out some arcane regulation at the last minute, and elicit credit for a fine—or a bribe, depending on how honest the inspector was.

<They're still working on breaching,> Sabrina advised as Arquette began going over the cargo with Cheeky.

<Any idea which of them it is?> the captain asked.

<Not totally. It seems to be coming from several of them at once. I kinda wonder if it's an NSAI loadout operating from their armor.>

<That seems most likely,> Fina chimed in. <It's too persistent to be managed by human operator—unless one of them is an L2 and moonlighting as a grunt in the AST.>

Cheeky directed Arquette to the crates flagged for delivery to the blackhole-monitoring facility that lay deep beneath Nunataq. "These are the specially sealed containers. I have no idea what's inside. Manifest had the 'Don't Fuck With This' mark on it."

"Smart woman," Arquette replied with a laugh. "You'd be surprised how many times we find a DFWT seal breached."

"Wow." Cheeky's mouth hung open out in surprise.

<Nice bit of research, figuring out that the locals have a different name for the Damage-prone/Fragile/Weapons/Tech label,> Fina commented as Arquette replied.

"Not corporate couriers like you—not usually, at least. Mostly, it's smaller independents who want to see if there's something they can lift for more profit than their standard fee."

"Seems stupid," Cheeky scoffed. "I mean, the seals are tamper-proof."

Arquette nodded, giving the captain a pointed look. "Doesn't seem to stop people from thinking they can slip something past us."

Cheeky shook her head while making a 'tsk tsk' sound. She knew what the inspector was doing, trying to make her nervous in order to catch her in a slip.

Lady, I've hauled more contraband past people like you than you can ever imagine. You stand zero chance of putting me off guard.

Arquette stared at her for another moment, then moved on to the next crate.

"So, what's going down on Sedna?" Cheeky asked. "I have to admit that I'm a bit worried about touching down on a world dealing with a nanophage."

"It's minor," the woman gave a nonchalant wave. "Just causes some issues in people's circulatory systems. It never got down to Nunataq."

"Really?" Cheeky frowned in confusion. "You quarantine a whole world for that?"

The inspector shrugged. "Seems like an overreaction to me too, but whatever. No one asks me."

"I hear that. I just go where I'm told, hauling whatever's on the manifest. Orders say we're to touch down on Sedna, we touch down on Sedna."

"Well…" Arquette straightened after examining the last crate. "Cargo all looks good. Let's take a little walk through the ship, and then you'll get to fulfill those orders."

<What's the word?> Cheeky asked. <Have they finished fishing around in our network yet?>

<Seems like it. Mostly it was a crosscheck of our log data with stated logs. They did try to get into some private personal files that we leave on as honeypots. I let them into some, and made a few too tricky for a surreptitious breach.>

<Hopefully that's the end of it,> Fina added. <This seems like a bit much, if you ask me. I kind of wonder if this inspection team does it to dig up dirt so they can extort ships.>

<Wouldn't surprise me,> Nance said. <We've wrapped up in

engineering. I'm escorting them back to the airlock.>

Cheeky sent an acknowledgment as she led the team through the ship, Arquette expressing no small amount of delight at the well-appointed galley, and greeting Fina cordially when she toured the bridge.

Half an hour after the inspection team came aboard, they were gone, much to the relief of Sabs, who deactivated stealth next to the airlock the moment the shuttle detached.

"Staying EM-silent is the worst. Especially when you are all chatting up a storm."

"Shouldn't we remove all the monitoring devices they dropped on the ship before you come out of hiding?" Cheeky asked.

"Already done," Sabs said with a nonchalant shrug. "Not like I had anything else to do. I've never seen such a well-mannered squad of goons."

The captain nodded as she considered the soldiers' actions. "They didn't say a word the whole time, did they?"

<You know, you're right. Not even a peep.>

"All the more evidence that something is going on down there," Cheeky said as she turned and began walking toward the bridge. "Let's hit dirt, and see what we're dealing with."

REPORTING IN

STELLAR DATE: 05.25.8950 (Adjusted Years)
LOCATION: Airthan Ring
REGION: Huygens System, Transcend Interstellar Alliance

Svetlana couldn't help a cheek-splitting grin as she strode toward Krissy, who stood next to a holotank in her president's office. The other woman still wore her admiral's uniform, but her demeanor had changed, exuding more gravitas than even before.

Which is something she's never really lacked to begin with.

"Job well done, Admiral." Krissy spoke first as they clasped hands, then touched shoulders in a brief embrace.

"You too." Svetlana nodded soberly. "Ended the Airthan Civil War *and* put down Orion, all while I was traipsing about behind enemy lines."

"I had a bit of help," the president replied with a wink. "And your Hoplite forces did more than you can imagine. Especially uncovering the DMG at Machete. Knowing that the Guard had that technology saved a lot of lives in other conflicts."

"Glad to hear it," Svetlana said. "If I were to be honest, I wasn't initially excited about being selected — well, I was, but at the same time, I wanted to be where all the action was."

"And now?" Krissy prompted, a smile teasing the corners of her mouth.

"Well, that was the sort of thing I doubt I'll ever have the opportunity to do again...just wander around behind enemy lines with no real worry over reprisal? You can't put a price on that sort of...experience."

"You sure you don't mean skiing?" Krissy asked.

"I only got to do two runs!" Svetlana laughed.

"Seriously...then I went ahead and got attacked and kidnapped. Not one of my better days."

"No, I suppose not." The president gestured at a couple of seats in her office, and the two women settled into them.

As Svetlana got comfortable, something strange happened. Her vision grew dim, almost as though a filter had been set in front of her eyes. Next, sounds grew indistinct, and her body felt numb. Then her arm moved of its own volition, sliding to the side a little on the chair's armrest before a leg lifted up and crossed over the other.

What the fuck is going on?!

Then, she spoke.

"I'm really proud of you, Krissy. You did so much. I'm impressed."

The president scowled at the compliment, and gave an uncertain smile. "Uhh, thanks, Svetlana, I'm just doing my job."

A smile crept over Svetlana's face, and she leant forward. "Can't a mother be proud of her daughter's accomplishments? I've watched you for so long, disappointed that you never achieved your true potential, and allowed yourself to be sidelined. But no more. You're the president of the most powerful human nation, heading up an even stronger alliance. As such, I decided it was time for us to become reacquainted."

As Svetlana voiced the words, a sense of horror grew within her—one matched by the expression on Krissy's face.

"No..." the president whispered. "How is this—you checked out!"

Svetlana made a dismissive swipe with her hand. "Do you think those girls from New Canaan could totally subvert me without giving away their secrets? I might not have been able to break free of their sway, but in my fruitless struggles, I learned how the bonds of my mental prison were created. Turns out that knowledge is very useful."

"So…is it you in there? What happened to Svetlana?"

"She's here too, just not in the driver's seat. And no, this isn't all of me, just a clone of sorts. Oh, and I'm sure you've discovered that you're alone here, now. No one is going to see or hear while I make a few adjustments to you. You know…as is a mother's right with her daughter."

Krissy leapt from her seat, reaching for her sidearm, only to freeze before she managed to draw it.

"Now now, Krissy." Svetlana rose, a sickly smile twisting her lips. "That's not how this is going to go at all. To be honest, all of this is rather serendipitous, but it's playing out just as *she* told me it would. Svetlana might have had her little romp in the PED, but this is where the fun really starts."

Over the next ten minutes, Svetlana screamed so much within the confines of her own mind, she thought she'd go mad. From the wide-eyed expression on Krissy's face, it was clear the other woman felt no better about the situation.

Once the procedure was over, Svetlana sat back down, and then something clicked in her mind, and she cocked her head, frowning slightly. "What were we talking about?"

"When?" Krissy laughed. "Before or after you went on and on about your exploits in the PED?"

"Sorry about that. So, what's next on the docket?"

The president stood and walked to her holotank. "I think it's time we plan the next phase of the war."

Svetlana nodded in agreement as Krissy flicked her wrist, and the tank focused in on a single star system. "New Canaan."

"Yes." Krissy bobbed her head. "It's time to finish what we started years ago."

A CLUE AND A PLAN

STELLAR DATE: 05.25.8950 (Adjusted Years)
LOCATION: ISS *Andromeda*, Amora
REGION: Car Almor System, Trisilieds Kingdom

Corsia leant back in her seat in the royal study, watching with approval as King Remal sent off the missive to the remaining rebel forces still operating in his father's name on the fringes of the Trisilieds Kingdom.

As much as she'd wanted to instruct the young ruler to tell the remaining lords to stand down or be destroyed, her advice had been to let them form their own nation. It could be entirely separate, or operate as a semi-autonomous region.

"Do you think they'll take us up on the offer?" Remal asked, uncertainty writ large on his features.

"Hard to say," Corsia replied. "I can't imagine that they want to keep fighting any more than either of us do. That being said, some people can be irrationally stubborn. At the very least, we made the offer to make peace."

"Are you really that tired of fighting?" he asked, giving her an innocently curious look—one that made her wonder how safe the young man would be once she left.

*Then again, his mother is a viper that **I'd** not cross. Now that she's freed of her husband, I think she'll protect her son better than I could.*

"You mean because I'm an AI?" Corsia asked.

"Yes, do you get tired at all?"

"Not in the same way you do, no. I do get *weary*, though. And I'm weary of fighting. I left Sol ages ago so that I could have a different kind of life, a simpler life, but that never really panned out. Things have been pretty much constant conflict since even before we left."

"How long has that been?"

"Well, I was in stasis for much of the journey. Probably...a little over a century awake since then."

"Stasis?" Remal asked, a look of surprise on his face. "I wouldn't have expected AIs to go into that."

"It was an idea the colony leaders had, for the AIs to feel more connected to the colonists. I rather liked it, to be honest. As amazing as Bob is, spending a few centuries with just him and a few other AIs would have been rather boring."

"I can't wait to see the galaxy," the new king whispered. "My people have spent so long cut off here. Well, not entirely cut off, but our beliefs and caste system don't make us very welcome in a lot of places."

"It'll take time to change that," Corsia warned.

She was about to provide him with some study materials to peruse when a message came in from Seraph.

<Mother! We just caught a courier ship that jumped in from Sol.>

<Really?> Corsia stood. *<Intact? Did you extract their data load?>*

<They blew their reactor, but I got most of the intel beforehand.>

<Don't make me come up there and drag it out of you.>

<An attack on New Canaan,> Seraph sent in a rush. *<They're planning one final assault in an attempt to force us into an armistice.>*

A grin formed on Corsia's lips. *<They don't know Car Almor has fallen yet, do they?>*

<So far as we can tell, no. They'd attempted to send a message to the former king before even realizing we were in orbit. I initiated the breach first thing—and good thing, too.>

<Prepare what you have and send it in a courier drone to New Canaan. Do we know when the attack is to be?>

A sigh came from her daughter. *<That was within the segment of data we didn't get, sorry.>*

<Better than nothing. Send an abbreviated message on the QC as well—wait. No, don't do that. Send the message to Jessica directly. I don't want the enemy to know we know.>

<On it,> Seraph replied. *<What do you have in mind?>*

Corsia turned her attention back to Remal. "Your Majesty, how do you feel about loaning me a fleet?"

A MIND'S EYE

STELLAR DATE: 05.25.8950 (Adjusted Years)
LOCATION: ISS *I2*, New Earth
REGION: New Sol System, Allied Occupied Space

Bob watched the *Voyager* settle into the forward docking bay, resting gently on its cradle—as he'd expect from someone as precise as Troy.

<*Bring her directly to Finaeus's lab,*> he ordered the ship's AI. <*I have brought his surgical suite online. Do you have neural map and data backups of her mind?*>

<*She put off the last few,*> Troy replied, the anguish in his mind flowing across the connection to Bob's.

<*Be calm, Troy. I performed a full backup before the assault on Airtha. No matter what that core-faction being did to her, I'm certain we can repair the damage.*>

Troy didn't respond, though a feeling of will-enforced calm flowed across the connection.

Bob watched, both through the sensors and his body—which filled the *I2* at this point—as a group of humans exited the *Voyager*, pushing a stasis tube floating on an a-grav support.

They moved quickly, as though time were of the essence. It was something humans were prone to...many AIs as well, if truth be told. But with Katrina in stasis, the only real added risk came from rushing.

Ironically, there were reasons for urgency, but the humans knew of none of them. He supposed it was possible that the general mood of exigency was affecting them, that they sensed things were coming to a head.

He felt it too. Darla had shared a few pieces of information with him when she'd passed through the New Sol System. It hadn't been much, but that was her way.

One thing she had insisted upon was that no one follow them to the core. She hadn't given exact reasons, but he suspected that the likelihood of capture would increase with a larger force. Then the rescuers would need rescuing, and before long, an all-out conflict would be underway in the core.

One we would likely lose, at this juncture.

He wondered if the humans would be comforted to learn that despite his additional knowledge and assurances, he was in no way mollified by them. Worry over the various people currently out of his reach occupied his mind at all times. It was only the fact that he had foreseen nearly all recent events that gave him any mental reprieve.

A few surprises had appeared, one being Cary's potency—and her recklessness. Still, her actions had benefited the Alliance, so long as the mental damage she'd suffered didn't adversely limit her future capabilities.

Bob kept a part of his attention on the progress of the four humans escorting Katrina to Finaeus's lab, aware that Troy was following along via the shipnet, watching them every step of the way.

<Perhaps you should utilize a frame,> Bob suggested.

<I don't know...I've always been a ship to her...well, for some time at least. Our relationship is built around that.>

<Troy,> Bob injected a note of humor into how he said the AI's human name. *<That is not the way organics work. They anthropomorphize you in their minds. If you show up in a frame—and you should be able to determine what sort of frame she'd appreciate—Katrina will be pleased. Trust me.>*

<Trust you?> The other AI laughed. *<Since when have you ever needed to implore someone to trust you? You never lie.>*

<I'm pleased that you think that. I do omit things, though. Some consider that to be a lie.>

<What are you omitting here? What could you possibly be

leaving out?>

<I can't tell you that,> Bob replied. *<If I did, then I wouldn't be omitting it in a way that would achieve the desired result.>*

<You're quite the manipulator, you know that?>

<Have you selected a frame yet?>

An annoyed sigh flowed across the Link from the other AI. *<Yes, it's being delivered to the ship in a few minutes. Will I make it to the lab on time?>*

<They're only just arriving with Katrina now. I imagine it will take some time to repair her mind.>

<Don't wait on me, then. You don't need the distraction.>

<You know it's impossible for you to distract me,> Bob replied.

Even though his response was technically correct, he did place a lower level of importance on communications from Troy, and turned his attention to the surgical suite, where a host of servitor-like bots stood ready to begin the work on Katrina's body—should it be required.

He gave a few words of assurance to the humans, impressed at the level of care and concern they still felt for Katrina. Few organics could tolerate one another for centuries. The fact that these four had remained close for nearly five of those was highly unusual.

The servitors brought Katrina out of stasis and lifted her free of the pod, setting her gently on the medtable while her crew looked on, sharing nervous glances.

<I will tend to her physical injuries after repairing her mind,> Bob informed them.

"Do you know if she'll make it?" the spider-woman asked.

<She will. At the worst, I can restore her mind to where it was a year ago. However, I do not think that will be the case. The physical structure appears largely undamaged. Allow me to work.>

The humans fell silent, and Bob stretched out two of his physical limbs—which appeared as little more than ephemeral strands of light to the humans—slipping them into Katrina's mind.

His own touch and senses provided far more information than the crude diagnostic tools of Finaeus's lab. It was clear that the being who had attacked her had been seeking something, and so it was not as destructive as he might have feared.

What was it looking for?

Katrina had lived a long and storied life, much of it spent with Xavia's memory lodged in her mind, a guiding force that had operated with two main goals: keep Katrina alive, and bring her to a place where she could kill Tanis.

It was possible, however, that the being had possessed other goals. Xavia had not been an agent of either Hades or Epsilon. Bob had never learned whether she'd operated alone, or was a part of a third faction.

The behavior of the ascended AIs Bob had encountered thus far had been inconsistent enough to lend credence to the idea that there were several groups, some allied, others at odds.

He had frequently wondered if Xavia had been the progenitor of the Caretakers, given Katrina's actions during her five centuries of waiting.

While wishing a short conversation with the ascended being had been possible, Bob began comparing Katrina's mind to the backup he had made before the assault on Airtha, layering in the differentials from Troy. He began to create a map of changes beyond those backups, examining her brain's digital and analog storage.

Some changes were new memories and experiences, the evolution of a mind. Others were more chaotic, things he was less certain were organic changes, and likely the result of the enemy AI's meddling.

Tallying the number of distinct chemical and structural changes to Katrina's mind, he began to see a pattern that was far from random destruction. Each alteration was to a remembrance, or a mindset change that resulted from that event...a deeper sort of mental manipulation than one often made.

Altering a person's memories in such a fashion was so pervasive that they became bedrock elements of personality and core axioms.

Bob dove into the revised events, playing them through, searching for similarities and reinforcements. It wasn't a thing he'd done in the past, not at the level required for this procedure. If he'd operated under the same sort of moral code as humans, his actions might have seemed like a violation of Katrina's deepest mind.

While he would have agreed in most circumstances, these memories were *already* not private—and some element in them wasn't even hers.

Try as he might, Bob was unable to discern what had changed. The humans, now joined by Troy in a frame, were querying his progress, and he was dismayed that his only response was one indicating further delay.

Of course.

As much as Bob hated to admit it, the very nature of a mind was to become myopic at times, to focus in on known issues and ignore subtle unknowns. In this case, he'd not availed himself of the tools at hand: the minds of Katrina's long-time crew.

Rather than tapping into their bodies directly, he loaded up the backups made of their minds before the assault on Airtha, and placed them in a simulation along with Katrina's.

It wasn't possible to play through their entire lives, because not all of them had been given memory mods at birth, but Katrina had. Her entire life was recorded in perfect clarity, while the other humans started as muddied impressions and reused token markers that doubled for hundreds of singular events.

Intellectually, he knew that humans intuited 'self', while he *knew* his own self. However, seeing it from their own perspective was an entirely different scenario. Eventually, Katrina's crew had all received memory mods, and their minds became much more ordered. But even so, it was difficult to spot what might have been altered in Katrina's mind.

I must go deeper.

Knowing that the alterations may be entirely in the impression and changes to core axioms, not the things she'd experienced, Bob simultaneously lived Katrina's entire life, alongside those of her crew, a thousand times over, then a million. He lived both versions, her backed-up mind, as well as her organic one.

Two things began to occur as he went through each one of her experiences in excruciating clarity. The first was that he'd never properly understood humans, the desperate frailty they lived with all their lives, the underlying knowledge that they were but one random mistake away from death shaping everything they did — or being willfully ignored.

It was one thing to know how ephemeral they were, but it was another to *feel* it, experience their rank terror in the moment when subconscious layers of fight-or-flight instinct kicked in, and they were saved — or not — by their own biological substructure.

In addition to a deepening understanding of others, Bob began to see a message layered into the alterations. It was not, as he had first feared, malicious in intent. It didn't change *who* Katrina was, but rather amounted to little more than the position of an individual finger on a glass during an inconsequential conversation, or the trajectory of a projectile round that missed the mark. Others were miniscule changes to her impressions of people, a touch more joy here, a little less sadness there. If anything, the core AI had made her life seem a sliver better.

Once he'd run through all the discrepancies, he walked through Katrina's life a hundred additional times, scouring every moment, looking for anything he'd missed.

When the process was complete, he found himself, for the first time in ages, in need of quiet repose. Through the process of spending centuries with this one woman, everything had changed for Bob.

I understand.

It took far less time to run the discrepancies through a million algorithms, hunting for their meaning, so he tasked an NSAI node to do it while he considered all the ways he'd been wrong about humans — and perhaps lesser life forms of every stripe, including most AIs.

He'd only processed a smattering of the changes he needed to make to his worldviews when the NSAI finished decrypting the message. It was painfully simple.

[They're watching, and I must be discreet. If you are reading this, you already have the message. Learn it well.]

In that moment, Bob learned something new: the true definition of 'speechless'. That another sentient being had given its life to send him through Katrina's in such unimaginable detail floored him.

After another full passage through her life, this time, savoring the cumulative experiences with his new perspective, he decided not to change any of the other being's alterations to Katrina's mind.

The medical servitors had completed the repairs to her body, and he spoke into the minds of those watching, which now included Captain Rachel, and a few others from the ship's crew.

<She is whole. The other AI did not damage her mind in any way.>

"Why did they stick their dirty fingers in her head, then?" Carl growled, clearly struggling to deal with the fact that his worry and anguish had been for naught.

And Bob *empathized* with the man.

<I am sorry you all were put through so much worry on my account. There was a message secreted in her memories, but that message was for me alone.>

"You alone?" Rachel's brow knitted together. "I hope you understand that you need to give us more than that."

<The other AI…it was a rebel of sorts. It said 'they' were watching, and that by finding those few simple words, I had also received the message.>

<Which was?> Troy pressed, speaking over the Link despite being in a frame.

<How to feel. She's waking now. Attend to Katrina, I must think.>

Bob retreated into himself, only a sliver of his mind on the *I2* and its surroundings in the New Sol System. He kept a thread of consciousness focused on Katrina, and when she had reached a state of calm, touched her mind.

<I forgive you, Katrina.>

<Bob?> Her response was startled. *<What do you mean?>*

*<I lived your life a thousand times, searching for what had been altered in it. I **was** you many times over. I feel your pain, I feel your joy. Your memories are now a part of me.>*

She didn't respond for over a minute, but he could see the thought processes within her. They vacillated through all possible reactions, from anger to fear to rage…eventually, they filtered through to understanding and acceptance.

At that point, she responded.

<I have to admit I feel a bit violated, Bob.>

<And for that, I am deeply sorry. I understand that too, now. You've made so many sacrifices for others, and I am sorry that you had to make this sacrifice for me as well, though I thank you.>

Another few seconds passed before she replied. <*And the forgiveness?*>

<*I know your soul, Katrina. The kernel of self-hatred that is nestled at your center. I understand that you can never be rid of it, that it is an important part of who you are. Yet at the same time, I understand **you**, and I don't know that, if I had been in your shoes, with your resources, I could have done any better. And so, because it is so difficult for you to forgive yourself, **I** forgive you.*>

A wave of emotion crashed over Katrina, and the woman began to sob.

She was alone in her quarters, and no one was there to comfort her, so Bob slid tendrils of his body out from within the deck below, up through her bed, and gently lay them at her side, one draped across her middle.

For a moment, she seemed scared, then laughed amidst her tears. "You could warn a woman first, Bob."

<*I'm sorry. Emotions...understanding what lesser beings need...it's new to me.*>

" 'Lesser beings'? Some things haven't changed."

~*I may have greater understanding, but I still am what I am. Would you like for me to withdraw?*~

Katrina turned toward his arms, and wrapped her own around them. "No, please stay. I feel...safer."

She fell asleep shortly after, drifting away into the blessed subconscious-reordering of mind that organics were granted.

He watched as her many centuries of experience with joy, grief, and everything in between helped her process recent events, and after a few hours, she truly was at peace. It was marvelous, and as Bob followed along, he finally understood his true purpose.

JUST A TASTE

STELLAR DATE: 05.25.8950 (Adjusted Years)
LOCATION: High Terra, Earth
REGION: Sol System, Hegemony of Worlds

Elena ran her tongue over one of her fangs before leaning forward and brushing it across the man's neck, lips trailing in the tooth's wake.

"I love that you love this," she whispered in his ear.

He moaned with pleasure before responding, "You have no idea. Blood games have fallen out of favor on High Terra for some reason. Takes forever to find a committed partner these days."

Elena dug both fangs into the side of his neck, raking them through the man's skin, and sending two trickling flows of red delight running down his neck.

One at a time, she licked up the streams of sticky substance, wondering how it was that she always ended up having to play a sucker when undercover. If she had any belief in fate, she'd have some questions for it.

So many questions. Maybe a kick in the groin, too.

Even worse, whenever she made love, her thoughts returned to the time she'd spent in the *I2*'s brig, to that final visit from Sera after the attack on the Scipian empress's ball.

Her former lover had admitted that she understood that Elena had been conditioned by General Garza, forced to do his bidding.

Elena had still been somewhat under Orion's thrall at the time, but her mind had been her own, and her thoughts lucid. The encounter had ended with Sera simply leaving, never to return, never to offer forgiveness.

Until several months ago when she'd returned—only it

hadn't been her, but Seraphina, a clone splintered off before those final betrayals where Elena had taken so much from Sera.

Seraphina was able to divorce her knowledge of those wrongs from the woman before her, and she'd guided Elena through the final stages of her rehabilitation, and brought her back into the Hand.

It was surreal in so many ways. The Transcend was changed from its former glory, a bastion of strength and power. Now it felt much like any other struggling alliance of disparate peoples.

Seraphina was also a harder woman than Sera, as though when Airtha had forged her, she'd left out a touch of the compassion that Sera possessed. Given the first iteration's propensity to shoot first and ask questions never, that made Seraphina a force to be reckoned with in the organization.

At the same time, she was *more* tender when alone than Sera had ever been. Ready to talk through why she felt a given way, to dig into the reasons behind an emotional response, and seek better understanding of herself.

Elena wasn't certain if it was a deliberately created trait in Seraphina, or the result of being a clone and constantly trying to discern what was a genuine reaction, and what was tainted by the knowledge of being a copy of another.

Either way, it turned out that Seraphina's propensity for introspection was just what Elena had needed to speed her own healing process.

She realized that, as she'd made love to the man beneath her, she'd been imagining it was Seraphina...or perhaps Sera. Sometimes it was hard to tell them apart in her memories. She hoped never to see Sera again, though. The dark-haired love of her life had chosen Jason Andrews, making it clear that she'd always been a fallback option, someone for Sera to sate her needs with while Jason was unavailable.

A spike of rage came over her, and she bit too deep, causing the man to shriek in pain. She sucked up the blood and let his nano heal the wound. Once the flow was stemmed, she pulled back.

"Sorry about that."

"Sorry?" The man laughed and shook his head. "You should do that more often. Make it real."

Elena wanted to tell the man he was pathetic, but truth be told, she loved it as much as he did. Even without the mods, she'd always had an appreciation for the taste of blood. Sera had never allowed any letting, but Seraphina was more forgiving of Elena's pernicious behavior.

"You sure about that?" she purred in his ear. "I might bleed you dry."

"That might get you in some trouble," he replied, tracing his hand down her chest, nails leaving white marks in her skin. "I'm rather important, you know."

Elena laughed, high and airy, shaking her long, red locks from behind her shoulders like waterfalls of blood cascading down around them. "Really now. I love a good chase...are you tempting me?"

He snorted. "Girl, the people I work for would find you and kill you in an hour if I told them to."

"Oh yeah? You a spy or something?" Elena kept her voice high, no trace of threat in her tone at all as she slid up to sit on his stomach.

"Something like that," he tried to get her back down, but she hooked her feet around the inside of his thighs while her knees tucked in against his chest.

"Military, then?" Elena giggled. "I love a man in armor. Do you wear that stuff? It's so hardcore."

He opened his mouth to reply, but in one swift move, she clamped her hands around his throat and spread her knees, driving them down into his biceps, pinning him in place.

"Don't bother trying to use the Link to call for help," she said, her voice still sweet and airy. "When I drank you, I seeded nano into your bloodstream. It would have seemed harmless at first, but...well...turns out, not so much."

He scowled at her, but his eyes widened as the realization that he was truly at her mercy settled in.

"Thought you were in control of the situation till a few seconds ago, didn't you?" Elena's voice began to drop, a hint of menace slipping into the words. "I breached your home's defenses before we'd finished the wine. You took a bit more work, but really, you're not as far up the chain as you think. High enough to know the things I want, not so high that your nano would pose a real challenge."

His surprise turned into rage, and he bucked against her, only now realizing that her seemingly light frame was a lot heavier than expected.

"You're not going to get away with this," he blustered. "I'm not telling you shit, and when they catch you...."

"I know you support Uriel's front-line guard detail," Elena said. "Not in direct contact with the hegemon herself, but you talk with the people who are. You hear things. You're going to tell those things to me."

"You're blood-drunk if you think you'll get anything out of me, you psycho. I'll not—"

His words cut off as Elena tightened her grip around his neck, severing his air supply.

"I wonder which you'll do first," she mused. "Pass out from lack of air to your lungs, or blood to your head? I guess that depends on your mods. Granted, you don't *have* to be alive for me to learn what I need." Elena's fingernails dug into the back of his neck, ripping into the skin and pulling it back from his spine.

Unable to even make a sound, the man couldn't do anything other than writhe—with less and less energy—as streams of nano flowed from her fingers into his spinal column. After a few seconds, she'd tapped his motor control, and his body went limp from the neck down.

"Now, I'm going to loosen my grip. If you scream, I'll slice your voicebox open, and we'll be done with that nonsense. Not that anyone can hear you where we are, but it'll just annoy me."

He gave a weak nod, and she relaxed her hands ever so slightly.

Starved lungs expanded, drawing in a deep breath before rapidly expelling it, working hard to re-oxygenate his bloodstream.

"So, I'm going to ask you a simple question…one I'm pretty sure you know the answer to. The AST is building up their fleets, that's easy to see. But I know your real defense is the mass drone fleets, the ones that take special, AI-driven control centers. I want to know where those control centers are."

"I don't know what you're talking about," the man said in a pleading voice. "You have to believe me, I literally just make sure Uriel's security is properly equipped for their work."

"Yeah, I know. Which means you service their armor and weapons, and make sure they have whatever gear is necessary. You even went with Uriel to Sirius not long ago. So…spill it."

He shook his head in defiance, and Elena leant forward, her hair creating a veil between them and the rest of the room.

Her eyes bore into his, and her words came out on a whisper. "Have you ever felt what it's like to have your spinal column shredded? To have your nerves ripped from place, one by one? It's like your entire body is on fire, beyond excruciating. Want to see what it feels like?"

She sank her fingers deeper into the meat of his neck, not seriously damaging anything, but putting the fear of it in his mind.

He still didn't speak, and she shrugged.

"OK, let's have at it, then."

She pulled her hands out of his flesh, and reached over to her handbag. The device she took from it was known as a scarab. It would clamp onto his neck and begin to thread filaments through his nervous system, tearing them apart and replacing each neuron with its own non-organic 'cell'. When complete, the device would fully control his body. Given enough time, it could do the same to a person's brain.

Or so Elena had been told. She'd never used one; never had to.

He shrieked at the sight of the thing, and immediately began gibbering. It took a few moments to begin making sense of his rapid-fire exclamations, but the moment she pieced it together, she slid off his body and began washing the blood off herself in the attached san.

"What was that?" she called out. "The drone control systems are on ships? Heavily shielded dreadnoughts?"

"Yes," he tried to nod, but grimaced from the pain. "And some on High Terra, but most on the ships."

She stuck her head out, giving him a dark look. "And the other part? You're sure they're planning a counterattack, sending the fleets away?"

"So far as I know," he said. "To the ISF's home world, New Canaan."

"What else do you know?" she asked while striding out of the san, moving toward the chair where her clothes lay. "Who is in command of the fleets, and when do they leave?"

"I don't know who the AST admirals will be," the man pleaded. "No one has mentioned anything about that."

"Very well," Elena said as she plucked at her dress, ensuring it fell properly past her hips. "Then you're of no more—"

"Hurom!" he shouted. "Admiral Hurom from Sirius is here on High Terra. He's in command of the Sirian ships, he'll know."

"Well then." Elena inclined her head. "Looks like you can be useful after all."

"Will you…free me?"

She gazed down on the helpless man, wishing there was time to wipe his memory, clean him up, send him on his way. But there wasn't, not if an attack on New Canaan was imminent.

"I'm sorry," she shook her head. "It's not going to be like that for you."

The Hand agent lifted the hem of her dress and pulled a lightwand from her thigh. The moment the beam came to life, the man on the bed began to shriek. His cries hastened her strike, and before he drew his next breath, his head lay in two pieces.

Elena reached into her handbag and pulled out a small container, a potent batch of nano that would dissolve the body, the bed, and any parts of the room affected by blood or DNA. Once complete, it would reconstruct the entire space just as it had been when they'd entered an hour earlier—minus the poor fool who had been sacrificed in the name of the greater good.

She would have felt guilty over it, but it was such a small drop in the bucket compared to what she'd done in the past that the murder barely registered on her conscience as she turned her focus to hunting down Admiral Hurom and finding out the AST's attack strategy.

Then maybe this will be over, and I can return to Sera…phina.

TURNABOUT

STELLAR DATE: 05.25.8950 (Adjusted Years)
LOCATION: ISS *Carthage*, Incandus
REGION: Sirius System, Allied Occupied Space

<Admiral.> Kerr's tone was filled with urgency as his voice slipped into Jessica's mind. <I've just received a message from Admiral Corsia, your eyes only.>

<Thank you,> Jessica said as she connected to the QuanComm system and accessed her queue.

A goodly number of messages were waiting for her attention—after being cleaned out only two hours ago, no less—but at the top sat one marked with the utmost urgency.

[Hegemony organizing counterattack on New Canaan. Mustering remaining enemy forces. Timing unknown. Data drone dispatched.]

"Fuck," she muttered aloud, and all eyes turned toward her.

"What is it?" Jason asked.

"Corsia just sent word, the Hegemony is planning an assault on New Canaan. She said they're 'mustering all remaining forces'."

The governor placed his palms on the table. "Then I must go. Did she say when?"

"Unknown," Jessica shook her head. "I'll reach out to Cheeky, and update her priorities."

"It could be a feint," Greer cautioned. "Don't pull out forces from across the galaxy on so little intel."

The field marshal nodded. "I know, but I can take what we have here, First Fleet from New Sol, and Carson's from Genevia. They won't have taken down our jump interdictors as well as we did here, so we should see them coming."

Everyone rose from the table at the same time, and she saw both Caldwell and Usef looking uncertain.

"You're both to remain on mission," she ordered them. "I want you to get into Sol, and be ready to hit those drone control centers. Even if this attack on New Canaan is real, we're smashing Sol the moment it's over."

"You might not even need to wait," Petra pointed out. "If they empty Sol to hit you, we can take advantage of the opportunity."

"But if you need aid," Greer gave Jessica an understanding look, "you call for it."

"We will," she promised, glad of the support. "Now, anyone that doesn't want to jump to New Canaan in the next thirty minutes, you'd better get the hell off this ship."

THE OLDEST ENEMY

STELLAR DATE: 05.26.8950 (Adjusted Years)
LOCATION: *Sabrina*, Sedna
REGION: Sol System, Hegemony of Worlds

Nunataq's spaceport looked like something time had forgotten.

Cheeky stood at the top of the ramp, looking out over the rows of cradles—most of them empty—and was reminded of ports deep in the PED, where rows of tired freighters hunkered down on ancient struts, none quite too certain if they'd ever take off again.

While that sort of port was entirely expected in the poorer end of Orion space, she hadn't expected to see it in Sol. Then again, Sedna was a relic, a terraformed dwarf planet beyond the protection of Sol's heliosheath—not the sort of thing that was done anymore.

"Place is like a museum," Fina said from her side. "Kinda exciting, if you ask me."

"Nance and Misha staying aboard?" Cheeky asked.

"Yeah, Nance took one look and declared that the place gave her the creeps."

The captain laughed. "Classic Nance."

"True that. Some things never change."

Cheeky glanced at her former captain and nodded. Clone or no, every time she looked at Fina, she saw the woman who had saved her life in so many ways. "Don't really want them to, either."

"Well, let's change the Hegemony a bit."

"OK, I'm on board with that."

The pair fell silent, and Cheeky's gaze swept across the field of ships once more, suddenly realizing that there was not a soul to be seen anywhere. No cargo handlers, refueling teams, or crews.

"Where is everyone?" she asked.

"No idea…Nance was right, it's a bit creepytown."

Cheeky snorted. "Well, let's go find us the portmaster, and figure out where our cargo's going."

<You really think that'll happen?> Fina asked.

<Stars no, but we're being watched, right?>

<Yeah, I imagine. Let's go to the tower.>

The pair of women walked down the ramp and ambled between the rows of ships, cutting across to the next, and then one more. A few hundred meters farther, and they reached the port's tower, a squat building with a single spire stretching up half a kilometer.

Cheeky wondered why it needed to be so tall when even with Sedna's curvature, the entire port could be seen from a hundred feet in the air.

Maybe someone is trying to compensate for being an itty-bitty planet.

As they approached the tower, the door opened, and a slender man stepped out. Cheeky queried the local network and saw that he was Deputy Portmaster Arens.

He gave a jaunty wave as they approached, his pleasant smile almost putting them at ease, but even the man's easy saunter couldn't make up for him being the only person they'd seen since landing.

<Cheeky, Fina, we've got a problem,> Sabrina said.

<What is it?> Fina asked as Cheeky stretched out her hand and greeted Arens.

<Just caught a few glimpses, but there's a group of soldiers moving in on us.>

<Shit,> Fina cursed. <Seal up, we'll be back as soon as we find out whether or not this dork is in on it.>

"What's going on here?" Cheeky asked, gesturing at the

nearest ships. "Where is everyone?"

"You've heard of the phage, right?" Arens asked, still wearing a half-smile. "Most everyone is holed up, waiting for the lockdown to be lifted. I honestly can't believe you landed."

"Job's a job," Cheeky replied. "Our load is for the folks running the black hole. Figure they're not really the sort who can do without."

"Oh yeah, that'll be tricky," the portmaster said, his smile finally disappearing. "See, you're at risk of contamination now, so you can't return to your ship. It'll require a special pickup from a hazteam to get your cargo."

"I thought the phage wasn't down here," Cheeky frowned. "And if that was the protocol, why didn't you broadcast it?"

"Because," a new voice said from behind them. "Then we wouldn't be able to divide and conquer nearly as easily."

Cheeky spun to see an AI frame step out from behind a cradle. As he approached, the weapons systems on several nearby ships came to life, all taking aim at the two women.

"And who the fuck are you supposed to be?" Fina asked.

The AI stopped a few meters away. "I'm the one who wants to know how you thought you could fool us with such an obviously fake delivery."

"Well," Cheeky shrugged as she glanced at Fina. "We certainly expected to fool Arens here. Now answer her question, who are *you*?"

"Little ol' me?" the AI asked before giving a slight bow and spreading his arms wide. "Why, you may call me Virgo, and if you're who I think you are, then my friend Prime and I are going to quite enjoy learning everything inside those heads of yours."

Cheeky glanced at Fina. "Either of those names mean anything to you?"

The other woman had paled noticeably. "There's no way. You died."

Virgo shrugged. "I got better."

In the distance, the sound of weapons fire echoed between the parked vessels. *Sabrina* was under attack.

Cheeky glanced at Fina and gave a small nod. *<You ready?>* *<Ready.>*

TO BE CONTINUED...

* * * * *

Pick up **Return to Sol: Star Rise**, the final book in the Orion War series, and see what it will take to end the war once and for all.

THE BOOKS OF AEON 14

Keep up to date with what is releasing in Aeon 14 with the free Aeon 14 Reading Guide.

Outlaws of Aquilia
- Book 1: The Daedalus Job
- Book 2: Maelstrom Reach (2020)
- Book 3: Marauder's Compass (2020)

The Sentience Wars: Origins (Age of the Sentience Wars – w/James S. Aaron)
- Books 1-3 Omnibus: Lyssa's Rise
- Books 4-5 Omnibus (incl. Vesta Burning): Lyssa's Fire

- Book 0 Prequel: The Proteus Bridge (Full length novel)
- Book 1: Lyssa's Dream
- Book 2: Lyssa's Run
- Book 3: Lyssa's Flight
- Book 4: Lyssa's Call
- Book 5: Lyssa's Flame

The Sentience Wars: Solar War 1 (Age of the Sentience Wars – w/James S. Aaron)
- Book 0 Prequel: Vesta Burning (Full length novel)
- Book 1: Eve of Destruction
- Book 2: The Spreading Fire
- Book 3: A Fire Upon the Worlds (2020)

Enfield Genesis (Age of the Sentience Wars – w/Lisa Richman)
- Book 1: Alpha Centauri
- Book 2: Proxima Centauri
- Book 3: Tau Ceti
- Book 4: Epsilon Eridani

- Book 5: Sirius

Origins of Destiny (The Age of Terra)
- Prequel: Storming the Norse Wind
- Prequel: Angel's Rise: The Huntress (available on Patreon)
- Book 1: Tanis Richards: Shore Leave
- Book 2: Tanis Richards: Masquerade
- Book 3: Tanis Richards: Blackest Night
- Book 4: Tanis Richards: Kill Shot

The Intrepid Saga (The Age of Terra)
- Book 1: Outsystem
- Book 2: A Path in the Darkness
- Book 3: Building Victoria

- The Intrepid Saga Omnibus – *Also contains Destiny Lost, book 1 of the Orion War series*

- Destiny Rising – *Special Author's Extended Edition comprised of both Outsystem and A Path in the Darkness with over 100 pages of new content.*

The Sol Dissolution (The Age of Terra)
- Book 1: Venusian Uprising
- Book 2: Assault on Sedna
- Book 3: Hyperion War (2020)
- Book 4: Fall of Terra (2020)

The Warlord (Before the Age of the Orion War)
- Books 1-3 Omnibus: The Warlord of Midditerra

- Book 1: The Woman Without a World
- Book 2: The Woman Who Seized an Empire
- Book 3: The Woman Who Lost Everything

Legacy of the Lost (The FTL Wars Era w/Chris J. Pike)
- Book 1: Fire in the Night Sky
- Book 2: A Blight Upon the Stars

The Orion War
- Book 1-3 Omnibus: Battle for New Canaan *(includes Set the Galaxy on Fire anthology)*
- Book 4-6 Omnibus: The Greatest War *(includes Ignite the Stars anthology)*
- Book 7-9 Omnibus: Assault on Orion
- Book 10-12 Omnibus: Hegemony of Humanity *(includes Return to Kapteyn's Star) (2020)*

- Book 0 Prequel: To Fly Sabrina
- Book 1: Destiny Lost
- Book 2: New Canaan
- Book 3: Orion Rising
- Book 4: The Scipio Alliance
- Book 5: Attack on Thebes
- Book 6: War on a Thousand Fronts
- Book 7: Precipice of Darkness
- Book 8: Airtha Ascendancy
- Book 9: The Orion Front
- Book 10: Starfire
- Book 10.5: Return to Kapteyn's Star
- Book 11: Race Across Spacetime
- Book 12: Return to Sol: Attack at Dawn
- Book 13: Return to Sol: Star Rise (2020)

Non-Aeon 14 volumes containing Tanis stories
- Bob's Bar Volume 1
- Quantum Legends 3: Aberrant Ascension

Building New Canaan (Age of the Orion War – w/J.J. Green)
- Book 1: Carthage
- Book 2: Tyre
- Book 3: Troy
- Book 4: Athens

Tales of the Orion War
- Book 1: Set the Galaxy on Fire

- Book 2: Ignite the Stars

Multi-Author Collections
- Volume 1: Repercussions

Perilous Alliance (Age of the Orion War – w/Chris J. Pike)
- Book 1-3 Omnibus: Crisis in Silstrand
- Book 3.5-6 Omnibus: War in the Fringe

- Book 0 Prequel: Escape Velocity
- Book 1: Close Proximity
- Book 2: Strike Vector
- Book 3: Collision Course
- Book 3.5: Decisive Action
- Book 4: Impact Imminent
- Book 5: Critical Inertia
- Book 6: Impulse Shock
- Book 7: Terminal Velocity

The Delta Team (Age of the Orion War)
- Book 1: The Eden Job
- Book 2: The Disknee World
- Book 3: Rogue Planets (2020)

Serenity (Age of the Orion War – w/A. K. DuBoff)
- Book 1: Return to the Ordus
- Book 2: War of the Rosette

Rika's Marauders (Age of the Orion War)
- Book 1-3 Omnibus: Rika Activated
- Book 1-7 Full series omnibus: Rika's Marauders

- Prequel: Rika Mechanized
- Book 1: Rika Outcast
- Book 2: Rika Redeemed
- Book 3: Rika Triumphant
- Book 4: Rika Commander
- Book 5: Rika Infiltrator

- Book 6: Rika Unleashed
- Book 7: Rika Conqueror

Non-Aeon 14 Anthologies containing Rika stories
- Bob's Bar Volume 2

The Genevian Queen (Age of the Orion War)
- Book 1: Rika Rising
- Book 2: Rika Coronated
- Book 3: Rika Destroyer (2020)

Perseus Gate (Age of the Orion War)
Season 1: Orion Space
- Episode 1: The Gate at the Grey Wolf Star
- Episode 2: The World at the Edge of Space
- Episode 3: The Dance on the Moons of Serenity
- Episode 4: The Last Bastion of Star City
- Episode 5: The Toll Road Between the Stars
- Episode 6: The Final Stroll on Perseus's Arm
- Eps 1-3 Omnibus: The Trail Through the Stars
- Eps 4-6 Omnibus: The Path Amongst the Clouds

Season 2: Inner Stars
- Episode 1: A Meeting of Bodies and Minds
- Episode 2: A Deception and a Promise Kept
- Episode 3: A Surreptitious Rescue of Friends and Foes
- Episode 3.5: Anomaly on Cerka (w/Andrew Dobell)
- Episode 4: A Victory and a Crushing Defeat
- Episode 5: A Trial and the Tribulations (2020)
- Episode 6: A Deal and a True Story Told (2020)
- Episode 7: A New Empire and An Old Ally (2020)
- Eps 1-3 Omnibus: A Siege and a Salvation from Enemies

Hand's Assassin (Age of the Orion War – w/T.G. Ayer)
- Book 1: Death Dealer
- Book 2: Death Mark (2020)

Machete System Bounty Hunter (Age of the Orion War – w/Zen DiPietro)
- Book 1: Hired Gun
- Book 2: Gunning for Trouble
- Book 3: With Guns Blazing

Fennington Station Murder Mysteries (Age of the Orion War)
- Book 1: Whole Latte Death (w/Chris J. Pike)
- Book 2: Cocoa Crush (w/Chris J. Pike)

The Empire (Age of the Orion War)
- Book 1: The Empress and the Ambassador
- Book 2: Consort of the Scorpion Empress (2020)
- Book 3: By the Empress's Command (2020)

The Ascension War (Age of the Orion War)
- Book 1: Scions of Humanity (2020)

OTHER BOOKS BY M. D. COOPER

Destiny's Sword
- Book 1: Lucidum Run

ABOUT THE AUTHOR

Malorie Cooper likes to think of herself as a dreamer and a wanderer, yet her feet are firmly grounded in reality.

A twenty-year software development veteran, Malorie eventually climbed the ladder to the position of software architect and CTO, where she gained a wealth of experience managing complex systems and large groups of people.

Her experiences there translated well into the realm of science fiction, and when her novels took off, she was primed and ready to make the jump into a career as a full-time author.

A 'maker' from an early age, Malorie loves to craft things, from furniture, to cosplay costumes, to a well-spun tale, she can't help but to create new things every day.

A rare extrovert writer, she loves to hang out with readers, and people in general. If you meet her at a convention, she just might be rocking a catsuit, cosplaying one of her own characters, or maybe her latest favorite from Overwatch!

She shares her home with a brilliant young girl, her wonderful wife (who also writes), a cat that chirps at birds, a never-ending list of things she would like to build, and ideas...

Find out what's coming next at www.aeon14.com.
Follow her on Instagram at www.instagram.com/m.d.cooper.
Hang out with the fans on Facebook at
www.facebook.com/groups/aeon14fans.